GREG WEISMAN

SCHOLASTIC INC.

ISBN 978-1-338-22567-9

10 9 8 7 6 5 4 3 2 1   18 19 20 21 22

Printed in the U.S.A.   40
First printing 2018

Book design by Rick DeMonico
Cover art by Aquatic Moon and interior illustrations by Samwise Didier

To my second-grade teacher, Sandy Voyne, who started all
this with a handful of spelling words . . .

PART ONE:

ABOARD WAVESTRIDER

CHAPTER ONE
A DREAM OF LIGHT AND MOTION

Aramar Thorne turned away from the Light.

It had called to him, and he had followed, sailing toward it across the sea—without benefit of ship, boat, or raft—until the surf and spray vanished from beneath his feet and he found himself ashore. And still the Light called to him. This strange Light came not from the sun nor the moons nor the stars, whose constellations his mother used to point out to him when he was six, after his father had vanished, and under which she had promised Greydon Thorne could be found. No, this was a new Light, a moving target with no fixed progression through the heavens— quite impossible to reliably track, let alone pin down. Still, without ever making a conscious decision to continue, Aram found himself walking toward it. He walked and walked through dusty desert, broken forest, swampy bog, and dense jungle, stopping only when

1

a great wall of a mountain seemed to rise up out of the ground to block his path. But the Voice of the Light still called his name, "Aram, Aram," all without ever making any actual sound that reached his ears. The Voice grabbed him like a fist around his heart and pulled him painfully into the air, and soon Aram Thorne was soaring, soaring through sunshine and cloud, through rain and thunder—until lightning struck so close, he could feel the hairs on his arm stand at attention and singe. But even this lightning paled before the bright, bright Light.

He had traveled so far to find it, find it so that the Light could save him, could return his father, bring Aram home to his mother, reunite him with Robb and Robertson and Selya and even Soot. Yet when finally he achieved it, the Light blinded, and Aramar Thorne turned away. It called to him: "Aram, Aram, it is you who must save me . . ." But he turned away. One last time, it called his name . . .

"Aramar Thorne, get your sorry bones out of that bunk!"

Aram woke with a start, sitting up abruptly and smacking his forehead painfully against the underside of the upper berth, only eight or nine inches above where he laid his head. It had been six months aboard ship, and he figured he must have a permanent bruise, given the number of times he had done the exact same thing, never learning from the experience. The strange dream of motion and Light began to fade instantly, and he struggled to hold on to even a fragment of it, but *she* was of another mind.

Ship's second mate Makasa Flintwill had evolved beyond any amusement she once enjoyed from seeing Aram bash in his own skull. The fact that the kid never woke up on his own, and rarely without her shouting at him for two solid minutes, was yet more proof he didn't belong aboard the *Wavestrider*. She was sick of the sight of him, but the captain—without ever actually giving the order—had all but made Aram her responsibility. Still, there was never any suggestion she had to treat the young fool gently. Tired of yelling at him, she grabbed his bare right foot and yanked him bodily off his bunk.

Landing hard on his behind, Aram winced sharply and glared up at his nemesis. Makasa was seventeen, only five years older than he was, but had he been standing at attention she'd still tower over him by a good half a foot. Right now, she positively *loomed*. He blinked twice, trying to focus. Backlit by the open hatch behind her, Makasa's sable skin blended with the belowdeck shadows and gloom and his own hazy consciousness, rendering her as little more than a silhouette. But there was no denying her solidity, her presence. She was five foot ten, lean and muscular, with kinky hair, cut extremely short to match the shape of her skull. Flintwill was the irresistible force, and unfortunately for Aram, he was no immovable object. She grabbed the front of his tunic and dragged him to his feet.

"Landfall in five minutes," she growled. "Pull on your boots and meet me in the hold in two."

*　　*　　*

3

He had to go up to go down. Having donned stockings and boots and splashed his face with water, Aram climbed into the open air. He glanced ashore—at the first land he'd seen in a week—then trotted across the deck to the hold, passing sailors about the business of making landfall, knowing that no matter how fast he moved, it would never be fast enough for *Wavestrider*'s second mate.

Swinging his body into the hold, he grabbed the outside edges of the ladder and slid down it smoothly. He'd learned that trick at least. His boots hit bottom. There was minimal light here, too, and it smelled of mildew and fish.

Makasa, of course, was waiting. She had her back to him but began barking out orders before he had even touched down: "That barrel and those four crates are going ashore. Help me with the barrel, then come back for the crates. And make sure you send up the right ones."

He didn't answer, which suited both of them fine. In his first few weeks aboard ship, he had tried out, "Yes, Miss!" and "Yes, Ma'am!" and "Yes, Sir!" They all made her grimace. Later, "Yes, Second Mate!" and even "Yes, Flintwill!" and "Yes, Makasa!" But none of them seemed to suit. So he had stopped addressing her by name or title. He had tried very hard to stop addressing her at all.

They tilted the heavy barrel to roll it across the hold, and he could feel and hear its contents sloshing about within. The question came out of his mouth before he could censor it: "What's in this thing?"

"Hardboiled chicken eggs pickled in brine," she said darkly, as if challenging him to deny it.

He screwed up his face in disgust. "Who would ever want hardboiled chicken eggs pickled in brine?!"

"Wait and see," she said, smiling for the first time all morning. Maybe for the first time all month.

He shook his head, something he had taught himself to do, because rolling his eyes seemed to particularly aggravate Second Mate Flintwill, and he didn't need to give her any more reasons to dislike him. They maneuvered the barrel onto the cargo net, which immediately formed a hammock around it, as the deckhands above used ropes and pulleys to raise it topside. Without another word, she climbed up the ladder, leaving him below.

He crossed back to the crates she had indicated. They weren't sealed, and he wrenched off a lid to satisfy his curiosity. Inside were old, scarred axe blades affixed to splintered or shattered wooden hafts, broken knives and sword tips, even rusty nails. He glanced about the hold of his father's ship. It was full of random stuff like this, useless junk that no sane man or woman could ever want. And yet it was exactly this useless junk that was Greydon Thorne's stock-in-trade. *Wavestrider* traversed Azeroth, landing in both Alliance ports and Horde—and everything in between. Captain Thorne trafficked in the obscure. A small trade here, a small deal there. If there was profit in any of it, Aram could hardly see how. He shook his head again.

He made four trips across the hold, placing each crate in the net, watching each one get raised into the light. This reminded him of . . . something. But he couldn't summon up a notion of what that something might be. He shook the dormant memory off and followed the crates into the air.

Achieving the deck, he was rewarded by a massive slap on the back that took the wind out of his sails, followed by a hardy "Mornin', Greydon-son!"

"Please, don't call me that," Aram said, catching his breath. He turned, unsurprised to see the robust smile of *Wavestrider*'s first mate, the burly red-bearded dwarf, Durgan One-God, who stood just a smidge over five feet tall and weighed easily thirteen stone. Just as Aram had rarely seen Makasa smile, it was even more rare to see One-God's expression form anything else.

"Aye, Aramar," One-God said with mock contrition. "Ye're yer own man, o' course. Bit of a puny man, but still . . ."

The five-foot-four Aram grinned down at the dwarf. Aram knew he was tall for his age, with every reason to believe he'd grow taller still. But it amused the first mate to call his young friend puny, and Aram didn't begrudge the dwarf his amusements—mostly because One-God was his favorite person on the ship, bar none. And that included Aram's own father, the ship's captain, Greydon Thorne.

"Ye got that little book o' yours?" One-God said cheerfully.

Aram patted the back pocket of his breeches. "Always," he said.

"Good. Might see somethin' worthy of its pages today. We've weighed anchor. Yer old man said tae go ashore."

For a split second, Aram felt *that urge*. The urge to throw his father's orders right back into the high-and-mighty Captain Greydon Thorne's teeth. Aram's relationship with his father was, well . . . complicated. But truthfully, Aram was dying to put his feet on solid ground again, so there wasn't much point in rebelling now. Besides, he could hear the voice of his mother, Ceya, in his head: "Don't cut off your nose to spite your face, child." He suffered through another friendly but painful whap on the back from One-God and headed for the gangway.

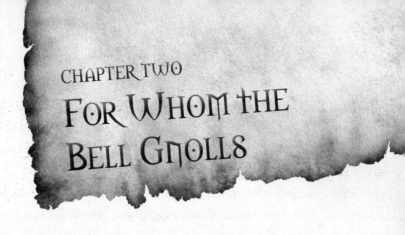

CHAPTER TWO
FOR WHOM THE BELL GNOLLS

Descending to within a few feet of the end of the gangway, Aram jumped sideways to land on the steep, sloping beach. This was no port, but a small natural harbor on the coast of Desolace that allowed the *Wavestrider* to sail virtually up to the shore. The barrel and crates were already on the sand, flanked by Makasa Flintwill and Aramar's father, Captain Greydon Thorne.

Greydon stood a hair short of six feet tall. He was slim but well muscled with thick dark hair and a thick dark beard, both just beginning to gray to match the tint of his light gray eyes. The bridge of his nose zigged and zagged from being broken multiple times. But the gray eyes smiled, and the corners of his mouth curved up in concert upon Greydon seeing his son come into view.

"You ready?" he asked Aram with a grin in his voice.

"For what?" Aram responded, scowling. As usual, the more his father smiled, the less inclined Aram was to reciprocate.

But for now the captain didn't seem to notice. He smiled in earnest, turned his head, and nodded up at One-God, who was watching from aboard ship. The first mate rang the ship's iron bell three times. Then all eyes but Aram's turned to stare toward the forest trees that crept up to the very edge of the shore.

Aram's own eyes flicked back and forth between his father and Makasa and the woods. Aram noted that Makasa was well armed. Her shield—an iron circle covered with layers of impact-absorbing rawhide—was strapped to her back; a length of iron chain crisscrossed over her chest; her cutlass was at her side, and a long iron harpoon was held loosely in her left hand, its blunt end at rest in the sand. In contrast, his father's ubiquitous cutlass was conspicuously absent from his belt, but he leaned on a fairly impressive war club of star wood and iron that easily came up to his navel. Suddenly, Aram felt unprepared to the point of nakedness. Yes, he had his sketchbook, but he longed for his cutlass instead.

Just then, Aram felt—more than he heard—a stirring of the leaves. Something melted out of the forest onto the rocks that separated wood from sand. And not one something but many somethings. They looked like massive dogs, brown fur with yellow accents and black spots, standing not quite erect on two feet, wearing ragged clothing of rough wool accented with bits of iron armor. And they were holding weapons. Lots and lots of weapons. Clubs and spears and axes and bolos and more clubs, all "decorated" with sharp iron spikes and barbs.

"What are you seeing?" Greydon asked.

"Gnolls," Aram answered breathlessly. He normally hated being quizzed by his father, but in this instant Aram was too riveted to remember to be resentful. He'd heard rumors of the monsters since he was a child in Lakeshire, but Aram had never actually seen a gnoll before. These matched Greydon's description of the species exactly—though the good captain had neglected to mention the kind of fear they'd inspire.

Greydon removed his worn leather coat and let it fall to the sand. He slipped the compass that hung on a gold chain around his neck down behind his white shirt. Then he took a step forward and with a lurch swung his own heavy club up onto his shoulder. In response, the gnolls . . . laughed. Or at least it sounded like laughter to Aram. It rose to a loud, chilling cackle, then reaching its crescendo, devolved into scattered chuckles and then into heavy panting, like the family dog, Soot, after a run along Lake Everstill back home.

The largest gnoll, a female, padded forward. Though in height she had only a few inches' advantage over Aram, she was solid as an oak, with massive shoulders, a short snout, and a grin of sharp, spiky teeth. She had pointed ears, one pierced by a feather, the other with a small gold ring. And she had her own massive war club similar to Greydon's—moontouched wood reinforced with iron—though unlike the clubs of her fellow gnolls, hers was free of pointy metal protrusions.

"Cackle here is matriarch of the Grimtail clan," Greydon whispered. "She and I have faced each other before."

"And lived to tell about it?" Aram asked dubiously, catching Greydon's sly smile and Makasa's angry scowl.

Cackle circled to the left. Greydon stepped forward and circled to the right. Aram spotted Makasa lift her harpoon half an inch off the ground, but the captain spotted this, too, and shook his head slightly, causing Makasa to lower the barbed iron javelin back to its resting position.

Aram tried to swallow but his mouth was dry as dirt. He tried to breathe but felt like he had forgotten how. He didn't much care for his father, but he didn't want Greydon Thorne to die fighting this monster. The anticipation of the clash made his heart pump rapidly in his chest—and still he was unprepared when both combatants suddenly rushed each other, war clubs swinging.

The two clubs smashed together with bone-crushing force, the iron reinforcement of the weapons ringing out louder than *Wavestrider*'s bell. Greydon pivoted and swung again, but Cackle leapt, her powerful hind legs propelling her above the horizontal arc of his attack. She brought her club down with her descent, but Captain Thorne tucked and rolled forward, leaving her weapon to strike empty ground with enough force to send sand flying in all directions—including into Aram's slack-jawed mouth and staring eyes. The boy choked, coughed, and spat. His eyes watered, and as he squeezed them shut and wiped the back of his arm across his face, he briefly lost track of the fighting.

He blinked several times, listening for the dull sound of wood impacting flesh or for a sharp cry of anguish, but all he heard was another bell-like striking of club on club. Finally, his vision cleared, and he saw his father swing up with his war club, missing Cackle's jaw by fractions of an inch. She stumbled back a step but recovered quickly, sweeping her own club across in an attempt to cave in Greydon's chest before he could bring his club down and block. But Captain Thorne was too fast for the gnoll, and his falling club didn't simply check hers—it *shattered* the matriarch's weapon into splinters, and snapped itself in half.

The two warriors stood a few feet apart, still grasping the hafts of their broken and useless weapons, breathing hard and glaring at each other. Aram tried to whisper, "What now?" to Makasa, but his sand-dry mouth only managed to croak out something unintelligible.

Makasa, nevertheless, shushed him angrily.

Then Captain Greydon Thorne threw his head back and laughed. The laugh seemed to echo behind him, and Aram whipped his head around to see Durgan One-God guffawing from aboard ship. Aram whipped his head back to study Cackle. Her lips parted to emit a low growl . . . which quickly built into the high-pitched sound that had clearly given the matriarch her name. Soon every gnoll on the beach was laughing and hooting along with Greydon and Cackle and the entire crew of the *Wavestrider*. In fact, only the stunned Aram and the grim Makasa seemed not to be in on the joke.

Cackle slapped Greydon on the back—hard but friendly and not at all unlike the slaps Aram had received from One-God—and pointed what remained of her club at Aram. Captain Thorne whispered something in her ear, and Cackle nodded while redoubling her hysterics. Aram felt the heat rise in his face, and seeing his boy's angry blush, Aramar Thorne's father swallowed what remained of his own laughter. His expression saddened for a moment, before he covered up a pain unknown to Aram and regained a mirthful mien. "Shall we trade?!" he called out boisterously.

"Yes, man!" answered the gnoll at full volume, between continued cackles and the occasional amused glance Aram's way. She waved toward her clan, who brought forth thick packets wrapped in giant gunnera leaves. A dangerous-looking male with multiple ear, eyelid, nostril, and lip piercings placed one of the packets atop the barrel and carefully unfolded the thick but supple leaf, revealing long strips of dried smoked meats.

"Boar jerky," said Cackle. "Finest the Grimtail make. Sixteen packets. And twelve of rockscale cod."

Captain Thorne stroked his beard, as Cackle rapped a paw-like fist against the barrel and listened to the sloshing of the brine within. Aram watched her mouth water, drool literally dripping into the sand. "This what I think?" she asked hungrily.

Greydon nodded. "It is." Then he pried open the top crate and picked up a battered axe blade. "And here are four crates filled with ready spurs."

Cackle smiled with all her teeth. "Thorns of Thorne," she said and laughed. But her eyes betrayed something else, a sudden nervousness that Aram noticed but failed to comprehend.

His father had a firmer grip on the situation. "So you see I bring much treasure to trade. But sixteen and twelve. You know that's not enough, Matriarch."

She growled again, and Aram saw Makasa adjust her grip on the harpoon. But Cackle's growl ended with a grunt and a wave, and soon more packets materialized from the jungle. "Twenty and twenty," Cackle barked. "No more. Final."

"Agreed!" said the captain, and everyone—on both sides of the trade—cheered. Even Makasa cheered, and even Aram found himself caught up in the moment—belatedly. His cheer arrived a second or two after the rest, causing more embarrassment when Cackle pointed at him, laughed, and asked, "Your boy a little slow?"

Greydon looked at Aramar and said, "Not slow. Just new."

Aram crossed his arms over his chest and scowled, as his father said, "What? New's not bad."

His son resisted the urge to roll his eyes at the old man and shook his head instead.

The barrel was pried open, and the stench from the pickled eggs almost made Aram retch—and even had the stoic Makasa looking a little green. But Cackle and the Grimtail howled with joy. The matriarch slapped away the paw of the large, pierced male and reached into the brine. Her talons emerged, gently clutching the first egg. She held it up as if it were a diamond to be admired. Then she dropped it whole into her maw. Her head rolled with joy at the taste. Aram forgot his nausea and stared in wonder.

"To the gnolls those eggs are quite the delicacy," Greydon said. Aram flinched. He hadn't noticed his father slip behind him. (For a big man, Greydon Thorne was surprisingly light on his feet.)

"So I can see," Aram said, trying to make his voice sound cold and uninterested. But his desire to distance himself from his father was fighting a losing battle against the boy's own curiosity. Aram watched the gnolls break open the four crates, watched them ooh and ahh over the broken blades and old horseshoe nails, and, before he could stop himself, was shooting Greydon a questioning look.

"The Grimtail have no ironworks," Greydon said as he slid his arms into the sleeves of his leather coat, shrugging it up until the shoulders fell correctly. "No forges like your friend Glade." Aram didn't care for Greydon Thorne referring to Robb Glade as his "friend," but he let it pass this once as his father continued: "But they can hammer a nail or an axe blade or a knife tip into a war club and triple the damage they can do to their enemies. To these gnolls, those bits of iron are worth their weight in gold."

Aram raised an eyebrow. "So you're cheating them. Tricking

them into taking worthless refuse in exchange for . . ." Here, he paused, confused. In exchange for what? For boar jerky? For codfish jerky? It seemed to Aram that those forty packets were hardly worth more than the barrel of disgusting eggs.

"No one's cheating anyone," Greydon said, with more patience than Aram probably deserved. Absently, *Wavestrider*'s captain pulled the compass and chain out from under his shirt and let it fall against his chest. He said, "This is what I've been trying to teach you. It's *what* you trade to *whom*. One man's junk is another gnoll's treasure."

"And one gnoll's smoked meat?"

"Is treasure of a kind to the centaur, tauren, and quilboar of Flayers' Point."

"Quilboar eat boar jerky?"

"Some do, actually. But mostly they take the codfish."

Aram shook his head with something like admiration. "You'll make a fortune on these trades, won't you?"

Admiration not being one of Aramar's typical reactions to his father, Greydon grinned happily—soaking up every stingy morsel his son offered up. "A *small* fortune," the captain said with a shrug.

"So if all of this was so friendly and honest, why did you and Cackle have to fight?"

"Gnolls don't like humans. Probably because most humans don't like gnolls. Cackle couldn't trade with me in front of her clan until I demonstrated I was worthy of her respect."

"Then . . . it was all for show?"

"Yes and no. You have to see folks for who they are, Aram, not for who the old men of Lakeshire have taught you to *think* they are. Gnolls are a warrior race. A cantankerous warrior race, at that. Even the pups know the difference between a pantomime and a real battle. So we went at it. For real. But you'll notice there were no spurs, no barbs, no 'thorns' in either war club."

"Yeah, but they were still war clubs! You still could've been killed!"

"Don't tell me you care," Greydon said, still smiling.

Aram merely looked annoyed. "I don't want you dead, Greydon." Aram knew his father hated it when his son called him Greydon. "I just wanna go home."

Greydon sighed. "I know, son. But here is where you need to be right now." He patted his boy gently on the shoulder and moved to join the cackling Cackle.

Only then did Aram notice that Makasa was nearby, had seen—and probably heard—the whole exchange. Aram met her glare. Then she turned away, but just for a second, Aramar thought she almost looked sad.

They remained on the beach, celebrating with the gnolls all through the night. One-God and the rest of the crew descended with a keg of Thunder Ale and joined the party. Captain Thorne allowed one packet of boar jerky to be opened and shared with the crew and the gnolls—though with a curt nod to Mose Canton, the ship's quartermaster, Greydon made sure the other thirty-nine packets were safely stowed aboard ship.

Curious now to try this "treasure," Aram tracked the progress of Jonas Cobb, the ship's cook, who walked among the crew and gnolls, passing out samples. Old Cobb was certainly taking his time—and an oddly circuitous route among the crowd—offering up strips of jerky to the gnolls lurking at the treeline. Then Aram watched Cobb disappear into the forest. He was gone for a minute or three—while the party at large was focused on One-God's fairly rollicking distribution of ale—and Aram was just rising to express concern for the ancient cook, when Cobb's white head reappeared a dozen yards from where he had entered the woods. He continued his distributions, eventually reaching Aram.

Aram tried a strip of the jerky. It was so tough he thought he'd rip his jaw out trying to bite off a chunk. But once it was in his mouth, he had to admit it was spicy and flavorful, and the smallest bite—no matter how determinedly he chewed—lasted in his mouth for nearly half an hour. He could see its value now. Or taste and understand it, anyway.

While he chewed, he took out his sketchbook—a small leather-bound volume of formerly blank pages of parchment, which he kept wrapped in oilskin cloth in his back pocket. It had been a gift from his stepfather, Robb Glade, and it had cost the blacksmith a pretty penny. Easily two days' work, if not a full week's. It was Aram's most prized possession, in part because he loved drawing, loved it more than almost anything. But also because the gift was tangible proof that Robb believed in his stepson's talent. Sure, both his mother and stepfather had insisted Aram learn the blacksmith trade. A man needed to earn a living, after all. But Robb also saw the value in Aram having a way to express himself, and no one was more delighted than the smith when Aram filled the first page of the book with his sketch of the burly, smiling Master of the Forge.

Aram flipped through the pages. The early ones were all of Lakeshire, his home. There were a few sketches of the town, a few landscapes of the shores of Lake Everstill, and one of Robb's forge. There were a handful of pictures of animals, but animals were less inclined to sit still. Nevertheless, there were a couple horses, a mule, and a one-eyed tomcat, whose picture was, from necessity, finished from memory. And, of course, two or three sketches of Soot. But mostly the book was filled with people. His family featured heavily. In addition to his stepfather, there were three sketches of his mother and two each of his younger half-siblings, Robertson and Selya—plus a sketch of all of them together. There was even a self-portrait of Aram, done with the aid of a looking glass and hours of obsessive sketching and rubbing out and resketching until the parchment of that page was thinner than an eyelash—and even so, it was Aram's least favorite sketch in the book. To everyone who saw it, it was a mighty good likeness. But Aram *never* felt he caught his own true self.

Ceya, Robb, Robertson, Selya, and Soot

About a third of the way through the book, the subjects of the sketches shifted from Lakeshire to the *Wavestrider*, starting with one lengthwise portrait of the ship itself. She was a fine, solid trading vessel, a converted small frigate, old but yare— and meticulously maintained. Patched, yes, in multiple places, but the work was excellently done. She was a hundred feet long, had three masts, a crew of thirty, and *no cannon*—for, according to her captain, his trading partners must always feel assured that Greydon Thorne and his ship came in peace.

Her most unique feature, which merited a sketch of its own, was the strange mahogany figurehead affixed to the bow: a winged creature of unknown origin—neither male nor female— carved and polished into smooth, dark facets, depicting few curves, mostly angles. To be honest, Aram thought the figure-head ungainly and crude when compared to some of the beautifully honed elves and human women he had seen on other ships in Stormwind Harbor. *Wavestrider*'s figurehead was not original to the boat and had been carved four years ago by ship's carpenter Anselm Yewtree, who once told Aram it had been made to Captain Thorne's extremely precise specifica-tions. But if any member of the crew knew the figurehead's significance, none admitted to it. And Aram refused to ask his father, at times convinced it would give the man too much sat-isfaction, and, at other times, fearing he would deny his son an answer.

Aram's book also contained multiple sketches of One-God and more than a few of Duan Phen and at least one of nearly

every other member of the crew. Even an unfinished sketch of the captain himself, which Aram had been feeling pretty good about until his father noticed his son drawing him and offered to hold still and pose. Aramar Thorne had slapped the book shut immediately and stuffed it back in his pocket.

The only person aboard ship Aram hadn't sketched was—no surprise—ship's second mate Makasa Flintwill. Even now, as she saw him slip the coal pencil from his shirt pocket, she growled at him once again. "You better not be putting me in that blasted book."

He repeated what he always told her, every time she made this same implied threat. "I promise I won't sketch you unless you ask me to." This satisfied them both, as both knew she'd never ask, and Aram had no more interest in preserving the bane of his onboard existence for posterity than she had in being preserved.

Besides, Aram was much more interested in sketching the matriarch. And then the pierced male, whom the other gnolls called a brute. And then a small gnoll pup. For the young artist, sketching them meant understanding them. Getting inside their skin, experiencing their musculature, feeling the structure of their bones in his mind's eye, in his hand, and on the page. On first impression, Aram had thought Cackle a monster. But now, he knew she was just another animal. Like Soot or the one-eyed tomcat. Like Durgan One-God. Like Aramar Thorne.

Cackle noticed him sketching the pup. She approached and leaned in over the sketchbook. He was distracted by the dank

ARAM

Matriarch Cackle

musty scent of her fur—until she barked out a laugh and barked out at Greydon, "Your boy so useless!" Aram started to color—though whether with anger or embarrassment, he wasn't quite sure.

But still snickering, Cackle was soon drawn back to the page. She stared at the upside-down picture of the pup in Aram's book. She stared at the actual pup crouching at their feet. She stared at the sketch again.

Then she grunted once and came around behind Aram, leaning so far over the boy's shoulder, he could feel her hot breath on his cheek and smell each and every one of the twenty-eight eggs she had consumed from the barrel. Her sharp, sharp teeth could easily and at any second tear his ear off—at the very least—but he didn't flinch. He knew her better now. He held still, and she stared again at the drawing of the pup. The matriarch's breathing slowed noticeably. "Flip leaf," she whispered hoarsely.

Aram turned the page, revealing a pristine piece of parchment. But Cackle growled at him. "No, not new leaf. *Old* leaf." Aram nodded and turned the pages back.

Makasa watched all this with one hand on her cutlass. One-God started to make a joke, but Greydon—recognizing that something special was happening—put a hand on his first mate's shoulder, and the dwarf fell silent, though he was still smiling. Greydon nodded in much the same way Aram just had. Even the giggling gnolls had fallen silent, focused on the matriarch and the boy.

Aram turned to the sketch of the brute. She glanced up at the actual brute briefly but then coughed out a laugh that seemed to say *the gnoll* was a poor copy of Aram's picture. "Flip leaf," she said again. "Old leaf."

Aram turned the page back, and Cackle saw herself in charcoal. She sucked in air and held her breath for a silent minute.

Then she exhaled and straightened. She looked up at Aram's father.

"Good magic," was all she said to him, and Greydon nodded once more.

Again she leaned back over Aram's shoulder, and again she said, "Flip leaf."

Aram turned back a page to the unfinished picture of Greydon. Cackle's brow furrowed. "You not finish."

"No," he said.

"You finish. You finish your father."

"I—"

"No. You finish, boy." She moved away, shaking her head and muttering. "Boy must finish. Boy must finish. Or else bad magic."

Greydon Thorne

ARAM

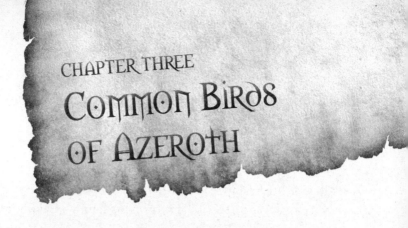

CHAPTER THREE
COMMON BIRDS
OF AZEROTH

"**B**last your hide, Aramar Thorne, *wake up!*"

Whap! Groan. Yank. Thud. Wince.

For the second morning in a row, Aramar started his day on the floor, rubbing his bruised forehead with one hand and his bruised behind with the other.

Makasa glared down at him. "Your father says it's time for your lesson. Get up and get on deck."

Most mornings, this was Aram's standing order, so—in spite of the second mate's aggressive sense of urgency—he felt slightly less of a need to rush than he had the morning before. He didn't dawdle, but he took the time to dress, wash his face, and brush his teeth. Still, minutes later, he was topside, his cutlass on his belt. He spotted the captain at the helm, one hand gently resting on the wheel. The other hand lifted up the compass on the chain around his neck. Greydon glanced down at it and looked . . . *disappointed?* He let the device drop against his chest and stared out across the Veiled Sea.

The *Wavestrider* was sailing south, skirting the western shore of Kalimdor. This was pretty much all Aram understood of their current location, beyond the salient fact that *wherever* they were, it was impossibly far from his family's Lakeshire cottage in the Eastern Kingdoms on the complete opposite side of the world.

Aram turned away from his father. There was a forest on shore off the port bow. The trees reminded him of home, and Aram wondered wistfully if the forest had a name.

As if reading the boy's mind, Durgan One-God said, "Locals call it the Last Forest. The Last Forest o' Desolace. An' maybe it was, once upon a time. It's home, as ye know, tae the Grimtail gnolls, but also tae the tauren of Ol' Ironhoof, some scattered orcs, trolls, and goblins, an' a handful o' nomadic quilboar tribes. Not tae mention a few other random beasties."

"Children of the One True God?" Aram teased.

One-God laughed, slapped Aram on the back, and said, "No one ever accused Eonar the Life-Binder o' lackin' imagination."

Just of lacking compassion, Aram thought, or sanity. How, he wondered, could a single "god" make such a hash of the world—with Horde fighting Alliance and with undead corpses like the Forsaken walking the earth, among other nightmares lurking along the edges of his rather tranquil Lakeshire upbringing?

No, Robb Glade was right when he used to say, "Azeroth was clearly shaped by a whole mess of titans and spirits, each with his or her own agenda, desires, and ass-backery." But Aram spoke none of this now. He liked One-God, despite the dwarf's odd faith in a single deity—a faith even One-God admitted no one else had ever shared. Why Durgan had chosen Eonar, while disavowing the rest of the titans, was a complete mystery to Aram—just as the idea of a seagoing dwarf who could barely swim was a mystery to Aram. But there was something about the dwarf's odd quirks that made him more endearing, and Aram had no desire to seriously challenge the first mate's beliefs and risk driving a wedge between them.

One-God wrapped a beefy arm around Aram's shoulder and spoke to him in a low—almost conspiratorial—tone. "See, the Life-Binder loves variety. Must be why She made me stout and strong . . . and you so blasted puny." He shook with laughter that built to a roar.

Aram rolled his eyes—then quickly glanced around in case Makasa might have seen him do it. And there she was, glaring, boiling. By the gods, Flintwill was exhausting. And everywhere. She was everywhere. Ubiquitous. Omnipresent. Probably omniscient and omnipotent, too. Maybe Makasa Flintwill *was* the One God. She certainly behaved as if she were. "Omni-annoying," Aram muttered under his breath, too softly for anyone else to hear. But Makasa's expression darkened further, and Aram swallowed hard.

Durgan One-God

ARAM

One-God's outburst had attracted attention across the deck, including that of Captain Thorne. He called out to Aram, "Get my cutlass from my cabin, son, and we'll start your lesson."

Aram turned and marched off, deeply resenting his father's command. In one sentence, Greydon had managed to pack in nearly everything Aram hated about his current situation. He was aboard *Wavestrider* against his will. Pressed into service like a galley slave at Captain Thorne's beck and call, without even enjoying the benefits—the camaraderie—of being a true member of the crew! Technically, his role was that of cabin boy. But Greydon Thorne wasn't the type of man to need or want a personal servant or valet, and Aram would hardly have passed muster in that position on any other vessel. Yes, he did odd jobs here and there—usually whatever Makasa Flintwill demanded of him. But his lack of function on a ship where function defined the perception of others couldn't possibly endear him to the rest of the crew.

No, Aramar Thorne's *true* role was that of "the captain's son," set apart from the other men and women aboard ship. No one—except Makasa—actually seemed to dislike him. But only One-God was open with him and free. The rest were, at best, guarded. *Of course, they'd never criticize the captain in front of his only son.* And the one time Aram himself had attempted to criticize Greydon Thorne, they had fallen silent fast. He was sure they thought he was trying to trap them. (It never crossed his mind they might love, admire, and respect the man.)

And just in case that wasn't enough, Aram was also subject to Greydon Thorne's own personal course of study: endless lessons in swordplay—interspersed with recitations and quizzing on the history of Azeroth, its races and cultures, even its flora and fauna—all held on deck with Aram's many shortcomings on display to every member of the crew, from Duan Phen in the crow's nest down to Old Cobb in the galley.

Aram entered the captain's cabin—slamming the door shut behind him—before realizing he wasn't there alone. Jonas Cobb was standing over Greydon Thorne's desk, having apparently collected a tray of dirty breakfast dishes, and Aram's violent entrance had practically made the old codger jump out of his skin. Cobb covered his embarrassment with a healthy dose of curmudgeon: "Whatcha doin', slammin' your way in here? That how they teach ya to be enterin' an *officer's* room in the sticks?!" And so on. The tirade continued for some time. Ultimately, Cobb departed the cabin, carrying the tray and a grudge against "brainless boys with no manners and no proper upbringin'."

Greydon's cutlass was in plain sight, hanging on a bulkhead, but Aram was in no hurry to return with it, so he allowed his eyes to wander about the room.

The captain's cabin was much like the captain's hold: full of worthless junk. Only *this* junk was on display. Despite the satisfaction it would probably give his father, Aram found himself trying to see these "treasures" the way Greydon would.

There was a crude clay model of some ancient city. All kinds of battered weapons, including the broken war club. Maps and charts with Greydon's notations and calculations on the desk. A large pewter beer stein full of dice. In one corner, deck upon deck of cards, each separately wrapped with twine. A carved wooden dragon. An ivory kraken. A small iron stallion, rearing up on its hind legs. A wooden crate full of rocks. No, not rocks. Something in the crate caught the light, and Aram knelt to investigate. One of the "rocks" was split in half, revealing it to be a polished geode of sparkling white crystal. Other geodes of blue, orange, and red held their own subtle beauty. He briefly thought about smashing open one more stone to see what it held inside. He stood and stepped away to remove the temptation.

A built-in bookshelf lined one wall. One book, larger than the rest, stuck out several inches. Aram glanced over his shoulder, half expecting Flintwill to be there watching him. When he found the room otherwise uninhabited, he pulled the book off the shelf and flipped through it, finding page after page of handmade drawings of common birds: wrens and sparrows, grackles and jays. Aram marveled. Someone had taken the time to sketch and even color each winged creature in meticulous detail. There were also notations about the birds' habitats and habits under each drawing. "This saltspray gull dives for fish off the coastlines of Kalimdor"; "that raptor nests in the Redridge Mountains," etc. The skills of the artist—someone named Charnas of Gadgetzan, according to the frontispiece—made him envious, and the fact that this Charnas had traveled all over the world to find all these birds made Aram, perhaps for the first time, consider his current journey as an opportunity rather than a punishment.

He could have spent hours going through the large tome, studying the linework, even memorizing its contents, but he was expected on deck. He started to put the book away, when a loose piece of parchment fell from its pages. He tried to catch it, as the page fluttered to the ground. But he missed.

He stooped to pick it up. It was another picture of a bird— not elegant like Charnas's bound images—but crude, a child's drawing. And not just any child. This was the work of a specific child: Aramar Thorne, age six. Seconds earlier, he could never have summoned the memory, but the parchment in his hand brought it all back in a rush . . .

Aram on the rug by the fire, drawing with charcoal and handing that drawing to his father.

"It's a bird," the boy had said.

"I can see that," Greydon had replied. "It's a fine bird."

"It's for your birthday."

"But it's not my birthday. It's yours. Or at least it will be tomorrow."

"No, my BIRTH-day is tomorrow. Your BIRD-day is today!" And Aram had laughed, finding this statement uproariously funny—to Greydon's and Ceya's mild amusement. But the more the child laughed, the funnier his parents found his joke. Soon they

were all rolling on the hearthrug with Aram's contagious laughter. (Some tickling may also have been involved.)

Aram was stunned. Greydon Thorne had kept the picture. This awful and worthless little drawing was a treasure Greydon had elevated to the level of Charnas of Gadgetzan by preserving it in that master's book.

Carefully, Aram placed it between the book's pages and returned the volume to its place on the shelf. Then he grabbed his father's cutlass off the wall and rushed out to join him.

The day's instruction started off well enough.

Warmed by the mere fact that Greydon had kept his childhood drawing, Aramar was more open than usual to his father's teaching. They began, of course, by crossing swords. Though Aram had, over the last six months, shown little interest in the cutlass, he had—almost despite himself—demonstrated some aptitude. So today, with a new willingness to learn, he countered or parried Greydon's first five thrusts. And then his next five. And his next.

The crew began to take notice. Makasa's scowl seemed more automatic and less pointed. Helmsman Thom Frakes nodded approvingly. Six or seven deckhands—Cassius Meeks, Desamir Ferrar, Mary Brown, Schuyler Li, the gnome Cog Burnwick, and others—gathered round to watch (whereas usually they were so embarrassed by Aram's performance, they made a less than subtle effort to turn away). One-God laughed, warning that his captain "looked tae be in danger o' workin' up a sweat." Pleasantly surprised by how well he was doing, Aram wondered—even hoped—that perhaps Duan Phen might be watching him from her perch in the crow's nest above.

As the sparring continued, Greydon began the day's lesson, starting with the gnolls: "They're a warlike people," the captain said, "prone to fighting, even among themselves. I've seen two gnolls pull out axes with serious intent over the question of which one's shadow is longest."

"Their shadows? But that's . . ."

"Exactly. So is there any point in trying to work with them, trade with them, befriend them? Perhaps it would be best to simply exterminate the lot of them. Put them down like dogs. I mean, after all, to us, they look and even behave like drooling, foaming packs of rabid mongrel curs."

"Wait, wait . . . ," Aram said while parrying another blow—this time with a bit less grace and ease. Aram knew where this was going, of course. This wasn't the first race of creatures his father had brought up using this approach. Greydon Thorne's point was always, *always* that there was something worthwhile—something to treasure—in every species. The trouble for Aram was trying to find the answer while simultaneously keeping his sword up. Aram wasn't good enough with a cutlass to allow himself to get distracted.

"Wait?" queried Greydon. "Why? What do gnolls have to offer us?"

Aram exhaled. His mouth was dry. But he managed to block another attack and squeak out, "Dogs are loyal."

Greydon—who was about to lunge—hesitated, a smile already tugging up the corners of his mouth. "Excuse me?" he said.

Aram heard the implicit praise in Greydon's change of tone and grew more confident. "You called them dogs, mongrels, curs. But our dog, Soot, was very loyal. Robb said Soot'd give his life rather than let anyone hurt the family."

"Meaning?"

"Meaning if we treated the gnolls like family, showed *our-selves* worthy, we might earn their loyalty . . ."

"And why would we ever want that?"

" 'Gnolls are a warlike people,' " Aram quoted. "So wouldn't we rather have those fighting skills on our side?"

One-God clapped his hands and shouted, "That's it!" Greydon shot his first mate an exasperated look, and One-God laughed, held up his hands, and said, "Sorry, sorry."

Still, it was clear Greydon was pleased, too.

Aram knew it and continued, "Besides, they have other positive qualities. They like to laugh almost as much as One-God—"

A laughing One-God couldn't resist piping in with, "Now, now, let's nae get carried away."

Both Thornes ignored him. "What else?" Greydon asked.

"Well," said Aram as he parried once, twice, and again. "They can appreciate art. At least the matriarch could. Any species that sees the value in something so, so . . ." He struggled to find the right word.

"Useless!" shouted Thom.

"Pointless!" shouted One-God.

"Fascinating!" called out Duan Phen from the rigging.

In spontaneous unison, nearly the entire crew sighed a mock "OOOOOOO" over the young female sailor's "fascination" with their captain's son.

Aram's cheeks blushed red, but he was not displeased. Duan Phen was petite and slim and almost boyish. But throughout the voyage, she had smiled at him now and then and had seemed pleased the time he showed her the sketches he had drawn of her from a distance. Feeling slightly triumphant at having "fascinated" her, Aram parried again and said, "Enriching. Any species that sees the value in something so enriching can't be all bad."

"Plus they make great jerky," Desamir Ferrar said, and everyone shouted their agreement.

Greydon was pleased. This was their best training session yet. He felt as if he and Aram had turned a corner—and, truth be told, Aram was starting to feel the same way.

So, of course, it couldn't last.

Greydon praised his son for his analysis and for his defensive skills. He instructed the boy to go on the offensive occasionally and then became more aggressive himself.

DUAN PHEN

ARAM

Aram kept up at first—until the quizzing on past lectures started: *"Which goblin cartel joined the Horde after the Cataclysm?" "In what season do the giant turtles of the Veiled Sea return to shore to lay their eggs?" "What's the cause of the ongoing strife between centaur and tauren?" "How do you tell the difference between the clinging vine and the blueroot vine?" "What is the most common food source of the sea otter?"*

The captain was relentless, unintentionally exposing gaps in his son's knowledge and, worse, exposing Aram's complete inability to think and fight at the same time.

"How do gnolls initiate trade with members of another species?" Greydon thought he was tossing his son an easy one: something that would be fresh in the boy's mind.

And, in fact, Aram knew the answer. But as he struggled to find the right words, his father saw an opening and slapped the boy's cheek with the flat of his sword. Aram turned scarlet and attacked recklessly. The captain easily parried his son's thrust, swung around, and slapped his nether-cheeks.

Now, Aramar's face shone an angry crimson. Blindly, he swung his cutlass around. It was a blow that had it landed could not have helped but slice a second smile into Greydon Thorne's throat. But the captain leaned away and the blade whistled harmlessly through the air. "Careful," Greydon said, seeing his son was losing control.

"Careful?" Aram growled. "How can I be careful when you're determined to shame me?!" (And with that, Makasa's scowl became pointed. Helmsman Thom Frakes shook his head sadly. Six or seven deckhands—Cassius Meeks, Desamir Ferrar, Mary Brown, Schuyler Li, the gnome Cog Burnwick, and others—made a less than subtle effort to turn away. Duan Phen retreated to the crow's nest. And One-God stopped laughing.)

"That's not what this is about," Greydon said, putting up his sword. "You need to be able to overcome distractions during a fight. Do you want me to coddle you?"

"So if I'm not up to the level *you* think I should have achieved by now, then my choices are humiliation or coddling?"

"No, it's—"

"Maybe the problem is I started training too late in life. Maybe twelve's just too old. Maybe you should have begun giving me this gift of your endless knowledge *when I turned six.*"

Greydon swallowed hard. His sword arm sank slowly. If Aram's goal was to cut him to the quick, he could hardly have done a better job with his cutlass.

"Son, you know there's nothing I—"

"That's enough for today, don't you think?"

"Yes," Greydon said hoarsely.

Aram turned on his heel and stalked away. He was still thinking of the drawing of that bird. Only now he saw it in another light. Not the warm firelight of the night *before* his sixth birthday. But the cold light of day on the morning of . . .

The boy woke, blinking his eyes a few times against the light— and then, in an instant, recalled what day it was.

Full of excitement, he leapt from his bed—practically shot out of it like a crossbow bolt—and ran to the hearth. There was no fire burning, which was strange for that time of year. But stranger still was the noise coming from outside. Cautiously, he ventured out in his nightclothes to investigate. His mother was sitting on the cold, wet turf outside, and the strange noise came from her. She was crying, sobbing. It was his birthday, and Aram's mother was crying.

Aram didn't know what to do. Even after Ceya had wrapped her arms around her son and drawn him in close, all he could think to do was pull away to find his father so that Greydon could help Aram's mother stop crying . . .

But that was something Greydon Thorne would never do. Eventually, Ceya had managed to explain that Greydon was gone, had left, had packed a rucksack and walked out the door to return to a seafaring life. Refusing to believe his mother, Aram was positive his father must have been taken, stolen away from Lakeshire by orcs or trolls or ogres. A few months later, an older boy from south of the village repeated rumors of murlocs living on the far side of the lake. Having never seen a murloc, Aram imagined his father at the mercy of devious monsters with razor-sharp teeth and claws, slick, oily green skin, and fetid breath. The boy spent days and days searching for the creatures' lair, though he never saw a single murloc, let alone any sign that his father was a prisoner somewhere, anywhere. It probably took two or three *years* before Aram was truly willing to believe that his father had actually left of his own accord, that Greydon Thorne had actually abandoned his wife and son—*on his son's sixth birthday*—by choice.

But what was once impossible to believe was now impossible to forget—let alone forgive. That abandonment loomed like a wall between father and son, and both of them knew it.

In his cabin, the captain of the *Wavestrider* hung his cutlass up on the wall. Then he sat down heavily in the chair behind his desk. He glanced at the charts in front of him and the course they plotted—then angrily shoved them all out of the way onto the floor. With a sense of desperation, he lifted up the compass that hung on the chain around his neck. Greydon gazed down at it and was once again disappointed. He let the device drop against his chest and stared into his empty hands.

CHAPTER FIVE
FLAYERS' POINT

"*Land ho!*"

To avoid a violent storm along the shore, *Wavestrider* had sailed into only slightly calmer waters farther out to sea, out of sight of Desolace and western Kalimdor. It had delayed their arrival at Flayers' Point by two days. And it had left Aramar Thorne more seasick than homesick for the first time in months. (When he first came aboard, the need to hang his head over the railing was a daily occurrence. But after a few weeks of acclimation, it had rarely troubled him until now.) The ship had swung around the storm and raced it to port.

So Duan Phen's cry from above made his heart soar—and not just because he liked the sound of her voice. He ran to the rail, while Thom Frakes—under Captain Thorne's supervision—guided *Wavestrider* into the harbor.

Docking beside one other small, lonely trade ship, the crew weighed anchor and quickly tied *Wavestrider* off. From the rail, Aram heard the clomping of heavy steps on the pier below. He turned in time to see the approach of muscle and fur, of hoof, snout, and horn. It took a second or two to see it as more than an upright bull, but of course it could only be a tauren. A large tauren male. "The harbormaster," whispered a voice by his ear. It was Greydon, who had silently taken a place at the rail beside the startled Aram. It took another second or two for the boy to connect his father's words with the creature.

Then the tauren harbormaster greeted the boat and its first mate with a snorting laugh and a deep growl. "One-God, you blasphemous saltbeard! Thought I warned you never to show your face here again!"

"Ye were serious?" a smiling One-God called from above, as deckhands extended the gangway.

"At the time!"

"It's my fault, Ridgewalker!" shouted Greydon, startling the somewhat mesmerized Aram again. "It's not that he's useful, but he's so blasted entertaining!"

Ridgewalker snorted his laughter and waved a thick arm. "Come ashore then! I may kill him later, but he'll give us a laugh or two first!"

"Stay close," Greydon whispered to his son. Aram, belatedly remembering he was still in an unforgiving mood, bristled.

"You want to remain aboard?" his father asked.

Reluctantly, Aram shook his head.

"Then stay close."

Aram hesitated—then nodded, following a few steps behind his father. Before descending, Greydon paused to confer with his three officers: "That storm could still make landfall, so I want to be gone by daybreak. Organize shore leave in shifts, but I want at least one officer aboard at all times."

Makasa, already heavily armed, scowled. "Captain, one of us should be *at your side* at all times."

Aram resisted the temptation to roll his eyes at Makasa's intensity but was caught off guard when One-God agreed. "She's right, Captain. They dinna call it *Slayers'* Point in jest. I'll stay aboard f'now, but ye keep Flintwill close."

The ship's third mate, Silent Joe Barker—a man of Gilneas, whom Aram knew to be afflicted with the curse of the worgen—crossed his arms as if the matter was decided and closed.

Greydon Thorne frowned—and looked as if *he* was resisting the temptation to roll his eyes, too. Gripping his cutlass, he was about to make it perfectly clear he required no minder. But eventually he nodded. It seemed this was a day for the Thorne men to compromise.

So Captain Thorne, flanked by Makasa and Aram, descended, followed by Meeks, Ferrar, Ribierra the boatswain, and Canton the quartermaster, carrying pallets of the gnoll jerky.

On the dock, Greydon touched his chest and then his forehead with his right hand, as a sign of respect to Harbormaster Ridgewalker. The tauren followed suit, then raised one bushy eyebrow, asking, "No One-God?"

Greydon shrugged. "Thought I'd leave him aboard for a little while. Might save his life for a few more hours, at least."

Ridgewalker chuckled, or at least Aram assumed that the tauren's double-snort was the equivalent of a chuckle. The harbormaster said, "Probably wise." He looked up at the *Wavestrider.* "Still sailing this wreck of a ship, I see," he said.

Resting his hand on the guard of his cutlass, Greydon smiled dangerously and said, "Don't you talk about my lady that way, Ridgewalker. Besides, you know better. She may have a few blemishes, but she's the finest ship on the water."

"She inspires loyalty; I'll say that much for the old girl." Ridgewalker's words were conciliatory, but he was no longer smiling and didn't much care for Captain Thorne's hand being on his weapon, whether in jest or not. Then he nodded toward the crewmen and their pallets. "What you selling today, Thorne?"

"Gnoll jerky."

"Smoked gnoll? Hmm. I'll have to try me some of that."

Aram's eyes bounced back and forth between Ridgewalker and his father, as the boy tried to determine if the tauren was joking. A smile crept onto Greydon's lips. He said, "Maybe some other time. This is gnoll-*made* boar and codfish jerky."

The tauren shrugged off his (perhaps feigned) disappointment with a sigh and stepped aside to allow the small contingent to pass.

"Was he kidding?" Aram whispered.

Greydon's eyebrows waggled. "I sincerely hope so."

"But you're not sure."

"But I'm not sure."

As they walked along the dock, Aram glanced back to see Old Cobb lead the first leave shift off *Wavestrider*. Most, including Li and Brown, headed for what passed for an inn right on the wharf—really just a wooden lean-to with three canvas "walls." But Cobb himself broke off, his white head disappearing into the crowd. Aram wondered where the old cook was going, then wondered when Duan Phen would get her leave—and whether he could find a way to ditch his father in order to "coincidentally" run across her ashore. This daydream was rapidly becoming more and more elaborate, until they approached the market, the sights, sounds, and smells of which commanded his immediate attention.

Flayers' Point was an old skinning camp that had evolved into a busy but isolated trading post for the locals of Desolace and the rare trader who knew enough to come ashore—despite the fact that the destination wasn't on any map. Aram's twelve-year-old eyes opened wide with wonder at every sight they drank in. Here, some humans and a few dwarves from the one other ship milled about. Three green, pointy-eared goblins ran past his waistline, skittering through the crowd like children, but bickering among themselves (in what he assumed was the goblin tongue) like cantankerous old men. A single female elf, tall and fundamentally graceful, glided past them, taking Aram's breath away and momentarily pushing all thoughts of Duan Phen from his head. Her light gray eyes signaled she was a high elf—a fact Aram only knew due to his father's training, which was in turn a fact he was reluctant to admit to himself.

Mostly, however, the marketplace was filled with tauren, quilboar, and the occasional centaur. Excepting Ridgewalker, it was the first time Aram had seen any member of these races in person, let alone up close. Initially, all seemed brutish and dangerous—if not downright insane—but though his father never spoke a word to him, Aram could hear Greydon's voice in his mind, reminding him to look closer.

The centaur were vaguely human-shaped from the waist up and all wild horse from the waist down, with bony protrusions and growths marring every visage. They took up the most space, and there were more than a few times Aram feared for the survival of his toes. But the four-legged creatures had a muscular grace and a keen awareness of their massive bodies. Aram watched a tremendous male with body paint of henna and thick dried mud navigate the thin aisle between one stall piled high with clay pots and another with tomatoes stacked in delicate pyramids. Not one pot was brushed. Not one tomato bruised.

There were tauren everywhere, but what struck Aram in the moment was how different they all were from one another. In his imagination, the bull-men had all been one and the same creature. But there was so much variation: horn size and shape, fur color and length, snout thickness and nostril width, even basic height and weight. No, this was not a race of identical Ridgewalkers. No two tauren were any more alike than Old

Cobb was like Makasa. Aram knew this observation should have been obvious, but it was a revelation.

Some of the tauren were using horned kodo beasts as pack animals. And again, Aram was forced to admit to himself that he only recognized the beasts as kodos thanks to his father's training, which also taught him that even the largest of these kodos were juveniles, as a full-grown adult war-mount would take up as much space as two or three centaur abreast.

Fierce creatures all, to Aram the fiercest seemed to be the quilboar. Certainly, the boar-men had the most intimidating visages, all snout and tusk. And by far they made the most noise. Grumbling and grunting constantly in low guttural tones as they marched past. Bellowing if they didn't like the price of an axe. Belching and farting like it was their birthright. Occasionally, squealing like pigs for no apparent reason at all. But even these monsters required a second look. Most had decorated their tusks with war paint in intricate patterns. One had even used gold filigree. Others laughed deeply between belches, making their protruding bellies rumble and bounce above their belts or loincloths in a way that made anyone within earshot grin, Aram not excepted.

Friendly with everyone and always offering up a ready smile, Greydon nevertheless remained constantly on alert. (Makasa did the same—minus the smile.) For as exotic and fascinating as it all was, one still had to stay on one's guard. There was no love lost between the three species. They shouted and cursed at one another, and like clockwork erupted into brawls every five minutes. Once, Greydon seized hold of Aram's arm and tugged him violently left—saving the boy from being flattened when the uppercut of a red-furred tauren lifted a coal-black quilboar off his feet and sent him crashing down on his back in the mud exactly where Aram had been standing.

Aram tried to say thank you, but no sound came out of his mouth. His father didn't seem to mind or notice. (Though Aram was sure Makasa's scowl indicated she minded on her captain's behalf.) Aram began studying his father, began watching Greydon Thorne work the crowd, greeting everyone as individuals—and many by name—even though a solid majority barely spoke the Common tongue.

Greydon effortlessly understood every language spoken. He even responded with a few words and phrases in Taur-ahe. And he knew all the forms. As he had with Ridgewalker, Greydon gestured to his heart and head for each tauren. But to the centaur they encountered, he slapped a fist hard against his chest, and to the quilboar he snorted loudly. These were the traditional greetings of the various peoples of this region, which—once again—Aram knew from his father's lessons on the deck of the *Wavestrider.* In fact, Aram was surprised by how *much* he knew, how much he had absorbed despite the fact that he had consistently been such an unwilling scholar.

As usual, his admiration for the clever and learned captain battled his disdain for the father who had abandoned his family—with no clear resolution to this inner conflict in sight.

Most of the stalls were manned by females, tauren or quil-boar. Greydon raised a hand to stop his crewmen in front of a double-size covered booth where a female tauren—seemingly twice as wide as she was tall and with fur that ranged from an earthy red down by her shanks to something almost akin to the color of blood near her horns—haggled with an ancient gray centaur male.

"No," she said in a low rumble. "Not enough."

"Always enough before," replied the affronted centaur. He had two asymmetrical bony growths emerging from his fore-head and left cheek.

"Before over. Not enough now."

Neither held out any goods or coin that Aram could see. In fact, as Aram glanced over the tauren's wide stall, he saw no goods visible anywhere.

The centaur backed up a few steps—then advanced the same distance. He reared slightly on his hind legs and stamped down with his forehooves, saying, "Before same as now. Enough always enough."

"Three more rawhide shields make enough enough."

He seemed taken aback. Then he stroked his long gray beard.

As if in response, she stroked her short red beard and repeated, "Three more would make enough enough."

He continued stroking his long gray beard in silence.

Finally, he slapped his left fist against his right pectoral.

She responded by touching her ample chest and ample forehead.

He turned and departed. Nothing else—not words, not shields, not gold, not a single copper—was exchanged.

Greydon stepped forward then and made his own double gesture of respect. "Lady Bloodhorn," he said.

Can a tauren blush? Though such a thing was never covered in his lessons, Aram began to think it possible, as the huge creature became practically coquettish before the smile of Captain Greydon Thorne. She actually giggled as she waved off his compliment, saying, "Calling Bloodhorn a lady. Such a bale-shoveler you are, Captain."

He laughed a snorting, taurenesque laugh. "Bale-shoveler? You know how to wound me, you do."

She snorted back. Then, placing her hands on the stall, she leaned forward and whispered, "Whatcha bring me, Captain Shoveler?"

"Gnoll jerky," he whispered back. "Nineteen packets boar. Twenty codfish."

She licked her lips and stroked her short beard. "Whatcha lookin' for?" she asked.

He leaned in again and whispered, "I don't suppose you have what I'm *really* looking for."

"Whadda ya think?" she replied.

Aram watched his father step back and—for some reason—check his compass. As usual, his expression quickly turned to disappointment. And as usual, that expression quickly vanished from his face.

"No," he said.

"No," she confirmed. "What's yer second choice, man?"

"Nineteen gold coins, twenty silver . . ." He grinned. "And three rawhide shields."

Her eyes opened very wide. Then she leaned her head back and laughed loudly. But her mirth didn't last. She leaned forward again and whispered, "Whatsa saltbeard gonna do with rawhide shields?"

"What's a lady to do with that much jerky? Eat it?"

"Sell it!" she roared, laughing again.

"Exactly," he said with a smile. "Sell or trade. That's the game, milady. Do we have a deal?"

"Deal," she said, touching heart and head to seal the deal.

"Deal," he confirmed with the same.

Aram stepped aside to allow the men forward with the pallets. But Greydon departed without another word, Makasa at his arm. The men followed, taking the pallets with them. Aram had to run to catch up.

A light rain began to fall. Greydon glanced upward and frowned, and Aram knew just enough of sailing to realize his father was worried the shower was a harbinger of the storm.

Their procession finally stopped beneath a high pavilion, where the races mingled and conversed around low wooden tables. Greydon took a packet each of boar and cod and opened them on a table. He turned to Aram and said, "Get comfortable. We'll be here awhile."

Humans, goblins, dwarves, centaur, tauren, and quilboar stopped by the table to sample the jerky. And, in fact, one gnoll's smoked meat was a treasure of a kind to the centaur, tauren, and quilboar of Flayers' Point. Some of them responded with near rapture at the taste. *And do quilboar eat boar jerky?* Some do, actually. But, as foretold, mostly they take the codfish.

No coin was exchanged, and—with the exception of one gray-blue quilboar, who tried to sneak another strip of cod and got a poke in the ribs from Makasa's harpoon for his trouble— no individual took more than one piece each.

By this time, Aram had taken out his sketchbook and pencil and was sketching their customers as quickly as he could. It helped that the jerky was so blasted chewy. Those sampling tended to linger as they gnashed, making them wonderful subjects for his art. He had drawn three different centaur, one dwarf, two quilboar, and two tauren before Makasa even thought to growl, "You better not be putting me in that blasted book."

"I promise I won't sketch you unless you ask me to," he replied mechanically. He was trying to draw the high elf from memory but was far from satisfied with the result.

Leaving the sketch unfinished, he turned the page and started sketching the muddy black quilboar who was currently chewing his way through a strip of cod. He tried to capture the way the creature's dark fur lay across his chest, the woven ochre lines drawn onto his tusks, the burly musculature of his shoulders. By the time the quilboar had finished and moved off, Aram was quite pleased with the result. Drawing from memory was never as satisfying to Aramar Thorne as having his subject right in front of him.

When the quilboar left, Aram glanced up to find a new subject. He spotted Old Cobb a dozen yards off, talking in the rain with some man. They were too far away for Aram to hear what they were saying, and the man—who had his back to the pavilion—was wearing a hooded cloak that hid everything about him beyond his broad-shouldered build and six feet in height. Aram, vaguely curious, watched Cobb and the man shake hands—the man wore leather gloves—and he thought he saw something glint in the cook's fist right after. The man then slipped away into the crowd and out of sight, as Jonas Cobb approached.

"How's biznus, Cap'n?" said Cobb in a tone more cheerful than Aram had ever heard the old man use before.

"We don't talk business here," Greydon said. "But I'm not complaining."

Second Mate Flintwill spoke sternly. "Would have thought to find you in a tavern by this time, Cobb. Your leave shift must be almost over."

"Heading for a little nip now, girl." He held up a silver coin. "Won this at cards, and it's burnin' a hole in m'pocket. See you all aboard ship." Cobb actually did a little dance in place, winked at Aram, and left without another word.

The boatswain, Johnson Ribierra, grumbled, "I'm guessing he had a little nip or twelve while he was at the Hearthstone board. You ever see that codger skip a jig like that before?"

Canton, Meeks, and Ferrar all stated they hadn't.

Aram wondered about that coin. It seemed to him that Cobb had gotten it from the hooded man, though perhaps the man had lost it to Cobb gambling and was only now paying his debt. Still, Aram was on the verge of mentioning what he'd seen to Makasa when Greydon sat down beside him, asking, "Do you understand?"

Aram turned toward his father. Greydon waved an arm to include their table, the pavilion, and by extension the whole trading post and their part in it.

Aram nodded hesitantly. "I think so. They sample our wares here and go to Bloodhorn to place their orders. Not sure where or when the money gets exchanged, though. And I don't understand why the whole thing's made to be so complicated."

"Because Bloodhorn is no peddler or mere trader. She's a . . . facilitator, a level above the rest."

"Then why the double-size booth in the marketplace? What's the point of a big empty stall?"

"You tell me."

"Uh . . . bigger's better? It signals her importance?"

Greydon nodded. "And why no goods to show?"

Aram thought about this one. "Because her stock in trade . . . is trade itself."

"Exactly. Good."

Aram smiled, pleased by the praise. Then he remembered who was offering it and his expression darkened. He lowered his head.

Greydon noticed and sighed. "There were reasons," he said.

Aram's eyes darted up. They both knew what he was talking about, though Greydon had never addressed leaving his family before, and Aram had always been too stubborn to demand answers. "What reasons?" Aram now asked, not wanting excuses.

"Not now. Not here. But I promise I'll tell you everything soon."

Their eyes met, Aram's pleading for an explanation; Greydon's, for patience.

"Soon," Greydon repeated. "You have my word."

Aram thought about this for a few moments. Then he nodded. In unison, both Thornes breathed spontaneous and identical sighs of relief. It made Aram smile, and Greydon ruffled his boy's hair and moved off to offer a roan centaur some jerky.

Aram knew nothing had really changed. "Soon" could mean anything, of course. But Aram's one nod seemed to release six months' worth of tension between them, and Aram felt a sudden sympathy for his father. For the first time since he was eight or nine years old, Aramar Thorne felt prepared to offer Greydon Thorne the benefit of the doubt. Maybe there were reasons. Honestly, they didn't even have to be great reasons. Certainly, they *couldn't* be very good reasons in hindsight. But if Greydon could explain why he *thought* he had needed to leave Aram and Ceya, then that might be enough. Under his breath, Aram whispered, "A halfway decent explanation plus three rawhide shields make enough enough." He smiled to himself and flipped back a few pages in his sketchbook to finish the drawing of his father. It turned out quite well.

Good magic.

CHAPTER SIX
THE WHISPER-MAN

Never in his life had Aram done so many sketches in one sitting. Night had fallen; torches had been lit, and his hand was starting to tire and cramp, but there was always some new fascinating subject stopping by the pavilion to sample *Wavestrider*'s—or perhaps he should say Lady Bloodhorn's— wares.

Even Bloodhorn herself had come, and Aram was trying desperately to finish his sketch of her before she departed. She was chewing on a strip of boar jerky and, with her mouth full, laughed her snorting laugh, claiming it "tasted like quilboar."

Then she leaned toward Greydon and whispered, "These packets are almost spent. Less jerky reduces price."

He smiled and shook his head. "Deal was made. These are your samples I'm passing out."

Lady Bloodhorn

ARAM

She laughed loudly, spitting tiny bits of jerky everywhere. "Had to try!"

"Of course you did, milady."

She practically twittered then, hiding her eyes behind one massive hand and punching him with no little force in the shoulder with the other. He grunted painfully, but maintained his smile.

Then she departed, but two large male tauren stepped up in her wake. The first slipped coins of gold and silver into Greydon's hand. The second held three immense rawhide shields, which Meeks, Ribierra, and Canton took possession of at a nod from their captain.

The two tauren then piled one pallet atop the other and effortlessly walked off with them. All that remained were the two open packets on the table. Greydon carefully counted out seven strips of boar jerky and distributed one each to Meeks, Ferrar, Ribierra, Canton, Flintwill, Aram, and himself.

Absently, the captain tore a chunk off with his teeth. The rain was falling in earnest now and leaking through the over-saturated cloth of the pavilion tent. A drop fell, spoiling a corner of Aram's sketch of Bloodhorn. Aram attempted to dry it without smearing the page, then closed the book, wrapped it, and pocketed it.

Greydon stuffed a wad of half-chewed jerky into his cheek and said, "You men, see those shields into the hold. Then you can take a few hours' shore leave. But be back aboard before sunrise. The storm's coming in, and we'll want to be gone before it arrives."

A chorus of "Aye, Aye, Captain" followed, and the four men practically raced off into the night.

"Might I sample your wares, good mariners?" a whispered voice said.

Aram turned back to the table. An overstrong scent of jasmine wafted across it. Cobb's hooded man stood there, his face still hidden, still shadowed by his hood.

Greydon, his hand resting on the hilt of his cutlass, replied, "Be my guest, stranger."

The hooded man bowed elegantly. He said, "I am much obliged to you, friend." His voice, elegant in tone, was a whisper, like windblown sand across a beach.

As the man's gloved hand selected a piece of jerky, Aram attempted to subtly lean over to look at the face hidden within that hood. But the man kept his head angled down, and Aram couldn't manage a better view without being obvious or rude. He noticed Makasa and his father were likewise trying—but from their expressions, it was clear they, too, were trying and failing. Makasa gripped and regripped her harpoon tensely. Aram swallowed hard, remembering he had left his cutlass aboard ship yet again. He suppressed a groan.

The man brought the jerky into the shadowed depths of his hood and inhaled deeply. "Mmmm. Smells positively divine," he whispered softly. Aram wondered how the hooded man could smell anything over the quantity of jasmine water he must be wearing.

The strip emerged whole and the man slid it into the pocket of his long cloak. "Still, I'll save it for later," he whispered. "I might lose my head over it—or at least my jaw."

"I'm afraid I don't understand what you mean," Greydon said, an edge of suspicion in his voice.

"Oh, just that I could easily find myself overspending, buying more than I need from our good friend Bloodhorn. But thank you." He didn't lift or turn his head, but continued in that same eerie whisper: "Fine-looking lad, there. Is that your boy?"

Aram felt a chill run down his spine. The jasmine seemed to sour in his nose. There was something underneath the flowery scent, something rotten—or rotting.

"My *cabin* boy," said Greydon, "yes."

"Ah. My mistake. I seemed to perceive a resemblance that perhaps does not exist. Not a nephew then? Or a cousin?"

Aram croaked out, "We're not related at all."

Greydon, unable to help himself, shot his son a look, as if needing to confirm the boy was following Greydon's lead and not denying their relationship. Then Aram could see his father mentally kicking himself for offering up that tell.

"No," the hooded man whispered. "Clearly an error on my part. You'll forgive me, I hope. No offense meant, of course."

"None taken," Greydon said in a clipped tone.

"Well, then, I'll take my leave. Safe travels, sailors." He turned abruptly, his dark cloak slicing through the air, sounding much like his voice. He vanished into the rainy night, leaving behind only the wafting jasmine and the dread it covered up.

"What was that?" asked Makasa.

"Not sure," Greydon said.

"Was he even human?"

"Maybe. Maybe once. Leave the rest. We're going back to the ship."

Greydon took hold of Aram's arm and guided him forward; Aram didn't resist. Makasa followed a few feet behind.

"That man," Aram said in his own whisper, "that Whisper-Man, I saw him earlier. Talking to Old Cobb. I'm pretty sure he gave Cobb that silver piece."

Greydon stopped and faced Aram. "Pretty sure or pretty blasted sure?"

"Pretty blasted sure. And there's something else, now that I'm thinking about it. When I went to collect your cutlass the other day, Cobb was in your cabin, standing over your desk. At the time, I thought he was just collecting your breakfast dishes. But—"

"But my charts and our course were laid out on my desk."

"Uh-huh."

Greydon and Makasa exchanged looks.

"Anything else?" Greydon asked.

Aram racked his brain. "Maybe. At the gnoll camp, Cobb disappeared into the forest for a few minutes. Might be nothing."

Makasa stared at Aram. "That's a lot of nothings. Why didn't you speak up sooner?"

"I don't know. I kept meaning to . . ."

"Spilled milk," said the captain. "Makasa, shore leave is canceled. Gather up the crew; get them back aboard. Find Cobb."

"Yes, sir. Soon as I see you back aboard *Wavestrider.*"

"No, Second Mate, you follow my orders now. I'll take Aram straight to the ship and send Silent Joe to help you. But we're not waiting for sunrise to leave this port."

CHAPTER SEVEN
SPIRAL

"Why tip his hand?" Greydon asked.

Aram was in the captain's lamp-lit cabin with his father, One-God, Makasa, and Third Mate Silent Joe. Two days had passed. It had taken less than an hour for the first and second mates to gather the entire crew back aboard ship—or rather the entire crew except for Jonas Cobb. As the storm built through the night, two more hours were spent unsuccessfully trying to track the old man down. Another two hours were spent consulting Bloodhorn and Ridgewalker. Both knew the white-headed saltbeard from voyages past, but neither could locate him now, despite their network of connections in the undersized port. By this time, even the most generous and unsuspicious member of the crew had to admit that Cobb's leave was long past over and that it wasn't like him to be this late. He had either deserted or been taken, or he was dead. Ultimately, Captain Thorne decided to leave his cook behind, and the *Wavestrider* had set sail three hours before the dawn. Maintaining a southerly heading out of Flayers' Point, they had stayed ahead of the storm.

Some of the crew had grumbled about leaving a man behind—storm or no storm—particularly as neither captain, mates, nor Aram had been forthcoming with their suspicions of Old Cobb. But within that elite quintet, no one harbored much doubt: Cobb had sold the *Wavestrider*'s secrets to the Whisper-Man. So Greydon had plotted a new course: one the cook could not have predicted or sold. He sent the ship spiraling north, back around the storm and far out to sea, hoping to lose any possible pursuers.

Thus far, the strategy seemed to have worked. But late into this night, one question still ate away at Greydon Thorne's gut. "We had no suspicion of trouble until the Whisper-Man came to our table. So why did he tip his hand?"

Durgan One-God snorted. "Maybe he's a fool."

Greydon shook his head. "He was no fool."

"Arrogant?" suggested Makasa.

"That's just another kind of foolish. It felt like he was there with a purpose."

"He seemed interested in the boy," she stated. Normally, Aram resented Makasa referring to him as a boy when she had five years on him. But Aram couldn't summon up much resentment while simultaneously feeling so guilty. The captain and

71

his mates had had no suspicion of Cobb because Aram hadn't revealed what he had observed. Makasa never seemed to stop scowling at Aram—not an unusual occurrence—but for once Aram felt he deserved it.

"Yes, I thought of that," Greydon said. "He did seem to want confirmation that Aram was my son. But aboard ship that was hardly a secret. Cobb could have told him."

"Maybe he di'nae trust Cobb," One-God said, "which'd make him a blasted sight less a fool than the four officers o' this ship." Aram didn't know whether to feel relieved or depressed that he wasn't included in that accounting.

Greydon nodded absently, taking One-God's suggestion as the most plausible yet offered, but he clearly remained unsatisfied. For perhaps the tenth time that night, the captain raised his compass, stared at it, frowned, and let it drop against his chest. For a while after, they were all as silent as Joe.

Eventually, Greydon said, "Here's another question: Jonas Cobb's been ship's cook since we formed this crew four years ago. Why betray us? And why now?"

"That's two questions," One-God said.

Greydon ignored him, asking his mates, "Did any of you sense dissatisfaction? Resentment?"

All three shook their heads. Greydon turned to Aram, who swallowed hard and said, "I just thought he was, well, you know, a sour old man."

"He was *that*," One-God said. "But he was *that* four years ago, too. By the Life-Binder, I'd lay odds he was that at birth."

Makasa asked thoughtfully, "If I might ask, did he have a standard five-year contract?"

"Yes," her captain confirmed. "The whole crew does, except Aram and you, Makasa." Aram hadn't known the crew had contracts. That side of things had never crossed his mind. Now, he wondered why Makasa *didn't* have a contract. But he knew it wasn't the time to ask.

"So he was only a year shy of receiving his full share of the voyage's profits?" she asked.

"Eleven months, to be precise. Why risk that?"

"Maybe he was promised a *bigger* share," said One-God, "once the pirates divvied up their spoils."

"So the Whisper-Man was a pirate?" Aram asked.

"Among other things," One-God said. Greydon and Makasa said nothing, though they had seen the Whisper-Man and One-God had not. But by now, all present knew that the Whisper-Man was most certainly one of the Forsaken, a corpse raised into undeath by the darkest magic.

Aram tried to imagine what would motivate an undead pirate. Dubiously, he asked, "And he wants *this* ship?"

They stared at him, each of their four faces presenting a different version of insulted annoyance.

"No offense," Aram said. "I've come to appreciate our cargo. But look in our hold. Wouldn't a pirate be disappointed? And wouldn't Cobb tell them as much?"

Contemplating this, they were all silent for another long stretch. Greydon checked his compass again.

Aram bit his lip and asked his father, "Is it possible I got it all wrong? I mean, I saw what I saw. But maybe Old Cobb went into the forest to, I don't know, empty his bladder. And maybe he *was* just collecting dishes off your desk."

"And the silver?"

"A gambling debt."

"And the reason he didn't report back aboard ship?"

"Uh . . . drunk in a gutter somewhere?"

Greydon shook his head. "I'd like to think better of the man, even if that made me the villain for abandoning him in Slayers' Point. I don't want to think any man or woman on this crew would be disloyal. Truth is, if I could convince myself the Whisper-Man had grabbed him up, it would ease my mind—awful as that sounds. But I can't get my head around any explanation save betrayal."

One-God and Makasa nodded. Joe crossed his arms.

More silence.

Then Greydon slammed his fist down on his desk and repeated: "Why tip his hand?!"

Eventually, Captain Thorne dismissed his mates—but asked Aram to remain.

Greydon unrolled a chart on his desk, using the dice-filled pewter beer stein and the wooden dragon as paperweights. Then he took out a pencil to plot a new course. Aram approached and was surprised to see his father wasn't working off a chart of Kalimdor, but one that encompassed all of Azeroth.

Without looking up from his work, Greydon asked, "What is home to you, Aramar?"

Aram hesitated before saying, "Uh . . . Lakeshire?" It almost seemed like a trick question.

"No, I mean what does home *mean* to you?"

"Um, my mother. My brother and sister. Soot—I mean, our dog. And . . ." For the first time he hesitated to say the name in his father's presence.

But Greydon said it for him. "And Glade. Your stepfather."

"Well . . . yeah."

"And that's right; that's good. If you take nothing else from this voyage, take that."

"I—I don't understand."

"You know Ceya wasn't born in Lakeshire, don't you?"

"I . . . uh, yeah. She was born in Goldshire."

"Yes. Born in Goldshire, raised in an Eastvale logging camp, and then she moved with *her* mother to the coast. She and I met in Stormwind Harbor, and it was only after we married that we decided to make our home in Lakeshire. I'd never been there. She'd been to market there a few times as a child. It wasn't home to either of us, but it became home."

"All right," Aram said, almost as if humoring a rambling child; he had no idea where this was going.

"The point is," Greydon said, looking up from his chart for the first time, "home isn't a place. It's the people with whom you choose to share your life. Family is what makes a home. Not the other way around. And there are all kinds of families."

Suddenly, the conversation seemed significant. Suddenly, it occurred to Aram that Greydon was finally about to reveal his "reasons."

"This ship is a family," Aram said. "I can see that. Contracts or no contracts, it's your family."

"One of them, yes. A person can have many families, Aram. Even a man like Robb Glade, a man who's never in his life traveled five miles beyond little Lakeshire, will have at least two families in a lifetime. The one he had as a child with his parents, and the one he has as a man with his woman, their children . . . and you. Oh, and the dog."

Aram flinched. It was one of Greydon's less noble habits to separate Aram out from his half-siblings, as if a decent, uncomplicated man like Robb wouldn't treat all three of his children equally. As if Robb didn't treat Aram as a son. (Frankly, Greydon's implication was that Robb equated Aram with Soot.) But this didn't seem the time to protest, so Aram simply changed the subject, trying to get to the heart of what he thought Greydon was trying to teach him—because Greydon was *always* trying to teach him something. "It's why Cobb's betrayal hurts. He's not just a cook betraying his captain. He's a man betraying his family."

"Yes. With this crew in particular. I should be wiser than to think that, but it is how I feel. In here." He slapped his fist against his chest, as if saluting a centaur—which instantly gave the gesture significance. Aram felt he now understood its origin. The knowledge excited him, and he felt the impulse to confirm the revelation with his father. But Greydon had leaned back over the map of Azeroth, and Aram saw him draw a long arcing line from southeast Kalimdor—over the top of Pandaria—to the southern tip of the Eastern Kingdoms and beyond.

Suddenly, Aram knew. Greydon was plotting a course home. Aram was stunned. "You're taking me back?"

Greydon didn't reply.

"You're taking me back to Lakeshire." It was no longer a question.

And still, Greydon neither spoke nor looked up at his son.

"Why?" Aram demanded. "I mean, why now? Because of Cobb? Because of the Whisper-Man?"

When Greydon answered, his voice was a whisper, too. "I think . . . I think maybe I made a mistake, bringing you on this voyage." It was a sentiment Aram would have agreed with for most of the six months he had been aboard. But in this moment it cut him to the quick.

"Look, I know I should have told you about Cobb sooner—"

"It's not that."

"Then what?"

"You're not ready. And there hasn't been enough time. Maybe there was never going to be enough time."

"What does *that* mean?"

"Best if you don't know."

Aram literally staggered back a few steps, as if Greydon had slapped him across the face—or maybe as if he'd punched him in the gut. Greydon glanced up. Their eyes met. Aram said, "Why did you leave us?"

Greydon stared. His mouth hung open stupidly. Aram, his anger and resentment rushing back in full force, thought his father looked like a hapless and helpless fish pulled from the sea. Then Greydon's eyes lost focus, and he repeated, "Best if you don't know."

"No. You promised. You gave me your word."

"The situation has changed."

"No. Keep your word, *Father.* Tell me why you abandoned your wife and child."

"I can't."

"Tell me why!"

"I won't."

Aram felt his blood rise. He stifled an impulse to pick up the pewter mug and hit Greydon with it. Instead, he stumbled for the door, yanked it open, and slammed it on his way out. It echoed throughout the ship.

He staggered across the deck to the railing, passing Makasa, One-God, Thom, and even Duan Phen without seeing any of them.

He pulled his sketchbook out of his pocket, flipping through its pages until he found the sketch of his father. He tore it out of the book, crumpled it up, and let it fall overboard into the dark water below.

"How's that for magic," he whispered.

ome sunrise, a bitter Aramar Thorne was already on deck. Not—for once—because Makasa had dragged him out of bed, and certainly not because he had finally taught himself to wake on his own. No, Aram was up because he had never truly been down. He hadn't slept a minute, so at the first hint of light, he'd given up, gotten up, and gone topside. There was a chill in the air, so he was wearing a gray woolen cable sweater that his mother had knit for him a year and a half ago—that is, a year before Greydon Thorne had come back into their lives six months ago, on a day Aram was now ruing more than ever.

Silent Joe and the night watch—doubled by Greydon since they'd set sail from Flayers' Point—were heading to their bunks, but the bulk of the crew was stirring, quietly going about their business. Having executed his change of course during the night, Captain Thorne had the *Wavestrider* heading southeast—but they were still far enough out to sea that no land was yet in sight. To the north, clouds were low and black. To the south, low and gray. But here and there the sun peeked out.

Aram leaned his back against the rail, staring daggers at the closed door to his father's cabin. He was soon distracted, however, watching Duan Phen lithely climb the rigging and the mainmast to her nest. As usual, she wore silk slippers and a silk cap, the latter of which hid the long silky raven-black hair Aram had seen her wash in a rain barrel exactly once. She was fifteen, third youngest on the ship after twelve-year-old Aram and ten-year-old Keelhaul Watt, the cook's assistant, now newly promoted thanks to the defection of his master.

In fact, Aram could hear Keely cursing Old Cobb from the galley. The kid may not have been much of a cook—Aram could smell a kettle of burnt oatmeal from the deck, even before the boy emerged to dump the culinary disaster over the side—but Keely was apparently a genius at serving up epithets for Jonas Cobb capable of searing the most steadfast ears and heart.

Thom Frakes was back at the helm. Others attended to their various duties. Aram watched with some amusement as an already furious Flintwill emerged from the officers' cabin and stalked her way below to the crew quarters, cracking her knuckles in anticipation of a confrontation that just this once would not occur. Aram counted to two score and six, until Makasa emerged again, wearing an expression of pure bafflement. She

MARY BROWN

OLD Cobb

Cog Burnwick

SILENT JOE

Keely Watt

ARAM

scanned the deck and finally spotted him by the rail. She looked so flummoxed, he nearly laughed aloud.

One-God also exited the officers' cabin, shirtless, shoeless, and bleary-eyed. He stopped in front of the rain barrel, removed its wooden lid, pulled himself up by the rim, leaned over, and dunked the entire upper third of his shaggy red-haired body under the water, holding it there for about ten seconds. Then he swung his head up and staggered back into the cabin.

He emerged again five minutes later, smiling and laughing and slapping anyone within range of his limited wingspan hard on the back. His mirth seemed to waken the entire crew, who began chattering and gabbing and even singing their morning away. Soon, One-God was leading them in his favorite sea chantey . . .

Can a good young man drown without leavin' his ship?
Why, o' course is the answer, o' course by me hip!
Fer a fair sailor ne'er needs the deep blue to drown,
Just a barrel of ale 'n a head that's unsound!

Can a battleaxe cut down a cabin boy clean?
Why, o' course is the answer, o' course by me spleen!
Still, the axe isn't why the boy never set sail;
It was layin' his neck 'cross the barrel of ale!

Can a great kraken pull a stout seaman to brine?
Why, o' course is the answer, o' course by me spine!

Though the tentacles sure di'nae drown him alone,
Fer the seaman drank ale 'til quite drunk as a stone!

Can a poor sailor's headbone be crush'd by a mace?
Why, o' course is the answer, o' course by me face!
But the skullcrusher isn't what fills us with dread.
No, the barrel of ale crush'd his weak unsound head!

Can a pandaren junk set a frigate aflame?
Why, o' course is the answer, o' course by me frame!
But the bears' breath o' fire di'nae cause us to wail.
Fer the crew o' the frigate drank pandaren ale!

Can the claws of a worgen shred Captain and Mate?
Why, o' course is the answer, o' course by me pate!
But the worgen's sharp nails wer'n't the officers' doom,
Since they both drank enough ale to lower the boom!

Can a mariner die on the point of a knife?
Why, o' course is the answer, o' course by me life!
But the point o' the knife ain't the reason he's dead;
'Twas the barrel of ale an' that damn'd unsound head!

Can a deckhand expire from the bite of a troll?
Why, o' course is the answer, o' course by me soul!
Though the teeth o' the troll are but half o' the tale,
Fer the 'hand an' the troll shar'd the barrel of ale!

Can an old saltbeard wander, forever at sea?
Why, o' course is the answer, o' course by me knee!
All the maps in the world canna help him be found,
Once that barrel of ale finds his head so unsound!

Cross as he had been, Aram found himself smiling and was still smiling when he felt a hand on his shoulder and turned to look into the sad gray eyes of Greydon Thorne. Aram's smile calcified instantly, then vanished entirely—which did not go unnoticed by his careworn father.

Still, Greydon was determined to make the best of things, saying in a low voice, "We might as well make good use of the time we have left. Go fetch your cutlass."

Aram brushed Greydon's hand off his shoulder. "No," he said. "I've had enough. I've learned all I care to learn from a man like you."

Greydon's son had not kept the conversation private. To the contrary, he had spoken loudly enough for all to hear. Makasa glowered. Others looked away. Even One-God had stopped grinning.

Greydon's brow furrowed. "Boy," he said, matching Aram's volume, "I'm your captain and your father—"

But Aram, louder still, cut him off: "You may be my captain, but you're NOT my father! Robb Glade is my father! And you know how I know? Because he was there!"

Stunned into silence, Greydon could only watch as Aram turned on his heel and crossed to the aft side of the ship.

Makasa approached and growled low into Greydon's ear, "Captain, that boy could use a good flogging."

But Greydon sadly shook his head. "For being right? No. He's not the one who deserves flogging."

Aram stood aft, glowering out to sea. And then something caught his eye at the horizon. It was barely anything: a blacker speck peeking out from black clouds before vanishing again. Then, sure enough, a tar-colored ship emerged from the approaching storm, still tiny in the far distance. Aramar called out, "Look, a ship!"

All eyes followed his voice aft, including Duan Phen's up in the crow's nest. Instantly, her voice echoed his discovery: "A ship! Captain, a ship!"

Within seconds, Greydon, One-God, and Makasa had joined Aram at the aft rail to stare out in the direction Aram was pointing. At first Greydon Thorne saw nothing. But the first mate handed his captain a telescope. Greydon held it up to one eye. "A destroyer," he said. "An elven destroyer."

"Runnin' from the storm?" One-God asked.

"Or chasing us?" Makasa countered.

Greydon continued to study the other vessel through the spy-glass. "It's riding high. No cargo in its hold."

"You keep your hold empty when you plan to fill it with someone else's goods," said Makasa, ever the ray of sunshine.

Aram desperately wanted to give his father the silent treatment, but he couldn't resist asking, "So you think that's the Whisper-Man's ship?"

"Looks like we'll find out," One-God said. "She's gainin' upon us. An' that's nae a ship we can outrun."

"No," said Greydon. "But if we're sharp and lucky, maybe it's a ship we can outsail."

He turned on his heel and began barking out orders. Another sail was hoisted for the wind to fill. Various ropes were tied off. Every member of the crew knew his or her job and performed with admirable efficiency, speed, and cooperation, as if each 'hand were another personal appendage of their captain. One-God, Makasa, and Silent Joe (who'd been roused from slumber, along with the rest of the night watch) were everywhere—climbing the rigging, crossing the deck, descending into the hold—exhorting the crew, each in his or her own style: that is, One-God with humorous bluster, Makasa with threatening intensity, and Joe simply by speaking more words in that hour than he had the entire voyage. The captain ordered some of the less valuable cargo to be thrown overboard to lighten the load. This was accomplished with Aram pitching in; he watched pallets of sandstone, barrels of musk oil, and crates of iron chain vanish into the deep—and couldn't help wondering what treasures and trade his father would have made of them all. Greydon gave more orders, and Frakes turned *Wavestrider*, hard rudder, off their previous course to catch more wind. She cut across the sea at a stunning pace. The ship was hale; the crew, experienced; the mates, reliable; their captain, sharp.

But lucky, they all were not. From the nest, Duan Phen called, "It gains, Captain!"

Greydon Thorne's telescope confirmed the obvious. The tar-ship had matched the *Wavestrider*'s course correction and was still gaining. Aramar Thorne, Durgan One-God, Makasa Flintwill, and Silent Joe Barker, silent once again, approached.

"How long?" Makasa asked.

Greydon checked his compass as if it might hold the answer. Then he checked the sun, only partially hidden by clouds. Aram watched his father's face, as the captain made the necessary mental calculations. "Tonight," Greydon stated. "About two hours after sunset we'll have a fight on our hands." He tucked the compass under his shirt.

"Nae, Captain," said One-God. "Two hours after sunset, them pirates'll have a fight on *their* hands."

Makasa, smiling grimly—or scowling mirthfully—nodded her agreement.

Joe said nothing, and his face betrayed even less.

Greydon turned to Aram. "Now, will you get your sword?"

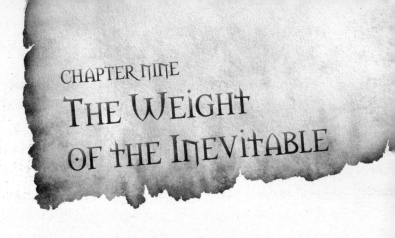

CHAPTER NINE
THE WEIGHT
OF THE INEVITABLE

The tar-ship chased the *Wavestrider* all through the day, gaining with each passing hour.

Captain Thorne had given up on evasive maneuvers. Instead, he and his mates were making sure the entire crew—up to and including the three youngsters, Aram, Duan Phen, and Keely—were armed and ready for what seemed an inevitable fight. Makasa strode across the deck with her shield strapped to her back, her iron chain crossed over her chest, her cutlass at her side, and her harpoon in her hand. She wasn't exactly Aram's favorite crewmate, but he had to admit her presence gave everyone more confidence, including Aramar Thorne.

In fact, Aram was tense but not overly afraid. Makasa, One-God, Silent Joe, Mary Brown, Anselm Yewtree, his father. He'd seen all of them fight at one time or another (mostly in tavern brawls) over the last six months, and he tended to agree with One-God that the elven destroyer's pirates had chosen the wrong ship, the wrong crew, to attack.

Then he thought of the Whisper-Man and shuddered.

Still, his greatest fear was of not holding his own in the fight, of proving himself a liability, of embarrassing himself by requiring rescue. Standing aft, watching the tar-ship until the light of day faded and the moonless night allowed no further view of their pursuer, Aram kept one hand on the hilt of his cutlass and wished by all the gods he had been a better student of the weapon.

He crossed the deck and heard Duan Phen call down, "I've lost sight of her, Captain!"

Greydon Thorne yelled up to her, "You'll see her again when she's upon us. Stay put and keep your eyes open!"

"Aye, aye, Captain!"

"Everyone, douse your lights! Not a candle glowing! And keep your traps shut, too! We're not going to make this any easier for those rogues!"

A chorus of "Aye, aye, Captain" followed, and rapidly the ship went dark and silent.

Thom whispered, "How long you figure, Cap'n?"

"Two hours. A little less."

Aram decided to make better use of the time.

He retreated to the near-empty hold—made his way down into its darkness quietly and carefully—and slid his cutlass from his belt to practice. It was pantomime, really. He imagined enemies, imagined their moves and countered. He'd parry, attack, parry, attack. And if the stale air of the hold had been the Whisper-Man, then, yes, the scoundrel would have been whispering his last words on this earth.

Yet as he sliced and stabbed, Aram had a hard time believing that these efforts were even the slightest bit worthwhile. It was child's play, shadow-play, a game. He stopped, his sword hanging slack in his hand. He thought of swallowing his pride and asking his father for one last lesson before it was too late. But he was sure his father had better things to do, and the last thing the crew needed to see was a demonstration of the "Greydonson's" pathetic level of skill. It could hardly fill them with confidence, and he knew enough to know that anything undercutting their confidence at this point could get them all killed.

"That's not my fault," he said aloud, to no one. He hadn't asked to be there, to be on this ship, to be in the midst of this crisis. Everyone else aboard had had a choice in the matter. Greydon Thorne was many things, but not a slave-master. He pressed no sailors. The crew had signed on voluntarily, had apparently signed contracts, had known the potential risks. But Aram hadn't had a choice in the matter. If he was a liability now, that was Greydon's fault, not his own.

Which changed nothing. He still didn't want to look bad. Nor did he want to die on this boat.

He sat on a crate, practically collapsed onto it. He began chopping at the wooden floor with the tip of his cutlass. Then he stopped, realizing it would dull the blade, which was the last thing he needed.

He tried applying some of Keely's curses to his father. But they rang hollow in his ears and tasted like dust in his mouth. He still had half a strip of jerky in his pocket. He tore off a bite and began chewing on it. *Two hours. A little less*, Greydon had said. Aram gave even odds the mouthful of jerky would last that long.

Chewing away, he leaned back, resting his head against the side of the hull. Down here in the darkness, he could feel the sway of the ship at its source. He knew he was below the waterline. He sighed heavily, shut his eyes, and chewed. "Just stay calm," he whispered to himself. "When it starts, just keep your eyes open and your wits about you." Greydon had said something similar more than once. He reminded himself that just because his father said something didn't make it bad advice. After all, his father was a skilled warrior. Not much of a father, but a skilled warrior. Aram remembered the gnoll fight. Remembered Greydon swinging his club against the matriarch. He remembered the matriarch. He felt the ship sway. He remembered her leaning over his sketchbook. He felt the ship sway . . .

She was saying he had to finish the drawing of his father. He looked up, trying to read the gnoll's face. But it wasn't Cackle; it was his mother, Ceya Northbrooke Thorne Glade. She said,

"Finish the drawing, Aram. Your father—both your fathers and I agree it's what you need. Finish the drawing."

"I finished it," he said. But he could feel that half-truth stick in his throat.

"Then show it to me," she said. It was Duan Phen.

"I . . . I can't."

"Why not?" Little Selya sounded so disappointed.

He didn't answer, felt ashamed.

"You tore it out, didn't you?" Makasa said. "You tore it out of the book and threw it overboard."

"I was angry. I didn't mean it." He coughed.

"Bad magic," said Cackle.

Choking on the bit of half-chewed jerky, Aram woke from his dream, coughing. He hacked up the wad of smoked meat and spit it out onto the floor. He could hardly believe he'd fallen asleep. With the ship on the verge of attack, he'd fallen asleep!

It was only then he heard it, or only then he became aware of it. Up on the deck. Shouting. The clash of swords. And light, light from above. Torches—or something—was burning, despite Greydon's orders.

The ship wasn't on the *verge* of attack. It was *under* attack.

CHAPTER TEN
THE LAST SMILE

Give the boy credit; he could have remained hidden below. But Aramar rushed topside just in time to witness the death of Cassius Meeks. A huge creature—eight feet tall, at least, and wielding a mace where his right hand should be—had, with one blow, ended Meeks's life. The deckhand's body collapsed at Aram's feet. Aram stared, first at poor Cassius and then up at the creature. Though Aram had never seen one in person before, he instantly realized it was an ogre—all bulk and muscle with huge rounded ears, ruddy skin, two tusk-like lower incisors, and a horn in the center of his forehead. The ogre could have taken a single step to his right and turned on Aram next, but instead he stepped to his left, swinging his mace-hand at Desamir Ferrar, who barely dodged the blow.

Keep your eyes open and your wits about you.

Aram's eyes could hardly have been open any wider, but his wits had all but fled his body, presumably in search of safer climes. He stumbled back a few steps away from Meeks's last ghastly staring smile. Then his eyes swept the deck. He saw One-God, a cutlass in one hand and an iron crow in the other, crashing like a wave through the mostly human pirates besieging *Wavestrider. Mostly* human. A female troll—six feet tall, with long hair, long pointed ears, orange-gold skin, and her own small tusks—wore strange undulating armor. She raised twin crossbows and peppered Thom Frakes with a bolt from each. He was slammed back against the half-open door to the officers' cabin. It gave way, and he fell backward through it and out of sight—as if departing the battle to take a little nap in an officer's bunk.

Frakes's "departure" chilled Aram to the bone. But there was little time to dwell on any single gruesome image. All the sights before Aram were quite as grim—but not all quite as unwelcome. Mary Brown ran a brigand through with her cutlass. The two O'Donagal brothers both did the same. The gnome Burnwick swung two short-handled axes, wounding one screaming pirate, who doubled over, allowing the gnome to end the noise with a second strike.

Then there was Silent Joe. Aramar had known Joe was a worgen, but knowing and seeing were two entirely different things. He witnessed *Wavestrider*'s third mate transform before his eyes. Fur covered Joe's body, and his face extended into a toothy snout, as he increased in mass to become a terrifying wolf-like beast that tore through the enemy with claw and fang.

Wavestrider's second mate was no less destructive. Makasa slashed with her cutlass, threw her harpoon—pinning a squirming enemy to the foremast until he slumped and was still—and with her now free hand unleashed the length of iron chain against two more invaders. A pirate rushed her from the left. Aram wanted to shout a warning, but—as usual in moments of crisis—no sound came forth. Makasa turned, exposing her back to the pirate. Aram watched in paralyzed horror as the villain's sword came down—only to see it blocked by a shrug of the shield she wore on her back. Then the length of chain swung around and shattered the man's stunned expression. He dropped.

Aram watched Makasa slide her cutlass through her belt to free her hand. He watched her stride forward two paces, yank her harpoon from the dead man on the foremast, and slash the weapon toward another foe.

And then Aram's eyes found his father. Greydon Thorne was on the forecastle, taking down any and all invaders within reach. *Wavestrider*'s captain was an artist with his cutlass and seemed nearly as strong as the worgen Joe. Not one pirate he faced could stand against him. Aram had once seen his father triumph in a tavern brawl, but that had been child's play next to this. Greydon Thorne was unstoppable, and Aram suddenly realized just how much his father had held back during their training sessions. Aram couldn't help feeling impressed—even proud—of his father. Though their eyes never even met, Greydon's agency somehow awoke the boy's own. Suddenly, his cutlass was up, his wits had—more or less—returned, and he rushed forward to meet the enemy.

His timing could not have been worse.

More pirates had been attempting to board the *Wavestrider* from the tar-ship lashed to its side. Those two mighty oaks, ship's carpenter Anselm Yewtree and ship's blacksmith Mordis Ironwood, were successfully stemming the tide. Then Yewtree reared back silently—a black shale dagger stuck in his throat—and the Whisper-Man boarded, wearing bone-spike shoulder armor over his familiar dark cloak. He relieved the carpenter of the dagger before the man could drop. Ironwood turned, swinging a crushing blow with his hammer that took the Whisper-Man's left arm clean off. *(There wasn't even any blood!)* But the Whisper-Man ignored the injury and ended the smith's life with a single elegant swing of the black broadsword in the pirate's remaining hand. Then, after sheathing his sword, the Whisper-Man calmly picked up his severed arm, which still clutched the shale dagger, and *reattached* it at the shoulder—before turning to face the oncoming Aramar Thorne.

Aram had already known that the Whisper-Man was an undead thing, one of the Forsaken. He had never heard of one who could instantly reattach a severed limb like this, but he tried to drive the thought of *what* he was facing from his horrified mind. In fact, Aram made a conscious effort not to hesitate against this strange spectral foe. He stabbed with his sword, which pierced the Whisper-Man—just below his sternum—sinking in a good inch and a half. In response, Aram's foe grabbed hold of the blade and pulled it free of Aram's hand by thrusting it deeper into the Whisper-Man's own chest so that the tip of the blade popped out of his back. Then his hooded face leaned in close to the unarmed, terrified boy and cheerfully whispered with cold, fetid breath, overly scented with jasmine, "Apologies, young squire, for what I'm about to do. But I'm told you might still be of some use."

He backslapped Aram hard.

Darkness.

Darkness, then suddenly . . .

The Light. The Light was so bright. The Voice of the Light called out to the heart of the boy, to the locus of sympathy in the center of Aramar's chest: "Aram, Aram, it is you who must save me . . ." But Aramar Thorne turned away from the Light.

Darkness.

Darkness, then gradually . . .

Cacophony: screams and the sound of fire, the clash of metal on metal, the horrible squish of steel through flesh. Dim light. The taste of blood and iron. Screams.

Dazed and bleeding from a cut lip, Aram blinked his way back to consciousness. The Whisper-Man's single blow had caused him to black out briefly and slide across the deck.

He struggled to get to his feet but couldn't immediately

communicate this instruction to his legs. Nor was he able to quite focus his eyes. He thought he saw the Whisper-Man turn back toward the tar-ship, yank the cutlass out of his chest, and signal with it. He thought he saw a tall, powerful man—almost as big and broad as a worgen—come aboard. He thought that maybe the Whisper-Man bowed slightly to this man, acknowledging him as his leader.

But that couldn't be. The Whisper-Man in service to another? What man could command that monster?

Aram's head finally cleared as a result of this new player turning from the Whisper-Man to pull someone else aboard with him. He shoved Old Cobb forward and shouted at him to earn his keep. Cobb's white head bobbed abjectly. "Aye, aye, Captain," the traitor said, before disappearing into the melee, allowing Aram to truly focus with clear eyes on the pirates' leader. Though Aram had never seen the man before, there was nevertheless something familiar about him. Something in the determined expression, in the bushy black eyebrows and the muscular gait. This pirate captain wasn't simply tall and broad—he was . . . *commanding.* He instantly *took possession* of the battlefield, killing Colin and Ainsley O'Donagal with one swing of his massive broadsword. Aram wanted to mourn the brothers but there didn't seem to be enough time. The pirate captain's presence was already turning the tide—even before he shouted at the ogre in a loud baritone, "Throgg! Stop wasting your time on these saltbeards and take the mast!"

Malus, the Whisper-Man, Throgg, and Zathra

ARAM

That command certainly got the ogre's attention. He responded with a deep but chastened, "Yes, Captain!"

But the ogre wasn't the only one to take note. Up on the forecastle, Greydon Thorne heard the voice of his opposite number and turned to confirm with his eyes what his ears had already revealed. Aram saw recognition in his father's face. Recognition and . . . *fear*. Actual, genuine fear of the pirate captain—which did more to sink Aram's spirits than the presence of the Whisper-Man, or the deaths of Cassius, Thom, and the rest, or the blow that had knocked him silly.

Still unable to find his footing, Aram did manage to roll over onto his hands and knees. His eyes found the ogre Throgg, who was in the process of unscrewing the mace from his wrist with slow and studied determination. He then placed it in an enormous quiver on his back. From the same receptacle, he pulled an axe, which he began screwing onto his stump with no apparent urgency whatsoever.

Greydon Thorne shouted, "Save the mast!"

The pirate captain turned at the sound of Greydon's voice, and Aram saw a now familiar expression of recognition on the invader's face as well. Recognition and . . . *what was that smile? Delight?* Aram shuddered involuntarily.

From various ends of the ship, *Wavestrider*'s captain and its three mates began fighting their way toward its center. The pirate captain moved to intercept Greydon Thorne, cutting his way through Schuyler Li and Black Max as if they were paper barriers, until Mary Brown and the worgen Silent Joe presented him with more of an obstacle—at least temporarily. The big man shouted past them, "I'll get you yet, you mad fool! Your quest ends tonight!" Aram saw his father flinch slightly, but Greydon made no acknowledgment, returned no insult. Captain Thorne just kept fighting his way toward the ogre and the mast.

Aram looked around for a new weapon. For good or ill, one wasn't hard to find. The swords of dead friends and pirates were scattered everywhere. He pried the closest cutlass from the tight fist of a slain raider and finally managed to stand, as the pirate captain shouted, "Don't let anyone throw anything overboard, or I swear I'll have your heads, you rogues!"

He heard and then saw the thunking toil of the ogre Throgg, who had finished attaching his axe-hand and was now using it to chop diligently away at the mainmast. Mose Canton sprang forward to stop him, but the Whisper-Man put his black sword through the quartermaster's back.

Greydon Thorne also heard the sound of axe on wood, and—cut off from the ogre by a trio of pirates—shouted, "Blast it! Save the mast!"

But the pirate captain, the Whisper-Man, and the troll created a perimeter around the ogre, and none was able to get past them to preserve *Wavestrider*'s spine.

Aram heard familiar cursing. It was Keelhaul Watt unleashing a torrent of expletives against his favorite target: Old Cobb. The cook was chasing Keely in circles round the mizzenmast. Both were armed with cutlasses, but Keely seemed to be attempting to kill Cobb either via vitriol or exhaustion.

In that moment, Aram was more furious than afraid. All this carnage, all this death—it was *all* the old man's fault. He had betrayed his ship, his crew, his *captain!* Jonas Cobb had betrayed Greydon Thorne, a man who made it a point of pride to find the good in everyone and everything. And Cobb had basically stabbed Aram's father in the back.

Aram attacked, but Old Cobb easily parried Aram's first strike and went on the offensive, apparently pleased to be facing a young adversary who wasn't running him ragged. The old man was surprisingly strong and nimble. It was all Aram could do to prevent the white-haired saltbeard from taking his head or running him through. Somewhere in the back of his mind, he realized that if Cobb was giving Aram this much trouble, then his father must have *truly* been going easy on him during all their daily lessons.

Keely rushed to Aram's aid, but the cook's assistant made the mistake of alerting his former master with a loud stream of invective. Cobb wheeled about and met Keely's advance with the point of his sword. Keely cursed Cobb one last time before falling to his knees and then onto his face, where he lay unmoving and silent.

A furious Aram redoubled his attack, hacking and slashing at the old man, and actually succeeded in driving him back a step or two. But Cobb recovered quickly, and Aram shortly found himself with nowhere to go, his back against the portside rail. He parried strike after strike, but each time Cobb seemed that much more likely to land a blow.

As something of a last resort, to throw Old Cobb off his fairly impressive game, Aram shouted, "Why?! Why did you do it?!"

But Cobb didn't seem bothered by the question. He growled, not unhappily, "Brainless boy, 'twas gonna be done whether I helped or no! Had t'pick a side, 'n I picked the one t'would save me skin!" The old man's cutlass caught the edge of Aram's weapon. Cobb whipped his sword in a tight circle and before Aram could blink, his found cutlass was lost—torn from his grip.

Cobb grinned as he leveled his weapon at Aram's throat, saying, "Course, Captain Malus's promise of a triple share didn't hurt, neither!" *Malus*, Aram thought. The pirate captain's name was Malus. It suited him a little too well for Aram's taste, particularly since it was likely the last name Aram would ever hear.

Cobb raised his sword to strike . . . when both opponents heard a final thunk of Throgg's axe and one loud crack. In grim unison, both turned to look up. The mainmast was timbering down right on top of them. Aram dove aside. But Cobb just managed to squeak out one of Keely Watt's favorite words before the thick spar smashed through the old cook's bones.

The whole boat shook. A pirate dropped a torch. Aram, back on hands and knees, was once again prying a cutlass from a dead man's hand. He looked up in time to see Throgg the ogre grinning at his achievement while the battle raged on all around him.

Malus, the pirate captain, had brought Mary Brown low but was still fighting the worgen Joe and now another of *Wavestrider*'s deckhands—thin, tall, and heavily freckled Crispus Trent. Glancing around, Malus shouted, "Where's their captain? I've lost sight of that madman!" No one answered, certainly not the "madman" himself, who was busy carving up another brace of pirates.

Furious, Malus took his anger out on the ogre: "Don't look so blasted proud of yourself. There are still men to kill." And as if to prove his point, he ran his sword through Crispus Trent.

The ogre looked disappointed, like a child whose father didn't appreciate his son's mud pie. The troll crossed in front of him while reloading a crossbow. She said, "If you be waitin' on praise from dat one, you gonna wait 'til doomsday. Might as well be gettin' ta work."

Grunting his acknowledgment of these basic facts, Throgg nodded once and swung his axe at Greydon Thorne, who had only just achieved the mast—too late to do it any service. Thorne ducked under the ogre's swing, put his back to the mast's stump, and kicked out with both feet. The ogre was caught off-balance and stumbled back a few paces, giving One-God the chance to smash his crowbar across the brute's neck. The blow seemed to anger more than injure the creature; he roared and attacked. One-God parried the ogre's axe-hand and shouted to Greydon, "Go! I've got this!"

So Greydon Thorne rushed toward his true target: his son, Aramar Thorne.

Captain Thorne grabbed the front of Aram's sweater and pulled him portside and aft. He glanced over his shoulder. The immense Throgg was driving the diminutive One-God farther away. The worgen Joe—now with the aid of Burnwick the gnome—was still attempting to keep Malus busy, but Makasa was advancing, slicing her way through one pirate after another. Greydon called, "Flintwill!"

She glanced his way, nodded curtly, and continued her advance.

Greydon pulled Aram over to the ship's dinghy. Then he looked his son in the eye and said, "Without the mast, the battle's lost." Aram didn't hear even a hint of defeat in his father's voice—just the cold, hard truth.

Still Aram felt the need to offer reassurance: "We can still fight. Beat them. Limp to shore. We've got two masts left."

Greydon didn't even bother shaking his head. He quickly shed his old worn leather coat and placed it over his son's shoulders.

"What are you doing?" Aram demanded.

His father's only reply was to pull the gold chain and compass out from beneath his shirt. He lifted them over his head and then placed them around Aram's neck. "Protect this compass at all costs," he said.

"The compass? I—I don't understand."

"And I don't have time to explain. I'm sorry. So sorry. For everything. But know that this will lead you where you need to go!"

Aram glanced around. There seemed to be so few of them left. It felt as if all he could make out clearly were the

Whisper-Man's shale dagger, the axe-hand of Throgg, the troll's crossbows, and Malus's sword.

Makasa, bloody from head to toe—and not a drop of it hers—materialized at Greydon's side. "Captain?"

He turned to look Makasa in the eye. "Protect my son at all costs. Now, both of you, into the dinghy."

Makasa took a second to register what he was saying, then immediately balked. "Captain, no! You need me here!" Gaining no purchase, she changed tack. "If someone has to go with the boy, let it be you. One-God and I will recover the ship and find you!"

"I can't go, Makasa, or these so-called pirates would follow." He looked from her to Aram and back. "There's more at stake than either of you realize. Now get in the blasted boat! That's an order, Makasa! That's your life debt!"

She immediately stopped protesting. After lowering her head and tossing her harpoon and chain in ahead of her, she climbed into the dinghy. Greydon, meanwhile, was hefting his stunned child into the boat after her. Aram tumbled in, nearly stabbing himself with the cutlass he held in his hand. He scrambled to his feet and found his father standing by the winch.

Their eyes locked. Aram shook his head. Greydon nodded . . . and released the catch.

Aram's footing rushed away from him. Honestly, he might have flown up and out of the thing, if Makasa's hand hadn't pressed down on his shoulder. Greydon's eyes pulled away, as the boat dropped with only Makasa and Aram aboard.

The dinghy hit the water with an impact that threatened to snap its timbers—or Aram's bones.

Makasa released the ropes, and the churning sea quickly tossed the dinghy—their *lifeboat*—a dozen yards from its glowing mother.

Glowing? Wavestrider *was aflame!* By the light of that fire, Aram could still see his father in silhouette. Captain Greydon Thorne turned from the rail to cross swords with the silhouette of the pirate captain Malus, their steel echoing across the water.

Malus's deep and brutally confident voice called out, "Finally, a reckoning!"

And Aram heard Greydon respond, his father's voice cutting through all the other noise. It held its own dangerous smile of confidence: "You have my full attention, you traitorous dog!"

By this time, they were hard to see. But underlit by the burning deck, their shadows played out the battle on a larger-than-life scale upon the remaining sails of the ship.

Suddenly, there was an explosion! *Had the fire reached the powder stores?!*

Aram would never know. The ocean pulled the little boat away, and *Wavestrider* was gone . . .

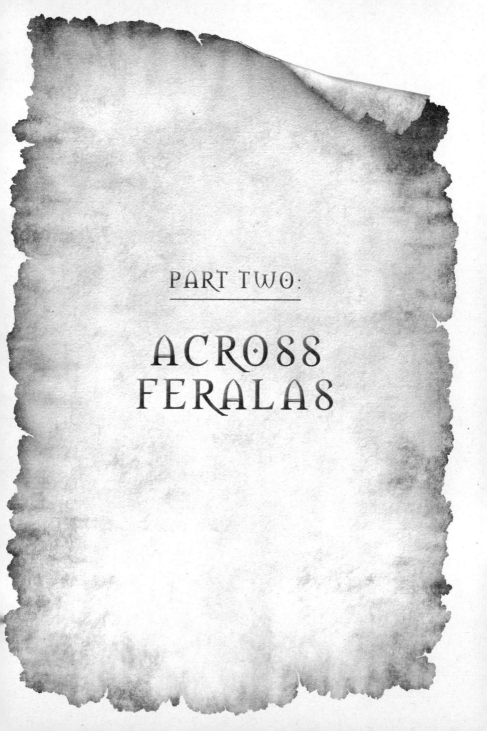

PART TWO:

ACROSS
FERALAS

CHAPTER ELEVEN
Grim Inventories

Aram sat low in the little boat, staring into the darkness. Soon, all that remained of the two ships was a glow on the horizon. He shrugged his shoulders, feeling the weight of his father's heavy coat. He inhaled, and the smell of leather and brine instantly brought a vision of the man before his eyes. A sense memory of Greydon Thorne that pierced his heart. Then far off to starboard, lightning caught his eye, striking the water with one crisp, jagged bolt, followed some seconds later by a crack of thunder. For as the tar-ship had caught up with the *Wavestrider*, the storm had finally caught up with those who had escaped its fate.

The dark clouds moved in, swallowing up the glow from the burning ship. The wind picked up; the waves became swells, each one threatening to capsize the boat.

Aram turned to face Makasa and shouted over water, wind, and weather, "What do we do?"

She grasped the sides of the boat with either hand. For the first time since he had met her, she looked her age: a seventeen-year-old girl with no authority, no power, no control. "Hold on," was all she said.

So Aram held on.

The Veiled Sea churned and tossed. Clouds bearing lightning, thunder, and stinging rain took up residence right above them. Huge waves lifted the little boat up and brought it crashing down with such force that Aram was sure the dinghy would shatter, splinter, disintegrate beneath them.

He kept his head down, his mouth shut, and his eyes open just a slit so that he could peer through the darkness and see Makasa's boots and know he wasn't yet completely alone.

It seemed like the storm would last forever . . .

Dawn found them on calm waters with nothing but the sun itself in view. Not a cloud, not a ship, not a hint of landfall was visible in any direction.

Aram exhaled—almost as if he had been holding his breath all through the night. Then he heard Makasa do the same. He looked up at her. She looked like a drowned rat, which gave him a pretty good idea of how he must look. In any case, she must have thought him fairly pitiable, because for once she spoke with a measure of gentleness. "We'll take turns sleeping. You first."

Aram nodded, but he didn't see *how* he was supposed to fall asleep in the cramped little dinghy. But he dutifully attempted to follow the order and laid his head and body down in half an inch of water at the bottom of the boat.

Within a minute, he was dead to the world.

The water pulled him down, but he was sinking, not drowning. Sinking toward the Light. At the bottom of the ocean, he found a barrel of pickled eggs. He wrenched off the lid, and the Light poured forth. Even through the water, he thought it would blind him. Before the Voice could speak, Aram turned away, and Jahid Khan, the ship's cooper, resealed the barrel.

But with the barrel shut, the Voice silenced, and the Light contained, Aram found he could no longer remember how to breathe underwater. He was at the bottom of the sea, and he could no longer breathe! He struggled to rise, to swim to the surface, but the pirate captain Malus wrapped Makasa's iron chain around his ankle, anchoring him to the barrel. He tried calling out to Makasa, but no sound came forth. Besides, she and One-God and Aram's father were already dead and drowned, chained to the barrel by the Whisper-Man, the ogre Throgg, and the troll.

He gasped for air . . .

And woke up, choking and coughing.

Makasa stared at him glumly.

"Your turn," he croaked.

*　　*　　*

A few hours later, Makasa had the oars out and was rowing toward the late-morning sun.

"Except," Aram asked, "*is* it late morning? Or early afternoon? Are you heading east or west?"

She glared at him. But she removed the oars from the water. "We'll know in a few minutes."

Aram glanced down at the battle-scarred dead man's cutlass he now carried. He wondered if anyone would ever again take up the practically virgin blade he had left behind inside the Whisper-Man.

He heard Makasa curse Old Cobb under her breath, in a manner that would make Keely Watt proud.

"He's dead, you know," Aram stated.

"What? Who? Old Cobb? How do you know?"

"He came aboard with the pirates. He killed Keely." Aram was about to say *he tried to kill me* but feared it would give the false impression that Aram had outfought the old cook, so he just said, "When the mast came down, it squashed him. I mean, Cobb."

She looked stunned. But finally, she uttered a single satisfied word. "Good."

But Aram's thoughts were already elsewhere. The mast reminded him of another loss—a loss of something he had never truly gained—a loss that threatened to break his already breaking heart. The more so because he hadn't thought of her once until now. He said, "During the fight . . . did you see Duan Phen at all?"

Makasa sat up straight on her wooden bench. "No. I heard

her shout her warning from the nest. Just a few seconds before the pirates' grappling hooks found our rails. I don't remember seeing her come down. I don't remember seeing her during the fight. What about when the mast came down?"

"I don't know," he said.

Makasa didn't know, either.

But this led her to a full inventory of the crew. They had originally set sail with thirty souls. Twenty-nine if you left out the soulless Cobb. She ticked off the names with seeming dispassion, answering out loud if she knew their fate. Pausing if she didn't. Sometimes Aram could fill in the blank by relating—as flatly as he could manage—what he himself had seen. Sometimes he couldn't.

But the final tally was as follows:

Second Mate Makasa Flintwill and Cabin Boy Aramar Thorne escaped aboard the ship's dinghy. (Two.)

Deckhand Mary Brown and Deckhand Orley Post were injured but still alive when last seen. (Two.)

Captain Greydon Thorne, First Mate Durgan One-God, Third Mate Silent Joe Barker, Ship's Surgeon Yakomo Hide, Deckhand Desamir Ferrar, Deckhand James MacKillen, and Deckhand Cog Burnwick were last seen alive, basically uninjured and still fighting. (Seven.)

Ship's Cooper Jahid Khan, Deckhand Ahnko, and Lookout Duan Phen weren't seen by either Makasa or Aram during the battle. (Three.)

Quartermaster Mose Canton, Boatswain Johnson Ribierra, Helmsman Thom Frakes, Ship's Carpenter Anselm Yewtree, Ship's Blacksmith Mordis Ironwood, Deckhand Cassius Meeks, Deckhand Schuyler Li, Deckhand Black Max, Deckhand Crispus Trent, Deckhand Willson Pariah, Deckhand Rose Haggard, Deckhand Quenton Miles, Deckhand Colin O'Donagal, Deckhand Ainsley O'Donagal, Cook's Assistant Keelhaul Watt, and Ship's Cook Jonas Cobb were confirmed dead by either Makasa or Aram or both. (Sixteen.)

They finished and fell silent. More than half the crew was confirmed dead and the rest—even the uninjured—had been left in dire circumstances. But there was also some hope in this inventory—barely.

Makasa said, "Hide's good. A true healer. He can work miracles." But she couldn't help adding, "If he's alive."

Trying very hard not to think about his father, Aram busied himself by inventorying their stores. The little boat was equipped with a small built-in chest, containing a hunting knife, a hatchet, a case of dry flints wrapped in oilskin, an oil lantern, a flask of oil, and a coil of rope. There were three oilskin maps, none of which would be of much use unless they sighted land. There was water and sea biscuits (hardtack), though not enough of either for a prolonged voyage. And there were four gold coins. In addition, Makasa had her shield, chain, cutlass, and harpoon; Aram, his "borrowed" cutlass, his sketchbook, his coal pencil, his mother's sweater, his father's coat, and the compass, which for some reason he had to "protect at all costs."

The compass! It could at least get them going in the right direction. Filled with hope, he held it up and glanced from the sky to the small device and back. *The stupid compass didn't work!* The sun made it clear its needle wasn't even pointing north. It was useless. Why his father thought it would *ever* get Aram home was beyond him. Why Aram had been commanded to protect it was a bigger mystery than his father himself was.

His father.

Greydon was his father, but during their last real conversation, Aram had denied him. And now . . . now Greydon Thorne was probably dead, leaving his son racked with guilt.

And it wasn't just the denial weighing on him, either. Aram had ripped up the drawing of his father, ripped it up and tossed it in the sea. He had been warned of bad magic. And it wasn't that he hadn't believed, that he was above such superstitions. No, he had willfully summoned the bad magic while in the midst of a childish tantrum. He stared overboard, as if he could find the crumpled sketch in the water.

Then he shook the idea from his head and took the sketchbook out of his back pocket.

Makasa stared at him, astonished, as he carefully unwrapped the oilskin cloth and carefully examined the book for damage. Almost as if it were required, she said, "You better not be putting me in that blasted book."

"I promise I won't sketch you unless you ask me to," he replied impatiently as he checked for water stains. With some relief, he confirmed the oilskin had done its job; the sketchbook remained unsoiled. He turned the pages, past his family and Lakeshire to the many pages of the crew of the *Wavestrider*. Here were faces he'd probably never see again—and faces he'd *definitely* never see again. He paused, touching an image of Duan Phen. Then he turned the leaves until he found the remnants of the page he had torn out. He ran his finger along that jagged edge of paper near the spine and felt the pain of his act of spite somewhere in the vicinity of his own spine.

Then he quickly flipped to the first blank page and reached under his still damp sweater to pull the pencil from his pocket. The tip was ruined. He took the knife from the stores to sharpen it. But his hands were shaking. If he kept up like this, he'd ruin the pencil for good. *Then how could he ever undo the bad magic?*

He sighed and put everything away. The knife, the pencil, the sketchbook in its oilskin cloth.

Makasa silently watched him. Then she glanced up at the sky. "Late morning," she said. She began rowing again, confident now that they were heading east toward Kalimdor.

He looked up at her and said, "Do you want me to take a turn?"

CHAPTER TWELVE
PAINFUL JABS

A sliver of a waxing crescent moon provided little light. A thin haze was enough to block out most of the stars. Neither of them rowed. There was no wind, not even a breeze. It was very still, and Makasa didn't like it. It set her on edge. Even in the darkness, Aram could see her grim visage, could hear her chewing furiously—as if with a vengeance.

They were both chewing—but not on hardtack. Rather, each had torn a small bite off that last piece of boar jerky that Aram still had in his pocket. (She had thanked him when taking hers. Being alone with him on the boat had—for now at least—made her something akin to gracious toward the boy.) After this, there'd be just enough left for each of them to have one last morsel for dinner the next night before they had to break out the hardtack.

The jerky was still lasting and flavorful. But it was also a somewhat bitter reminder of all they'd lost. And, of course, it was salty. But it generated enough saliva so they could hold off on reducing their water stores for a while.

Makasa's hands moved to the oars as if she thought she might row without the sun to guide them. Aram glanced down at the compass, but even if it had somehow miraculously begun to work, it was too dark for him to read it.

Suddenly, Makasa reached down and pulled out her harpoon. Aram stared at her as she stood up in the little boat, ready for battle—though against what was unclear to Aram . . . and ultimately even to Makasa. Then, for just a second, she looked . . . embarrassed. It was an expression Aram could barely recognize on her face. He didn't think he liked it. Where was the grim disciplinarian and warrior who had made his life miserable for six months? That was who they needed now. Not this unsure seventeen-year-old girl. *She* wouldn't do either of them any good.

Her expression reverted to something like contempt, which was both more familiar to Aram and more comfortable on her face. But even here the difference was palpable: the contempt she felt was directed inward. It spoke of self-doubt and self-recrimination. She felt foolish. She was about to sit, when the giant tentacle shattered the calm sea and rose two stories out of the water!

Makasa actually laughed!

She stabbed at it with her harpoon. Drew her cutlass and slashed it halfway through.

Aram was on his feet, too—though less steadily. He had his cutlass out in time to slash at a second tentacle that attempted to encircle the boat from the other side. Makasa sunk the harpoon into it to hold it steady, then brought her sword down like a guillotine and chopped the thing clean in two!

The kraken rose then . . . its massive cranium surfacing, perhaps to see how this little midnight snack could have brought such pain—and *that* was its big mistake. If it had simply raised more tentacles and sunk the boat, there was little Makasa or Aram could have done. But curiosity, it seems, isn't just a problem for cats.

Makasa yanked her harpoon free of the sundered tentacle and with all her might, jabbed the weapon right into the monster's great eye. A chilling scream bubbled up from the water. Flintwill yanked her harpoon free again, eager to strike another blow. But the creature descended, tentacles and all, leaving only the one severed tip, which lay across the dingy between Aram and Makasa. Together, they heaved it over the side.

Makasa sat down, smirking. "We were lucky," she said. "It was just a baby."

"*That* was a baby?" Aram squeaked, appalled.

"Aye. An adult krakcn can pull an entire ship into the deep. That little one found us too big to swallow."

At first, he couldn't tell if she was serious. Then he remembered that despite her grin, she had no sense of humor. He cautiously sat down and asked, "What if it runs and gets mommy?"

Makasa's grin vanished. She raised her harpoon. Aram smiled.

Makasa rowed toward the rising sun, positive it would take them to land eventually.

Aram studied her, questions running through his mind. Finally, he managed to summon up the courage to ask, "What's a life debt?"

Her angry eyes met his like two crossbow bolts. She didn't answer for a long time, as if willing him to abandon the question. He didn't turn away. She was stubborn, but she knew blasted well that he was, too.

She said, "Your father saved my life, so by the custom of both Stromgarde—the land of my ancestors—and of Stranglethorn Vale—the land of my birth—that life belonged to him. That is my life debt."

"*You* needed saving? How? What happened?"

"That is none of your business."

"Is that why you didn't have a contract on *Wavestrider*?"

"That is none of your business, either," she said. But a few seconds later, she added, "Yes. He offered, but I refused."

She rowed on. But Aram could see it weighing on her. Eventually, she said, "Greydon Thorne told me he didn't believe in life debts. He valued my service, he said, and was glad to have me at his side. But he swore he'd never call on me to pay back what I knew I owed him."

"But he did."

"Yes. He did."

"Is that disappointing?"

"I owe what I owe. What he might have said once changed nothing."

"But is it disappointing?"

She glared at him. "You'd like to hear I'm disappointed in the man. It would justify your own petty disappointment. Justify your own abysmal behavior toward him. But what I might or might not say changes nothing."

Aram felt his face flush, but he didn't look away. "This isn't about him or me," he lied. "I'm trying to understand you."

"You will never understand me."

"And you'll never understand me, either. But answer the question."

"I don't take orders from cabin boys, no matter who their fathers were." She quickly corrected herself: "Are."

The reality of that "were" rocked him—hard. *Was Greydon lost beyond hope?* He couldn't face that, not now, not yet. He struggled to remember the point he was trying to make. The thought coalesced in his mind, and he rephrased his question, asking her, "Had you come to believe him?"

She didn't answer.

"Had you come to believe him?" he repeated.

Another long pause, then she whispered, "Yes."

The sun was sinking. Aram had taken a turn rowing, but Makasa had taken the oars again, determined to cover as much distance as possible before night fell and navigation became impossible.

"Shouldn't you be able to navigate by the stars?" he asked her.

She scowled. "Shouldn't you?"

"We both know I was a poor student. What's your excuse?"

She grumbled, "They all look alike to me."

"Seriously?"

"He was teaching me," she barked. "Then you joined the crew."

This shut him up. Was this why she resented him so much? Was Greydon like a father to Makasa? A father who abandoned her for Aram the way he had abandoned Aram for the sea?

"Sorry," he said quietly.

"You never tried to understand him."

"He never tried to explain." And that much, Aram knew, was true.

Six months ago—after being gone for six years without a letter, without a word, without anything—Greydon Thorne had returned to Lakeshire. Aram and Robb had been working the forge together when Ceya had come in and asked Robb to return to the house for a few minutes. It was an unusual request for the early afternoon. But Robb could see something in her face and, after telling Aram to keep at it, departed with her.

An hour passed.

Then Robb came back to send Aram into the house.

Aram entered their cottage. A strange man was sitting by the hearth, staring at Robertson and Selya, who were playing with wooden soldiers on the floor. The man looked up, and instantly father and son recognized each other.

Greydon stood. "Aram . . ."

Aram was paralyzed. He couldn't move, couldn't speak. Finally, he turned toward his mother.

"Your father's back," she said helplessly.

Robb returned after closing the forge. With growing resentment, Aram listened at the dinner table as Ceya and Robb explained their life to a man who deserved no explanations. To a man who offered none in return.

Ceya Thorne had waited two years for Greydon to come home. Two years. But he did not come home, sent not so much as a letter, a word, a copper, anything.

During that time, Ceya had come to rely on the kind blacksmith. During that time, she had come to care for him. After two years, she gained her freedom from her first marriage from Magistrate Solomon, who was more than willing to declare Greydon Thorne dead at sea.

Ceya married Robb Glade. Robb became Aram's stepfather— and eventually the father of Robertson and Selya.

Robb admitted to Greydon that there had been some tough times between him and Aram. Robb was no glamorous sailor like Greydon Thorne. But he'd won the boy over eventually.

Greydon had nodded. Had professed to understand. He all but said, "I forgive you." As if he had any grievance to forgive, any right to forgive.

But he never asked for forgiveness himself. At least, not then, not from Aram. And he never explained anything. Even after he had promised he would.

Aram felt his bitterness rise again. What had changed after six months? Greydon had offered no explanations, had given Aram no choices. Had stuck him in a boat with a woman who hated his guts and had ordered him to protect a broken compass. It'd be laughable, if so many better men and women hadn't died in the minutes prior to this second parting.

Perhaps more frustrating was that he couldn't safely hate his father, either, not while he thought Greydon Thorne was most likely dead. Not while he felt so much culpability in that death.

Aram dangled his fingers in the water. Something passed beneath it. He thought of the kraken and yanked his hand out again. But this was no kraken. It was a sea turtle, big as the dinghy, with some kind of moss on its shell that glowed slightly green in the dark. It passed beneath them with nary a ripple to be felt. And then another passed, and another. They were heading east like the boat, but at a more northerly angle. He knew what this meant, but because the knowledge came from Greydon Thorne, it took him a good minute and a half to swallow his resentment and speak.

"Follow those turtles," he said, pointing.

"What? Why?" Makasa looked over her shoulder in the direction Aram indicated.

"This time of year, they head to land to mate and spawn."

"How do you know that?"

"How do you think?"

She looked at him. Then she nodded and adjusted course.

CHAPTER THIRTEEN
BETWEEN A ROCK AND A WET PLACE

It was a hazy morning. They had lost sight of the turtles, but by this time there were other signs they were on course for land. A pod of sea otters frolicked nearby, diving and surfacing, using rocks as tools to smash open clamshells held against the thick fur of their chests. The otters' presence was significant, for, as Greydon had once informed his son, sea otters were never actually found too far out to sea.

Better still (for the intelligence on this point came not from Greydon Thorne but from Charnas of Gadgetzan), Aram began to see the occasional saltspray gull and knew this common bird of Azeroth dove for fish just off the coastlines of Kalimdor. (Aram strove mightily to ignore the fact that he would never have seen Charnas's book and learned this fact if not for Captain Thorne.)

Makasa was rowing, keeping up a steady pace and a steady course. Aram had taken Duan Phen's role as lookout, eyes on the horizon, scanning desperately for land. As the sun rose higher, the haze began to burn off, and Aram had to squint and shield his eyes. It brought something to mind—less a memory than a sensation—but he couldn't quite put his finger on it.

Finally, just before noon, he pointed and called out, "Land ho!" Makasa turned to look over her shoulder. She turned back with a grim smile and redoubled her rowing efforts.

But for hours they seemed to make little progress. When Aram took his turn at the oars, he could feel the current working against the boat, against them. In addition, clouds were starting to form. The wind was picking up and the sea was getting choppy. Aram tried to follow the otters, rowing toward any he could spot with a quick look over his shoulder. He hoped they knew how to thread the currents and could lead them home. Well, not home, but to land, at least.

Maybe it worked; maybe it didn't. But by the time Makasa took over, it did seem as if they had gotten closer to landfall. The wind was in their favor now, too, and it blew hard and cold enough to cut through his father's coat and his mother's sweater and chill the sweat on his skin from his recent exertions. He shivered.

Come evening, as the sun sank behind them, and the clouds gathered, they lost sight of shore. But by that time, Kalimdor had filled the eastern horizon. They knew their heading, and Makasa kept rowing.

And rowing. And rowing. And rowing. Aram took another turn. He rowed and rowed and rowed. Then Makasa again. It began to rain softly. And then not so softly. The wind blew bitter cold in earnest now. She rowed on.

And then, finally, there it was. The sliver of moon emerged from between two dark clouds and revealed the shore, practically within reach. He alerted Makasa, and she looked over her shoulder for a good long while. When she turned back toward Aram, she didn't look happy.

"There's no safe place to land."

Aram looked again with new eyes. She was right. He had been focused on the shore's proximity. Not on the nature of it. As far as he could see, there were only dangerous rocky shoals and promontories.

"What do we do?" he said.

"We should wait for daybreak, if we can. Row along the shore until we find a safe haven to land the boat."

He nodded. They had a plan. But as One-God loved to say, *We plan. The Life-Binder laughs.*

The wind had changed direction. Makasa Flintwill successfully fought to maintain their distance from the coast but ultimately admitted it would soon become a losing battle. If they didn't try to land the craft now, the next morning could find them miles off shore again. Though the jerky was gone, they had plenty of hardtack yet. The problem, however, was water. She didn't think they could afford to wait two or three more days for landfall, and she couldn't guarantee this coming storm wouldn't set them back far more than that. And that's assuming it didn't get truly violent and swamp them.

"Then we try now," Aram said.

She nodded and rowed with even greater purpose than before.

They drew closer and closer to shore. The sea churned with increasing fury. Aram briefly wondered why he wasn't seasick. But a gift is a gift. The rain came down hard now, pelting them, soaking them through. Lightning lit the sky. And now, Aram could hear the crash of the waves against the rocks before them.

Makasa looked over her shoulder at every other pull of the oars. She had found her landing spot and was fighting to maintain her course. It was a small target, no less rocky than the rest, but not built up as high as the surrounding coastline.

"Just before we hit the rocks, we abandon ship and swim for shore."

Aram nodded.

"And take off that coat," she said.

"What? No! It's *his* coat. He gave it to me."

"And he wouldn't want it to drown you. You can't swim in that thing. Not here. Not now. It'll drag you down, and you know it."

Aram tried to object. But no thought occurred that wouldn't be a flat-out lie. Slowly, reluctantly, he took off Greydon Thorne's coat and laid it gently on the bench beside him. Then, careful not to lose his father's other gift—useless as it was—he slipped the compass and chain beneath his sweater.

Makasa watched all this while rowing. Then she gave a new order: "Divvy up the stores now. Anything that might be useful needs to be secured to our bodies."

Makasa's shield was still strapped to her back, and both of them still wore their cutlasses. Aram slid the sheaths of the hunting knife and the hatchet through his belt, which he tightened an extra notch. He pocketed the case of flints, two of the gold coins, the three folded oilskin maps, and the flask of oil. He wrapped the rope around his chest in much the same way Makasa's iron chain was wrapped around hers. He gave her the remaining two gold coins and divvied up the wrapped packets of hardtack; they each stuffed as much as they could into their clothes. There was still one packet left, so Aram opened it. He fed half to Makasa as she rowed, then ate the other half himself. All that remained were the lantern and the water.

"Leave them," she said. "If we can't find water and firewood ashore, we're doomed anyway." That was Makasa's version of optimism.

The roar of wave crashing against rock became a din.

"Get ready," Makasa said.

He gripped the sides of the little dinghy, prepared to launch himself over the side.

"When I say 'now,' you jump, swim, and then climb. Don't

wait or look for me until you're safe ashore. Because I will not be waiting or looking for you, boy."

Aram nodded, but perhaps it was too dark for her to see.

"Do you understand me?" she demanded.

"Aye, aye, Captain," he said aloud, just to see her scowl one last time.

She took another fierce pull on the oars, then another and another. Then she dropped them, quickly reached down for her harpoon, and shouted, "NOW!"

As Aram launched himself into the cold sea, the last thing he saw of Makasa was her standing erect and throwing her harpoon with all her might.

Then he was beneath. Almost immediately his clothes drank up the seawater and began to weigh him down. Makasa had been right. The coat would have drowned him for sure.

As he fought against the downward drag of what he *was* wearing, again and just for a moment, he was struck by déjà vu, but he had bigger concerns now. He swam.

He knew what direction to head, knew he was close, but as he fought to advance, he couldn't tell if he was actually getting any nearer to the rocks. He needed to achieve those rocks, of course, but he needed to achieve them himself—not be tossed and broken against them. So with each stroke, he reached forward hoping to skim hard stone with his fingertips. Hoping to find a purchase.

This went on for several minutes that felt like an eternity. His clothes pulled him down; his legs kicked him forward; his arms swept ahead. The moon must have vanished behind the clouds again, for he could see nothing. But every time he surfaced for breath, he could yet hear the crashing of the waves ahead, so if nothing else, he knew he was still swimming in the right direction. There was no hint of Makasa anywhere. But she had made it clear enough that this was an every-mariner-for-him-or-herself situation.

And still he couldn't reach the shore. He hadn't quit, wouldn't quit, but a piece of his brain told him his legs were slowing down. His arms were heavy. He was sure he must be within yards of the land—had probably been within yards of it from the moment he dove off the boat—and it seemed ridiculous that he could get this close and nevertheless drown. That possibility was too embarrassing to endure. If he died, Makasa would never let him live it down. It was perhaps a preposterous thought, but it powered him through one last push.

His hand brushed the rocks. He gasped for air and grasped for solid ground. He still couldn't see anything. He kicked furiously and managed to grab hold of a pointy outcropping. But just then, another wave smashed him against the wall of stone. He banged his crown hard—it dazed him. He nearly lost his grip but managed to hold on. He believed he could feel a liquid thicker than water dripping down his scalp and burning his eyes. He tried to pull himself tight against the rocks, so that he wouldn't be thrown at them again. A breaker crashed over his head just as he had risen up to take a breath, and he inhaled salt water, choked and coughed and spat. He felt light-headed.

He tried to remind himself that he was too close to safety to die now without eternal humiliation . . . but that no longer seemed to matter. He still held tight to the outcropping and tried to pull himself up, but his arms, his clothes, his body were too heavy. And the thought crept in—whispered—that now it would be so easy to just let go, to just allow himself to sink into the deep. He fought against the thought. But he couldn't quite silence it, and he couldn't quite pull himself clear of the sea, either. He kept fighting but became more and more convinced it was a fight he was destined to lose . . .

Something grabbed him by the collar and pulled him up—though neither swiftly nor smoothly. His body scraped over the pointy outcropping, tearing at sweater, shirt, and skin from his collarbone down to his hip. But in the end he was lying across wet turf with the toe of Makasa's boot poking into his kidney.

He rolled over onto his side. Their eyes met. She was scowling at him, and he thought he'd never seen a more beautiful sight. He knew that scowl and knew what it meant. She and Aram had never gotten along or even vaguely liked each other. But Makasa Flintwill was a creature of duty and loyalty. Despite what she had said before they left the dinghy, she had a life debt to repay to his father, which meant she could no longer stop protecting Greydon Thorne's son than breathing the air.

It was only then that he noticed his father's coat, the sleeves tied in a tight knot round her waist. *Abandon her captain's son? She couldn't even abandon his coat!*

He flopped over onto his back and started to laugh. The laughter made him choke and gag, but he was so relieved he couldn't stop. Eventually it settled into sporadic chuckling interspersed with only the occasional cough.

The last thing he remembered was Makasa muttering, "Fool." She laid the coat over his chest. Then he fell sound asleep on the rain-soaked ground.

CHAPTER FOURTEEN
THERE It WAS

They both woke with the dawn. Or rather, Makasa woke to find Aram lying across her left foot. She kicked him off and, as he groggily blinked his eyes against the rising sun, berated him for being incapable of waking on his own power. For a moment, it felt like they were back aboard ship. Their eyes met, and he recognized a certain pleasure they both felt in the familiar old habit of him disappointing her and her disparaging him for it. But the moment passed. The ship was gone. She fell silent abruptly. They rose together and began to look around. Specifically, Makasa said they needed to find water.

They found Makasa's harpoon first. Her throw had carried it to land—barely. It was embedded at an angle in soggy turf mere inches from the rocky ledge. Aram looked down to see how close it had come to being lost to her—and found the remains of the dinghy, splintered wood at this point, lodged among the shoals directly below. He pointed it out to Makasa, and she seemed to derive some satisfaction from her accuracy. She had aimed the boat and the iron spear at the same low point along the promontory, and both had hit their mark. She yanked the harpoon out of the ground with something akin to a chuckle.

They tried to get their bearings. Makasa stated, "We're in Feralas." Then she added grimly, "Ogre territory."

Aram thought of Throgg and shuddered internally. He tried to calm himself by reviewing what Greydon had taught him about Feralas. For humans, this was basically the far edge of the world. Feralas was a trackless wilderness of uncharted rain forest, with practically every inch of it under the control of ogres. Aram had never seen an ogre before the attack on *Wavestrider*. If they were all like Throgg, he and Makasa were still in serious danger.

So much for calming himself. To cover his fear and seem busy, he pulled out the three maps. The first was of the known world, all of Azeroth. But obviously, it was a bit stingy on local details. The second was of the Eastern Kingdoms. Nostalgically, Aram scanned it for Lakeshire, but before he could pinpoint the location of his home, Makasa growled, "Feralas is in Kalimdor."

"I know," he replied, but he quickly unfolded the third map, the map of Kalimdor. He located Feralas to the south of Desolace and to the northwest of the mountains that separated it from Thousand Needles. Looking up from the map, he could just make out the peaks through the dawn haze, which was already burning off. In fact, the air was warming rapidly. Aram pulled off his torn, damp sweater and tied the sleeves of it and his father's coat around his waist.

That revealed the compass. Unable to resist, he tried it again, comparing it to both the sun and the Kalimdor map. It still wasn't working, didn't point north. In fact, it pointed to the southeast. A thought occurred to him. And desperately he dropped to his knees and—ignoring Makasa's impatient "What are you about now?"—laid out all three maps on the ground to compare them . . .

And there it was. Lakeshire was southeast of their current position. Captain Thorne's compass wasn't pointing north. It was pointing toward home. What had Greydon said?

. . . *Know that this will lead you where you need to go!*

Where *else* did he need to go? Home. To Lakeshire. To his mother and brother and sister and Robb. Aram was somehow sure of it: the compass somehow knew the way home.

Of course, that wouldn't make getting there any easier. Nevertheless, Aram felt his soul lighten. He had seen the compass as a burden—and because he had thought it broken, a ridiculous burden at that. But now he could view the compass as a gift. A last gift from a father he'd never see again.

He wiped a dirty, salt-encrusted arm across his eyes, stinging them into further tears. Then he pushed the feelings down and away. He couldn't face them now.

Makasa repeated: "What are you on about?"

Having choked back his emotions, Aram stared at the map, trying to find something, anything, to say other than the truth of what he was feeling. And again, there it was.

Gadgetzan (capital of the Steamwheedle goblin trade cartel—and home of the helpful Charnas) lay to the southeast, practically in a direct line between where he knelt and Lakeshire.

He said, "Here's Gadgetzan. As the crow flies, it's the nearest large port, and it's neutral territory. We won't have to worry about the Horde. I can find a ship there." He pulled a gold coin from his pocket. "Use this to book passage home."

She studied the map, shook her head. "Gadgetzan's not close at all. We should head for Feathermoon Stronghold, up the coast to the north. There's a military outpost there controlled by the night elves. By the Alliance. Some trade, too. Even something akin to civilization, at least by the standards of Kalimdor."

"The odds of me finding a ship to the Eastern Kingdoms from there are pretty slim."

"The odds of you surviving a trek across Feralas are slimmer. There are gnolls here. Murlocs. Bears, hippogryphs, yetis. And don't forget the ogres."

"We're trekking across Feralas, no matter which way we head."

"The coast and the interior are hardly the same thing. You have no idea the kind of terrain we'd be crossing, inland across Feralas."

"I probably don't. But if we go to Feathermoon, I'm no closer to home. You'd be stuck with me still. But you get me to Gadgetzan, and you can consider your life debt paid."

Makasa started to object—but fell silent. Aram watched her convince herself that finally throwing off the burden of Aramar Thorne—after six months aboard ship and three nights aboard that dinghy—would make her happy. He could almost see the idea of Gadgetzan lighten the soul of Makasa Flintwill, too. She pulled out a packet of hardtack, opened it, and offered half to the boy. "Well, what are we waiting for?" she said. And they trudged off.

Following the compass, they maintained a southeasterly heading. The shores had been rocky and bare, but within ten minutes they were trudging through a dense rain forest. The air was thick; the vines were thicker. The canopy of trees rose above them like ceilings of great halls in the stories of castles his mother had told him as a young child. He had never seen so many different shades of green. He felt an immediate urge to climb a tree, to leap from branch to branch above the loamy turf, to somehow *paint* the colors of the forest into his sketchbook. He longed to explore Feralas—not by crossing it—but in an upward spiral. His pace slowed. He approached the mast-like tree with the bittersweet memory of a climbing Duan Phen filling his thoughts. He would ascend this tree in her honor . . .

"Keep up," Makasa barked at him, breaking the spell for the moment.

He trudged on behind her. This environment might be one Aram had never experienced before, but it was one in which Makasa felt right at home. She used her cutlass like a machete but didn't care for what that was doing to its blade. Aram offered her the hatchet. It was small for the purpose, but Makasa Flintwill was a young woman of precision, and so it served her well enough.

Mosquitoes buzzed around Aram's eyes and ears, driving him nearly insane. And the farther in they marched, the larger the mosquitoes seemed to grow. Soon they were as big as hummingbirds, big enough for Makasa to chop one or two in half—right out of midair.

The going was slow. The forest became less and less romantic. Sweat poured down Aram's brow. It mixed with the dried blood on his forehead, and when he wiped another arm across his face, it came back bloody—and for a second he panicked, until he remembered the smack on the head the night before. His mouth was dry, and he was starting to feel a bit light-headed again.

"Water," he croaked.

She looked back at him, over her shoulder. She scowled, of course. But then she nodded and knelt down. She tore up some thick vines and then snapped one in half. "Open your mouth," she said. "Tilt your head back."

He was dubious but complied, and she poured the liquid contents of the vine into him. It was warm but otherwise surprisingly clean and fresh tasting.

She snapped another vine open and drank herself.

He reached for another vine that was growing up the side of a tree. She slapped his hand away. "Not that kind," she said. "Note the difference in color."

"They're both green," he groused angrily. All thoughts of the differing hues he had so recently admired seemed a trivial annoyance just then.

"The difference in shade, then. See, this sea-green vine runs along the ground. That's what you want. Those pea-green tree vines that grow near fadeleaf contain traces of poison. Probably not enough to kill you, but enough to make you too sick to walk or fend for yourself. And if you think I'm prepared to carry you out of here on my back, you've got another thing coming."

Aram suspected that if push came to shove, Makasa would, in fact, carry him out on her back, but he didn't want to poison himself to test his theory, so he simply nodded.

She pointed to the vines running slightly downhill along the ground. "Also, these should lead us to an actual water source."

And they did: a small streambed overflowing from the recent rain, where both knelt and drank their fill. Aram washed the blood from his face and looked at his reflection in the water. He had a not insignificant bump on his head, but he was otherwise not too worse for wear. They followed the stream for a time.

Makasa, who had ever been on the alert, seemed particularly watchful now.

"What is it?" he said.

"We need something we can use for canteens," she said.

He didn't see how that was possible, but soon Makasa stopped in front of a stand of tall spur-covered plants bearing large spur-covered fruit, which Makasa called "palm-apples." She cut two largish ones off the plant, borrowed the hunting knife, sat on a log, and went to work, carefully carving out a cork-size hole high up on each palm-apple. She gave one of the palm-apples to Aram and picked out two sticks. She instructed Aram how to use his stick to mash up the soft fruit within the husk. Periodically, they'd stop to pour out yellow palm-apple juice into their mouths. It was sweet as nectar—but lighter, more refreshing. Still, it was a long and painstaking process that took them a good hour. But when they were done, they had created two canteens out of the husks.

She held them underwater, and Aram watched the air bubble out. She pulled them up and handed one to him. He poured a short sip into his mouth. The water was cool and tasted of sweet palm-apple. She handed him a cork, and he sealed the receptacle. He held it upside down to test it. A tiny bit of water trickled out, but for the most part, Makasa's creations were a complete success. And, as they walked on and the stream twisted to the southwest, they became essential.

None of Makasa's knowledge or skills particularly surprised Aram. He didn't much enjoy her company, but he had never once doubted her abilities.

They kept walking. The heat and humidity rose with the sun, despite the fact that the canopy of trees provided them with near-constant shade. Makasa seemed not to notice, but Aram was sweating like a pig and rapidly tiring. After another hour, he was relieved when Makasa stopped, giving him the mistaken impression they might rest. But instead, she squatted down near flattened grass to study some fresh, stinking scat on the ground. Aram, who had perhaps imbibed a bit too much palm-apple, felt his gorge rise—but managed to swallow it back down.

Suddenly, Makasa whispered, "Stay here!" and took off at a run, her tall body bent nearly in half to avoid hanging vines.

Aram had only a vague idea of what she was up to. But he drew his cutlass and stood at the ready for her to flush out, well, whatever she was attempting to flush out.

Minutes passed. The palm-apple canteen in one hand and the cutlass in the other were both starting to get heavy. The heat was oppressive, and he began to grow drowsy, his eyes drifting closed and jerking open, his head sinking slowly and jerking back up.

Then he heard the distinct sound of metal cracking wood! *That* woke him up. Then he heard another—stranger—noise. At first he couldn't fathom what it might be, but as it approached, he realized . . . *it was Makasa!* And she was . . . *whooping?* Yes, Makasa Flintwill, no more than a hundred yards away and closing, was swinging her iron chain over her head and *whooping* like a lunatic. It wasn't exactly a dignified sound, and a week ago he would never in a million years have imagined it emanating from his current traveling companion. But there it was.

Then there *IT* was! A great boar—easily two feet high, two feet wide, and four feet long—was bearing down on Aramar Thorne. Its curved white tusks—backed by a massive head and brawny shoulders—seemed more than equal to Aram's cutlass. But he stood his ground.

The boar lowered its bristling head to better aim its tusks at Aram's guts—when Aram heard metal whistling through the air.

Suddenly, the boar seemed to grow a harpoon haft out of its back.

The boar stumbled and rolled, took Aram's legs out from under him, and deposited the boy on his face, reopening the cut on his forehead.

Still, the end result was boar meat for supper.

But not venison. Because despite her prowess as a hunter and tracker, Makasa never even noticed the huge stag watching their proceedings from the trees.

CHAPTER FIFTEEN
THE FEAST OF LORD BLOODHORN

They dubbed their meal "Lord Bloodhorn," and the good fellow served them well.

Makasa had prepared the meat, while Aram—raised beside a forge—collected wood and started a small fire. He also went searching for water and found another small stream not far away, where he drank, washed again, drank again, and filled both canteens.

The night cooled off considerably, but they were comfortable beside the fire, eating their fill. Aram even grew complacent, lying back on the green turf with his hands folded behind his head, his eyes closed, and a sated grin on his face. But with a kick to his thigh to get his attention, Makasa reminded him to remain on the alert for predators—not to mention ogres.

Nevertheless, killing her own supper seemed to have put Makasa in a better mood than usual. It didn't suddenly make her a sparkling conversationalist, but she, too, gave off an air of contentment, which to Aram was a considerable improvement over her typical demeanor.

He pulled out his sketchbook and began sharpening his coal pencil with the knife. For a time she just watched him work. In fact, she waited so long to get around to saying her standard, "You better not be putting me in that blasted book," that Aram nearly forgot to reply. But he summoned up his, "I promise I won't sketch you unless you ask me to," as he tried to sketch his father from memory.

It didn't come easy. The coat helped a bit. He pulled the collar around his face and inhaled deeply, and perhaps imagined the smell of his father surrounding him. But he still couldn't get his efforts to come out right. *Was that his father's nose? And that didn't seem at all like Greydon's smile.*

He frowned at the sketch. He realized his memory of his father's features was already dimming. It had only been four days. What would he remember of Greydon Thorne in a month? By the time Aram made it back to Lakeshire, would the man be reduced to the kind of shadow he had been to his son six months ago?

Six months ago, Aram was told to put his brother and sister to bed. Selya had been fussy. Every time he had started to leave her room, she had said, "Don't go, Aram." He stayed with her until she fell asleep, so it was nearly an hour before he returned to the hearth to find his mother, Robb, and Greydon speaking in low tones— about him.

They quieted when Ceya noticed Aram and gently touched both men on their shoulders.

Greydon stood abruptly. "I'll be at the inn," he said. No one made any attempt to convince him to stay at the Glade cottage. He turned to his former wife. "Think about it. I'll be back in the morning."

He left without another word.

"Think about what?" Aram asked.

"He's leaving for Stormwind Harbor tomorrow," his mother said.

Aram darkened. "Well, he has been here a whole day."

"He wants you to go with him."

"What?"

Robb said, "He wants you to join his crew for a year."

Aram's heart raced. Childhood dreams of the sea momentarily filled his vision. How many years had he dreamed of exactly this? Of sailing beside Greydon Thorne? Of exploring the great wide world of Azeroth?

But almost immediately those childhood dreams seemed childish. Irresponsible. Irresponsible like Greydon Thorne. A man who could go to sea and leave his wife and child behind, with no word, no coin, no concern. That wasn't the kind of man Aramar Thorne wanted to be. And, anyway, if Greydon really wanted Aram, wouldn't he have asked his son himself?

Aram became aware his parents were staring at him. Waiting. Finally, he said, "He never mentioned that to me."

His mother said, "He wanted to make sure he had our approval first." Robb rolled his eyes, and Ceya acknowledged, "He wanted my approval first."

"Well, tell him no," Aram said quickly.

"Why?" said Ceya and Robb, almost in unison.

"Because. Because I'm apprenticed at the forge."

"We can get you out of that," Robb said with a wry smile. "I know the blacksmith."

"Then tell him no because I don't know him. Because I don't want to go. I don't want to leave you two or Robertson or Selya. Besides, I love Lakeshire. This is my home. I'm not a sailor. I'm a blacksmith."

Aram watched them both nod absently. It seemed settled. And then it didn't.

"He'll be back in the morning," Robb said. "You don't have to decide right now."

"It might be different if he stayed for a while," Aram said. "But I'm not going to change my mind about him in one night. He abandoned us. I don't trust him. I don't like him. He should have stayed dead."

Ceya bit her lip.

Robb shook his head. "Don't say that, boy."

"Fine. I'm sorry. But it is what it is." It is what it is was one of Robb's favorite truisms. Aram thought he'd scored a couple points with it.

"Go to bed," Robb said crossly.

Aram rounded up Soot and took the dog to bed with him. A few minutes later, his parents retired to their room, which had a common wall with the chamber he shared with his brother. Robb and Ceya were up late talking. Aram couldn't make out their words, but he could hear his mother crying and Robb trying to comfort her. Her son thought Greydon Thorne responsible for her tears, and they made him angry with the man. Well, angrier. He was sure he'd never fall asleep, but the rhythm of Soot's breathing beside him eventually lulled him into slumber . . .

He should have stayed dead. Had he really said that?

He thought he could feel his heart crumbling to dust in his chest.

Talk about ridiculous. The way his feelings for Greydon could swing between extremes was truly preposterous to Aram, even perverse. But it was what it was. Aram missed his father. And the guilt of leaving him behind to die, of tearing up his picture, of harsh, harsh words said and thought and felt, rushed back at Aram like the seas crashing over the rocks of Feralas.

"By the gods, I'm a brat," he said. He saw Makasa's eyebrow rise half an inch and belatedly realized he had spoken out loud.

"You're just realizing that now?" she said with a happy growl.

"Yeah, actually."

This answer seemed to surprise her. She sat up. She bit her lip, an unconscious gesture that stunned Aram, and not just because this woman—who seemed completely devoid of anything resembling maternal feeling—had, for one brief moment, actually reminded him of his mother. No, what stunned him most was the sense of indecision that bite on the lip represented.

She said, "He wasn't perfect. But he . . . loved you." Saying the word *love* out loud seemed to leave a bad taste in her mouth, but she forged on: "You were all that mattered."

"That's not true," Aram said, a knee-jerk reaction. But he softened. "I mean, I wasn't *all* that mattered to him. There was something else."

She started to protest, but he stopped her. "He *told* me there was something else. He just never got around to telling me what. Then he was out of time. And now, we'll probably never know."

She actually nodded.

He said, "But the thing is, I always pretended that because something else mattered to him, that meant I didn't. And I know that's not true. I've always known that. But . . ."

"*But*, by the gods, you're a brat."

He shrugged his acquiescence.

They were silent for a time.

Aram watched her. She had turned her thoughts inward and that introspection made her look young. It made her look her age. She was seventeen but behaved as if she were thirty. Usually, her inherent competence and cranky disposition lent credence to the illusion. But not just now.

"You loved him," he said.

"What?" she barked back at him, suddenly outraged. She stood and pulled her harpoon out of the ground as if she might skewer him with it.

"Sorry. I'm asking. *Did* you love him?"

Her hand gripped and regripped the iron weapon. When she spoke again, he thought he could hear that her throat had gone dry. "I *respected* him," she croaked. "I wanted him to respect me."

He thought, *Yes, that's all true. But that's not the whole truth. She offered him a life debt but hoped—thought—they'd moved beyond it. That much she's already admitted.*

The rest now seemed almost obvious—or obvious enough that he wondered why he hadn't seen it months before. *After two years aboard ship, standing beside Greydon Thorne, Makasa had come to love him like a father; I know she did. I was his son, but—whether she knew it or not—she wanted to be his daughter. It was one reason why she and I never got along, could never get along. I came aboard and took her place. It didn't help that I didn't seem to want it. Nor that I didn't seem to deserve it.*

He said, "I mattered to him. I know that now."

"A bit late," she said, scowling again and staring down at the fire.

"It was hard to see," he said. "Because no matter how much *I* mattered, it was *you* he valued."

Her eyes snapped up to meet his, to test them for sincerity. But that was an easy test for Aram to pass, because he sincerely believed Greydon valued Makasa more than any person in Azeroth.

"Get some sleep," she said, not unkindly. And then more harshly and in character: "We're up at dawn and walking."

He left the sketch unfinished for the time being and put the pencil and book away.

Days passed. Nights, too. Lord Bloodhorn lasted them a good long time, and Makasa was even able to dry, tan, and sew a crude pack from his hide. Many of their meager supplies were transferred to this pack, including the canteens and oil flask.

Their long march had begun to climb uphill and carry them above the canopy. The area should still have been lush, but tree after tree had been cut down, leaving only stumps. Makasa examined them and declared with certainty that the damage had been done by axe blades too large to have been wielded by anything smaller than an ogre. Thus, they were constantly—exhaustingly—on the alert and continued to sleep in shifts. Aram awoke one night to find Makasa stabbing at a rock viper that had slithered within five inches of his neck.

Without the shade of the trees, the heat and humidity grew oppressive. Other plants were scorched and withered by the bright, unforgiving sun. And the lack of flora had clearly had an effect on the fauna. Makasa had flushed out no more game and had seen little sign that more game existed—other than the poisonous snakes, which she was afraid to cook and eat because she couldn't be certain the snake-flesh would be free of venom. No more palm-apples were to be found, either. Fortunately, despite the heat, water wasn't a problem, thanks to the occasional runoff from the frequent rains. But when it came to food, they were rationing out the hardtack again.

Aram had taken to checking the compass with frustrating regularity—frustrating because it told him so little. He studied it, even sketched it. The casing was brass; the face was white with initials—marking north, south, east, and west—filigreed in gold. The needle was a sliver of crystal, which consistently pointed southeast. To Makasa, he said they were maintaining a direct route to Gadgetzan. It wasn't a lie—their map of Kalimdor confirmed his claim—but in his heart, he felt each step was really bringing him closer to Lakeshire. But there was nothing to consult that could reveal how many days they'd have to walk before reaching Gadgetzan or whether there'd be a ship there to take him home. Nevertheless, whether ascending or resting, he continued to consult the compass, as if maybe *this time* new information would be provided.

* * *

Makasa observed this new habit and came very close to adding it to her long list of things to harass Aram about—but she didn't. At first, she couldn't quite put a finger on why. Eventually, however, she knew: Greydon had checked the compass in the exact same manner. And every time he checked it, the result was the same facial expression of frustration bordering on disappointment that Aram was offering up now. Makasa Flintwill missed her captain, and Aram was bringing the man back to her in some small measure. So she said nothing, lest he stop.

A part of her still prayed that Captain Thorne had somehow defeated the pirates and retaken *Wavestrider*, that the ship had limped to port and was now undergoing repair of the mainmast, that it would set out in search of them soon. But the former second mate knew she'd never have allowed Aram to talk her into heading inland—away from any chance of regaining their ship and rejoining its crew—if for one moment she truly believed any of that fantasy possible. No, Makasa was too practical to lie to herself. By now, Greydon Thorne and the rest of the crew were dead at the pirates' hands.

Assuming the pirates *were* pirates at all. Makasa had her doubts on that score. There were still too many unanswered questions. For starters, she was forced to agree with Aram's earlier observation: in possession of Cobb's intelligence, it seemed unlikely that a standard pirate crew would have much interest in *Wavestrider*'s cargo. The ship itself was a prize, but she had witnessed how little concern the pirate captain had had for leaving said prize undamaged. *And what about that pirate captain?* He had known Captain Thorne, and Thorne had known him, had called him a "traitorous dog." *What was their history?* And when Greydon Thorne had told her and Aram, "There's more at stake than either of you realize," what had he meant? *What was at stake?* She longed to know but despaired of ever finding out. Maybe the pirates *weren't* pirates at all. Yet it changed nothing.

The "pirates," meanwhile, made landfall in Feralas. The tarship, called the *Inevitable* by its crew, was anchored off the coast, while a longboat carried its elite toward shore.

Malus, their leader, watched as the muscle of the group, the ogre Throgg, rowed fiercely, using—in lieu of his missing hand—an iron clamp tightly screwed into the rapidly splintering wood of the oar's handle. They'd be lucky if the oar made it to shore intact, and it frustrated Malus that—short of rowing himself—he could get no one else to take on this mundane chore. Their swordsman, the undead Reigol Valdread, had made a great show of offering his services—only to tear his left arm completely off his shoulder with his very first pull of the oars. He was all whispered apologies as he reattached the arm. But Malus could clearly hear the amused insincerity in Valdread's barely audible protestations of regret. Malus had then looked to their tracker, Zathra, but the troll simply curled her lip into a scowl and said, "Da sea be no place for a sand troll. I not be rowin' for you, mon." That left only their sorcerer, Ssarbik. But Malus hadn't even bothered to ask the strange robe-enshrouded arakkoa, now hissing relentlessly to himself through his sharp, curved beak in the boat's stern. To begin with, the foul creature's birdlike body and feathered limbs weren't well suited for the task, and neither was his arrogant demeanor. Ssarbik barely paid beak-service to being under Malus's command. And Malus was too practical to fool himself into thinking otherwise. So he watched Throgg row and watched the oar handle splinter.

The longboat drew near the rocky coastline. From the deck of the *Inevitable*, Zathra had spotted bits of wreckage among the shoals, and now that they were closer, she was able to confirm they were the remains of a small boat or dinghy.

"The dinghy from Thorne's ship?" Malus demanded.

She glared at him. "Now, how I ta know dat?"

"How long has the wreckage been there?"

"Get me closer, and I tell you."

Malus seethed at her casually insolent tone. This group was deadly and efficient. The successful attack on—and sinking of—the *Wavestrider* had demonstrated that. But they were hardly a cohesive unit. Ssarbik, of course, had his own agenda. Zathra was a mercenary, a professional. She took the job and would complete it. But she had no interest in Malus's cause, and he knew it. And Valdread? Like the troll, he was for hire, accepting gold in exchange for his services and his sword. But truth be told, Valdread had only signed on out of sheer boredom: not a motivation Malus could count on if things got uninteresting—or *too* interesting. He hadn't forgotten or forgiven that Valdread had nearly blown the entire operation by approaching Greydon Thorne prematurely in Flayers' Point. No, only Throgg the Truly Dim was truly loyal to his master.

In fact, loyalty all but defined the ogre. Even his missing hand was a symbol of that quality, having been taken years ago as proof of allegiance to the orcs of the Shattered Hand clan.

Throgg rowed as close to shore as he dared without scuttling them on the rocks.

Crouching in the bow, Zathra leaned forward, her sharp eyes taking in every detail of the wreckage.

"Been dere a week," she said. "It be da boat from da ship . . ."

"Or a startling coincidence," whispered Valdread.

"I do not believe in coinccidenccessss," hissed Ssarbik. His sibilant voice—unusual even for an arakkoa—grated on everyone aboard, even the Whisper-Man.

"No place to land," Throgg stated. "Throgg head south 'til we—"

But already the arakkoa had begun his chant: "We are the Hidden, the voyagerzz of Shadow. We ssserve and will conquer. What we conquer will Burn. Bend to the masster'ss will. Bend to the Hidden. Bend. Bend."

The water darkened and swirled around the boat. The air seemed charged with static. Shadows in the bottom of the boat twisted and writhed. Throgg and Zathra growled low in disturbed unison. Malus scowled, the hair on his arms prickling up to attention. Valdread's opinion was unknowable under his hood.

And still, Ssarbik intoned, "Bend. Bend. Bend."

With a lurch, the dark water lifted the boat upward. It landed with a crack of its keel upon the shore, just above the dinghy's wreckage—and, in fact, smack atop where Makasa's harpoon had struck earth. Malus couldn't help noting that the damage to Throgg's oar hardly mattered now that the entire longboat had been rendered unsound.

Valdread removed his hood, revealing blanched-white skin stretched tight over his skull-shaped head with its somewhat permanent skeletal grin. "Well, that saved some time," he whispered.

Throgg unclamped himself from the oar and stood up in the boat, tipping it. The others were quick enough to leap clear— all but Ssarbik, who was tossed out, face first, into the mud.

Scampering up and trying to cover the indignity with fury, the arakkoa hissed, "Fool! You will sssuffer!"

"Enough," Malus said. Ssarbik might not like it, but Malus was still in command. "We haven't the time to fight among ourselves. Zathra, earn your keep."

"Dat be some trick, mon. Since da mud-bird here wiped out deir traces wit dis boat and his clumsy self."

Ssarbik wheeled on the troll, but she leveled a crossbow between his eyes, and the arakkoa shrunk back, hissing.

Malus tried not to smile. "Find new traces," he said.

Zathra scanned the surrounding area. Then she smiled and strode toward the edge of the rain forest. They followed.

At the treeline, she nodded to herself and said, "Here. Dey entered here, headin' southeast."

"What's southeast of nothing?" asked Valdread. His lidless eyes surveyed their surroundings and found them wanting. He raised his hood again.

Malus considered. "If you march far enough, Gadgetzan. But why head toward Gadgetzan when Feathermoon Stronghold is so much closer?"

Throgg shrugged. "Maybe they don't know where they are."

Malus waved him silent. "Just because you don't know where we are."

But Throgg took some umbrage and would not be silent even for his captain. "Throgg know where we are. This is Feralas. Ogre land." He twisted the clamp off his wrist and replaced it with a machete.

"They follow the compasssss," hissed Ssarbik, catching Malus's eye.

"Perhaps," Malus said, before turning to Zathra and asking, "What's their lead?"

"Seven, eight days."

"Send it ahead," he ordered.

"*Her,*" the troll corrected. "She be a she." Zathra tilted her head, clicked her tongue several times, and began stroking her body-armor lovingly. "Wake up, little one," she said, with something like affection. The armor clicked in response and moved and then abruptly skittered off her torso and down one leg. Throgg and Ssarbik took a step back. Malus didn't, *only* because he refused to show weakness. Valdread leaned against a tree and yawned.

The sand troll knelt beside her pet: a three-foot-long, tan scorpid with black markings. She stroked her the way a human child might stroke a kitten. The creature brandished her stinger and emitted a few clicking noises. Zathra clicked back. The others waited impatiently.

When the troll finally spoke, her dry desert voice had a loving quality that was almost disturbing. "Skitter, my sista. Follow deir trail. Find dem. Den return ta me."

They clicked at each other a few more times—and then Skitter whipped around and skittered into the rain forest.

Zathra was still smiling after her scorpid when Malus said, "Lead the way."

And so, their tracker led the way, noting bends in the leaves and hatchet-hacked vines that marked their quarry's path, while leaving not a trace herself. Not that it mattered. The ogre followed the troll, using his machete-hand to hack a wider lane for himself and the others. Captain Malus went next, and the arakkoa scampered after him, as if not trusting their leader otherwise. Valdread took up the rear, one hand on the hilt of his black sword. The cracked longboat and the *Inevitable* itself were left behind, practically forgotten, as the Hidden vanished into the forest, hot on the trail of Aramar Thorne.

CHAPTER SEVENTEEN
MURKY DEPTHS

Since fleeing *Wavestrider*, they had been three days at sea and fourteen, now, hiking across Feralas, and most of the latter uphill. Lord Bloodhorn was but a memory, and they were almost out of hardtack. The land they traversed continued to be barren and devoid of even small game. And Makasa was on the verge of testing out the moss on the rocks for sustenance.

The days were hot, even steamy. But the nights were cold— and colder still since firewood had grown scarce. Aram would wrap himself tight in his father's coat and still find himself shivering.

Even water was becoming a problem. Their palm-apple can-teens had started to rot and had to be thrown away. There was still the occasional brook but no way to carry water with them. Aram didn't like to leave their southeasterly course, but Makasa was no longer willing to risk abandoning a water source. The next time they found a trickle, she insisted on following it upstream, even though it bent to the northeast.

Aram checked the compass and sighed but didn't argue. They marched on.

The sound swelled so gradually, it was practically a roar before it registered on their brains, and they had practically stumbled upon the river before they understood what they were hearing.

The river's churning rapids carved a deep, forbidding gorge into the canyon. There was plenty of water here—but reaching it was not without its danger. Makasa—as usual, making the decision for the both of them—skirted the edge, hoping for a safer way down eventually.

Aram pointed to a crevasse. "What about there?!" He had to shout over the din of the flow.

She said nothing until they were closer, but she didn't like the look of it and shook her head. Makasa was far from timid and might have been willing to try her luck if she'd been alone. But the burden of watching out for the Greydon-son had made her cautious. If he fell—or even if she did—she knew the boy would never survive.

They continued on, Aram a few steps behind Makasa. The low roar of the river filled Aram's ears, but something higher pitched began to play along the edge of his consciousness as he walked along the edge of the gorge. *What was that? Shouting?*

He leaned over the side, scanning for the source of the strange noise. He saw nothing. And at times he couldn't even hear it.

Makasa, who had walked on, glanced back to see Aram grasping a rock and bending almost horizontally over the gorge. "What are you doing?!" she shouted. It startled him, and she watched with horror as his grip on the rock seemed to slip. But he held on and still persisted to lean over the edge.

She stalked over to him, ready to pull him back by his earlobe—when she heard it, too: some strange cry emanating from below.

"There!" Aram called out, pointing with his free hand down into the gorge. It was some kind of creature, small—probably only a few feet tall—and green, entwined and trapped in what looked like an immense spiderweb at the river's edge below. No, not a web. Nets, fishing nets. The river kept tugging the beast under the water before it would emerge again and scream. On either side were jagged rocks, churning up more white water, and every time the current pulled the poor thing under, the nets stretched or tore, taking it closer to a braining against the stones.

"What is it?!" Aram shouted.

"A murloc!" she shouted back.

"That's a murloc?!" It wasn't at all what he'd pictured as a six-year-old, searching Lake Everstill for signs of the "devious monsters" and his missing father. "I thought a murloc was more . . . terrible!"

"They're terrible enough! Let's go!"

The creature's head emerged then above water and screamed plaintively. The words themselves were unintelligible, but Aram knew a cry for help when he heard one.

"We can't leave it like that!" he shouted.

"We can! There's no way down here! Besides, murlocs can breathe underwater. The thing's in no danger of drowning!"

"It's in danger of getting crushed on those rocks!" And just then the nets chucked the murloc against them. It cried out sharply in pain. "See!" Aram shouted, and then raced off, saying, "C'mon, there was a way down back here!"

Makasa tried to grab him—but he was too fast and just out of her reach. Growling angrily, she followed him back to the crevasse.

She overtook him there before he could start down. "No!" she yelled, grabbing hold of his shirt. Then something caught her eye. She turned. It was a stag. A massive buck. Ten, twelve points, at least. Only ten, fifteen yards away with no cover in sight. *Here* was enough meat to feed them for weeks. She released Aram and turned to pull her harpoon out from between her back and her shield.

But as she turned, Aram descended, wedging his arms on either side of the slim crevasse and lowering himself down a foot at a time.

Makasa felt helpless. She tried to keep an eye on the stag while calling back over her shoulder for Aram to *"STOP!"* But the boy didn't stop. The deer tilted his head at her, staring her down, as if waiting for her to decide.

Roaring louder than the river, she drove the harpoon down into dirt with both hands and turned her back on the animal. She could just hear him run off as she dropped onto her stomach and reached her long arm down, grabbing hold of Aram's hair, which was all she could reach.

"Ow! Let go!!"

"Listen—"

"No! I have to try to save it!"

She didn't let go of his hair, but she swallowed hard. "Fine! But first give me the end of the rope! Or were you planning to fly back up here after your daring rescue of the slimy thing that's probably going to eat you?!"

This gave him pause. He nodded and wedged his shoulders against one side of the crevasse and his feet against the other. Then he slowly reached for the rope that was wrapped around his torso.

"Careful!" she barked, startling him.

"Stop doing that," he said. He unknotted one end of the rope and handed it up to her.

She finally let go of his hair, took the rope, and wrapped it around her hand a few times. "Now unwind it!"

"We don't have time!" He glanced down, but from this angle he could no longer see the murloc.

"Do it, or I'll rip out your scalp!"

Slowly—because slowly was the only way he could manage it in his current position—he did as he was told. As it slackened, Makasa sat up and slung the rope around her back. "Now tie the other end around your waist, and I'll lower you down!"

Now he understood and quickly obeyed. He also tucked the compass under his shirt, as he'd seen his father do before taking action of any kind.

He carefully rappelled down the crevasse, with an angry, grunting Makasa acting as his anchor above. This was actually something he'd done before—at the Lakeshire quarry back home with his friends Stitch and Willy—so he made good time to the bottom.

Once his feet touched down on a thin strip of rocky terrain between the wall of the gorge and the rushing river, he waved up at Makasa and untied the spent rope, leaving it hanging. Then he rushed upstream, hoping the murloc was still alive to save.

Its screaming confirmed it was. Aram couldn't reach the creature, but he grabbed hold of the nets and tried to pull them in. But the panicked murloc hadn't yet seen its savior and was fighting the nets—and inadvertently fighting Aram.

Aram pulled again, but the murloc and the current pulled back; he stumbled forward, his left leg sinking up to the knee in the rushing water. He looked down and couldn't see the river bottom. Aram was still off balance, and one more tug of the current submerged him completely. The water was dark and murky, cold and deep. It dragged him forward. He surfaced, gasping for breath and glimpsing the white water and rocks ahead.

He fought the current, flashing back to the night he'd swum to shore and nearly drowned. And for one brief moment he thought, *This time, the water might win . . .*

But a hand grabbed his shoulder and pulled him back onto gravel. Aram sucked in air and looked up at a furious Makasa looming over him. Now, he flashed back to her yanking him out of his bunk aboard *Wavestrider.* Some things never change.

She helped him, practically pulled him, to his feet. They turned as the murloc—who seemed to be mostly one big head with gangly arms and legs—surfaced briefly and screamed again. But now, the creature's large soulful eyes locked onto Aram's. For the first time, the murloc became aware of his rescuer and smiled hopefully.

Makasa said, "If we're going to do this, let's do this."

Together, they both grabbed hold of the nets and pulled with all their might . . .

With Makasa's strength added to his, the effort was more than enough. Nets and murloc came flying out of the water, slamming into Aram, who slammed into Makasa. They all went down in a pile on the edge of the river.

Makasa, with Aram's armpit covering her eyes and a murloc foot stinking of fish right under her nose, growled, "Get. Off. Me."

They scrambled off. The murloc, still tangled to some degree in the nets, bowed to his rescuers over and over. "Mmrgl,

mmrgl, mrggl mrrrgl, Murky, mrgglll," he said, which meant exactly nothing to the two humans. Still, it was obvious the small green creature was grateful. He clapped his two-fingered hands and scampered about nervously back and forth on his webbed feet, tangling himself even more hopelessly. The fins on his cheeks flapped up and down. He seemed eager to approach Aram but kept pulling back, afraid—or too wild and undomesticated—to trust the human entirely.

"You're welcome," Aram said. "Do you speak Common?"

"Mrgle, nk. Murky mrrrgl mmmurlok."

"I guess you only speak murloc."

"Mrgle. Mrgle, mrgle," said the murloc.

"I'm Aram," the boy said, pointing to himself. Then he pointed to Makasa. "This is Makasa."

The murloc pointed to Aram and said, "Urm." Then he pointed to Makasa and said, "Mrksa." Finally, he pointed to himself and said, "Murky."

"Murky? Your name is Murky?"

"Murky, mrgle!"

"Wait? Murky or Murgle?"

"Murky! Murky!"

"Murky. Got it."

"Mrksa" actually rolled her eyes. "Let's get out of here," she said.

"Right," Aram said, turning to Murky. "Follow us. We have a way up and out. I think."

Murky hesitated. He didn't seem to understand. Wasn't sure if he was wanted.

"It'll be okay," Urm told him. He approached Murky slowly and then patted him on his slimy head.

Murky seemed to like that and rubbed his head against Aram's stomach. It left behind an oily stain and the distinct aroma of old fish. Aram had to fight off the urge to vomit, even as he tried with little success to wipe his hand off on his pants.

But the combination of Aram's soothing words and gentle actions had certainly worked its magic on the murloc. Murky was nodding enthusiastically as he began to gather up his nets.

Makasa growled, "Are we really waiting for this thing?"

Suddenly, Murky began jumping up and down excitedly. He reached down into his net and pulled out one very large salmon, then held it up over his head in triumph!

Then, with much ceremony, he knelt in front of Aram and handed him the fish.

Aram smiled up at Makasa with his own bit of triumph. "Looks like we eat tonight."

CHAPTER EIGHTEEN
URUM'S TALE

Makasa had left the rope tied to a rock atop the crevasse and used it to climb up. Then Aram followed, half climbing, half being pulled up by Makasa. He turned to lower the rope back down to Murky, but the little murloc had used his claws to scamper up the crevasse right behind Aram. So all three were back atop the gorge and exhausted.

Night was falling. They found a copse of ironwood trees that hadn't yet been chopped down and made camp. Their fire was small and burned poorly; the wood was too green. But they were able to cook Murky's salmon on a flat rock and share it among them.

Murky initially declined his share, pantomiming that he wanted his rescuers to have it. Instead, he tried to eat the oilskin that had been wrapped around the box of flints. "Mmmm,

mmm," he said, trying to put a brave face on his feast. But ultimately, he spit it out at Aram's feet, shook his head, and said,
"Mlggr, nk mmmm, mrggggl. Murky mrrrgll." Aram handed
Murky a piece of fish, which the murloc took but made a face
over. He used his claws to delicately remove any sign of char-
ring before swallowing the remains down.

Aram said, "You'd have liked it better raw, huh?"

Murky smiled at him but said nothing. Aram was never
entirely sure how much they understood each other. With two
fingers, he reluctantly picked up the slimy, saliva-covered oilskin and laid it near the fire, hoping it would dry.

And hoping he would dry, too. His plunge into the river had
soaked him to the bone, and the night was getting cold. He
huddled as close to the fire as he could get without setting himself ablaze. And as he stared, he thought of *Wavestrider* aflame,
and his face darkened.

It was then that Murky tried to get his attention, calling out,
"Urm. Urm." It took Aram some time to realize Murky was trying to say his name, and thus a lesson in pronunciation began.

"Urm?"

"Aram."

"Urm . . ."

"No. AIR-am."

"UR-um. Urum."

"Close enough," Aram said. "So you can *understand*
Common?"

"Mrgle," said Murky, nodding.

"You're nodding. So 'murgle' means yes, right?"

The murloc shrugged ambivalently. "Mrgle. Mrrrrgggl mrglll mmmrggl."

Aram sighed.

But Murky wasn't finished. He began talking rapidly. "Urum, mrgggl. Murky mrrrgl mrrgggll, mrrg, mrggllrm Murky n mmmurlok, mmmrrggl, mrgle?"

Aram smiled and shook his head. "I'm sorry. I don't understand."

So Murky began to act out his tale. He picked up his nets and started walking in place.

Aram attempted to follow along. "You took your nets and went for a walk . . ."

"Mrgle, mrgle."

Makasa stared at them both, unsure which one was crazier.

Murky then began throwing out his nets.

"You went fishing."

"Mrgle." Murky clapped his hands together. Then he climbed into his nets and intentionally tangled himself up in them.

"You got tangled in your nets . . ."

"Mrgle."

". . . And that's when we found you."

Murky's face fell. He shook his head, waved his arm back behind him, and said, "Nk, nk. Mrrrrgg mrrrrgglll, mrglllle mmmrgg." Then, still completely tangled in his nets, he started clomping halfway round the campfire and growling, "RRRgrrrs, RRRgrrrs."

Makasa had to leap forward to keep him from dragging the nets through the fire itself. "Stop," she shouted at him.

He clapped his hands, pointed at her, and shouted back, "Mrgle, mrgle! Mrksa RRRgrrr!"

Suddenly, he threw his arms around himself and wrestled himself to the ground. Then he looked up at Aram and said, "Mrrrgle?"

"Sorry," Aram said, "you lost me."

Murky frowned and looked at Makasa.

"Don't look at me," she said. "I wasn't even paying attention to you, murloc."

Aram turned to her with a reprimand. "Why not? *He* taught us both to pay attention to everything. To everyone."

They both knew exactly whom Aram meant by *he*. Aram saw Makasa look down, actually chastened. A girl again.

Murky was now trying to disentangle himself from his nets. With little luck. Aram stood and went to his aid. The murloc seemed to appreciate the help but seemed equally determined to help Aram help him. He wouldn't keep still, and Aram wasn't having any better luck setting him free. "Wait, Murky, don't move. I've almost got it . . ."

Finally, a frustrated Makasa told Aram, "Out of the way!" She grabbed the nets and lifted them up to her full height. Murky hung there by one last tangled foot. Aram rushed in and pulled the foot loose. Murky dropped, landing on his head. Aram knelt down, apologizing. Makasa swung the nets clear of murloc, boy, and fire. Then she sat back down in a huff.

Aram was concerned the murloc had been hurt, but Murky seemed cheerful. He pointed at what remained of the fish: nothing but bones, the head, and bits of skin. "Mmmmrgl?"

"Be my guest," Aram said.

Murky scooped up the remains and practically inhaled them, bones and all. Aram was half-prepared to see the murloc spit it all out as he had the oilskin. But Murky swallowed, smiled, and lay down on his stomach with a contented sigh. He propped his head up and stared at Aram with the biggest puppy-dog frog eyes the boy had ever seen.

"I think he's in love," said Makasa ruefully.

"He's just grateful," Aram shot back. Murky made Aram smile, and he pulled out his sketchbook to capture the murloc and that feeling. He flipped past the unfinished memory sketch of his father, pausing over it before shaking his head and turning the leaf to a blank page.

While Murky tended to his nets—rolling them up into a thick belt that he tied around his small waist, so that the belt became something more like a vest by the time he was done—Aram began sketching the murloc in detail: the huge head and eyes, the cheek fins, tiny nostril holes, and crooked toothy smile. The little body, so small it barely seemed capable of supporting the weight of Murky's head, and the musculature that actually did make it capable. As usual, sketching brought Aram closer to his subject, showed him the biology they had in common. Aram's own smile began to mimic Murky's as he started

Murky

AFAM

another sketch, this one showing the murloc in a familiar pose—entangled in his nets.

"Mrgle, mrgle," Murky said, resting what passed for his chin on one hand. Then he pointed at Aram and said, "Urum. Mrrrgl mrrg, Urum." He pointed at the nets and himself. Then he pointed at Aram again. "Urum mrrrgl mrrg."

Aram had a sudden epiphany. "You want to know my story?"

"Mrgle, mrgle," Murky said and shrugged again. Suddenly, Aram was less certain of his epiphany. And besides . . .

Which story is that?

On his last morning in Lakeshire, Aramar Thorne had risen early, determined to go nowhere.

But his parents—all three of them—had made their own determinations. Ceya, Robb, and Greydon were all waiting for him by the fire, and Aram could instantly tell by their expressions—different as they all were—that his cause was already lost. Not that Aram was ready to accept that loss—or at any rate, not that he was going to make it easy on any of them. Yes, there might have been a part of him that was curious, excited even, to travel with Greydon. Truthfully, he had dreamed of following—or perhaps chasing—his father to sea for years. But he hated that he was being given no choice in the matter now. So he suppressed that part of himself and argued, debated, whined, wheedled, pled, and flat-out refused.

Greydon largely stayed out of the discussion, but it hardly mattered. Ceya and Robb were adamant that Aram needed time to get to know his father, to understand him, and to see the world.

Aram appealed to their practicality, to their emotions, to their sense of justice. He wouldn't even shy away from questioning their concern for him or from claiming they'd always wanted to get rid of him so that they could have their own little family without any reminders of Ceya's old life with Greydon. If it seemed helpful to his cause, he said it. If it seemed hurtful, but helpful to his cause, he said it anyway.

Ceya had tears in her eyes, but it changed nothing. She said, "Aram, I know you're angry and frightened."

"I'm not frightened," he had said.

"Yes, you are. We're asking you—telling you—to leave everything you've ever known. Who wouldn't be frightened?"

He glowered but said nothing.

"But this is something you need to do or you will always wonder. You need to go out and explore that piece of you that is just like Greydon Thorne—"

"I'm nothing like him!"

"Oh, Aram, you grow more and more like him every day. If I thought you could see that, I might let you stay."

"Fine, I see it."

She smiled then through her tears. "Nice try, clever boy. But you need to open your heart to him again. I know he hurt you, hurt us. But you need to know him to know yourself. And you need to see all of Azeroth—open yourself to its strangers and their customs—*before you can decide that Lakeshire is truly your home. And you need . . ." She trailed off.*

"Need what?"

"The rest you need to discover with time."

"How much time?"

"A year. After that, if you want to come home—"

"I don't want to leave, so of course I'll want to come home!"

"After a year, you can come home."

So there had been a little packing and a lot of good-byes. Robertson seemed as angry as Aram and actually threw a cup at Greydon's head over breakfast, which—if it accomplished nothing else—at least made Aram smile.

After that, Greydon waited outside.

Selya was inconsolable. And the more she cried, the more their mother cried. Soot began to howl.

Robb Glade finally picked up Aram's rucksack and walked the boy out.

Greydon, trying not to look too pleased, stood at the crossroads a dozen yards away.

Robb knelt beside Aram and busied himself squaring Aram's sweater on his shoulders. "Don't spend the next year being stubborn," he said. "Or angry or bitter or any of those things. Any son of mine knows better than to starve his own fire that way. The forge needs to be fed to stay hot enough to melt iron. Hot enough to make something strong. So make yourself into something strong by feeding your forge with everything you can. Understand?"

"No," Aram said gloomily, though he thought he probably did.

"All right, you can starve it for one day. I don't blame you, I suppose. But by sunrise tomorrow, you open your eyes and feed that fire, Aram." The big man was squeezing back tears. He cuffed the boy gently—though not too gently—then stood abruptly, went inside, and shut the door.

Leaving Aramar Thorne alone with his new captain.

Aram stared at Murky and sketched the gigantic pupils of his big eyes onto the page.

"Urum?" Murky prompted.

"You want my story . . ."

"Mrgle."

Aram glanced at Makasa, who was watching him intently. Finally, he said, "Makasa and I were on a ship. Pirates attacked. Everyone died. We escaped. That's my story."

Murky seemed unsatisfied. Even Makasa seemed unsatisfied. But that, Aram decided, was all "Urum" had to say tonight. After finishing the sketch, he closed the book, turned over, and tried to sleep.

Watching with glowing silver eyes, the stag heard all of this, his curiosity piqued.

But the scorpid had witnessed none of it. As soon as Skitter had spotted Aram and the others sitting around the campfire, she had turned right around to fetch Zathra and the rest of the Hidden.

CHAPTER NINETEEN

POINTS

Come the morning, Makasa seemed in a better humor. She graciously thanked Murky for the salmon and wished him well before saying good-bye.

Murky looked stricken. "Nk, nk. Murky mrrgggrl mmmrgl mmgr Mrksa, Urum, mrgle?"

Aram smiled. "I think he wants to come with us."

"What? No! Absolutely not!"

"Why?"

"I've enough trouble looking after your sorry rear. We don't need another mouth to feed, especially one we can't even understand!"

"I'm starting to understand him a bit."

"That's not the point," she growled.

"Well, what is the point?"

"The point?! The point?!" She was shouting, which was bad enough. But then her voice lowered to a whisper, which for Aram was somehow even worse. "The point is Captain Thorne is dead. Our entire crew is dead. These lands are crawling with ogres, blasted snakes, and nothing to eat. You and I are lost and probably doomed. And so the life debt I *still* owe to your father, will *forever* owe to him—even though he's gone—grows more difficult to guarantee with every passing minute. I can't take it, Aram. I can't take on one more responsibility. I swear I'm at my limit. That's the point." She blinked back tears.

"The point is," Greydon had said, "home isn't a place. It's the people with whom you choose to share your life. Family is what makes a home. Not the other way around. And there are all kinds of families."

Aram did something odd then. Something spontaneous and honest but bizarre to anyone who had known him and Makasa or had *ever* seen them together. He embraced her. He wrapped his arms around her—chain, harpoon, shield, and all—and hugged her tight. She stiffened, and her own arms hung at her sides at first, but gradually she raised them and hugged him back. She laid her cheek atop his head and exhaled something suspiciously like a sigh. He thought, *We both loved him.* And her thoughts mirrored his. There was no need to say the words aloud. For once, each just knew what the other was thinking: they were brother and sister, mourning the same father. Both had their eyes closed and were quiet.

"Mmmrrglllmmm." Murky hugged them both around the legs, breaking the spell.

Makasa instantly pulled away, wiping her bare arm across her eyes.

Aram wiped his eyes with his dirty sleeve. He shrugged and smiled at her.

She scowled and turned away. But her next words were, "Fine, he can tag along. But he's *your* responsibility, Urum."

"Sure, Mrksa."

Murky skipped in place. "Mmrgl, Mrksa! Mmrgl, Urum!"

Makasa Flintwill shook her head, but Aram could tell she was at least a little bit amused. She marched on. They followed.

At home, Aram had a sister, a little sister. And a little brother. But he knew now that Makasa had truly become his big sister. Family. It had probably been true for months, though the realization was fresh. He hadn't recognized it, because he had always been the oldest of his siblings, the one who took care of and watched over—and, yes, on occasion, teased—the younglings. But that was Makasa's job with him.

He knew how she felt. His stewardship of Robertson and Selya had never been quite so dire, but there had been times—like on trips to the quarry—when trying to keep an eye on both had nearly driven him mad.

He caught up to Makasa and asked, "Do you have any brothers or sisters?"

"Why?" she asked suspiciously, without slowing down.

Ignoring the question, he instead volunteered, "I have one younger brother, Robertson, and a baby sister, Selya."

"I have three older brothers," she said. "Adashe, Akashinga, and Amahle."

So that's it, he thought. *I'm not used to being the youngest, and she's not used to being the eldest. No wonder we're always tearing at each other.*

"Had," she said quietly.

"What?"

"Had three brothers. They're gone now. Dead. All of them. I'd be with them, too, if not for your father."

She risked a glance at him. He swallowed, too stunned— thankfully—to offer up a look of pity, which would have truly set her off.

Murky came up on the other side, saying, "Murky mrrrgllle mmrrrrggg mrrrgll, Mrksa."

She stared at him, then offered up an unsure "Thank you?"

The murloc nodded, satisfied.

Aram was staring at the ground as they walked, three abreast, in silence. He knew he had led a sheltered life. The attack on *Wavestrider* was literally the worst thing that had ever happened to him. The only other thing that even registered on the scale was Greydon's desertion. And those two things were bad enough for any child's lifetime. But he had been so self-centered, it had never even occurred to him to consider Makasa's story and what she had been through. She had the same tragedy of the *Wavestrider* to equal his—because hadn't Greydon been as much her father aboard that ship as Aram's?— and she had an entire past Aram knew nothing at all about. Nothing except this: she had had three older brothers, who were all now dead.

He said, "Do you want to—"

"No!" she said fiercely. But then she added more softly, "Not now."

So they walked on, following the gorge and the river, across the ravaged land of tree stumps and seared grass.

Late that afternoon, Murky proved his worth to Aram—and even a little bit to Makasa—by leading them down a steep but walkable path to the river to drink. They had skipped breakfast and lunch, so Makasa broke out the very last of the hardtack, reluctantly sharing it with Murky. "That's it," she said. "No more."

Murky started to unfold his nets from around his waist. Both Aram and Makasa considered this sensible. Another fish dinner would do nicely. But twelve seconds later, Murky had hopelessly tangled himself in the mesh again.

While trying to negotiate his freedom—twisting the net over, sliding it under, and pulling this limb free of that loop, tugging that limb free of this loop—Murky suddenly screamed. Aram thought at first that the murloc was in pain, but as soon as he could get a hand free, Murky pointed up to the top of the gorge, shouting, "RRRgrrr! RRRgrrr!" They looked but saw nothing.

Murky growled in frustration and reached for Makasa's cutlass. She slapped his hand away. "Don't touch!"

"Mrksa mrrugggl!" He swung an imaginary sword around. "Mrksa mrrugggl!" He then pointed at Aram's cutlass and said, "Urum mrrugggl!"

They both got the message and drew their swords. "What did he see?" Aram asked.

"I don't know," Makasa said, scanning the cliffside. "But I trust it scared him. Stay on guard." She glanced back at Murky. "And get him out of that net, or we're leaving him behind for whatever's out there!"

"We're not leaving him behind, when he's the one who warned us," Aram said, knowing she had no real intention of leaving anyone behind.

She did, however, seem to be all right with the idea of cutting him free of the net. This also made Murky scream in horror: "Nk! Nk! Murky mmrrgggleee mrrugggl mgrrrl nk mmmurlok!"

"A murloc must always protect his nets," said a booming voice behind them. Makasa and Aram both wheeled about. A tall figure in dark hooded robes was standing behind them, close enough to make Makasa curse herself under her breath for allowing the stranger to draw so near.

The newcomer's face was hidden by his hood, instantly reminding Aram of the Whisper-Man. But this *clearly* wasn't him. If the hood was any indication, this stranger had a preposterously wide head. And although he stooped, bent nearly halfway over and leaning on a walking stick, he was still taller than Makasa by at least half a foot.

"Have no fear," he said. "I mean no harm." He spoke softly, but this was no Whisper-Man; his voice was fuller, warmer.

It was a still-tangled Murky who whispered, *"Kuldurrree,"* while bowing very low.

Aram didn't understand, but Makasa hadn't put up her sword, so Aram kept his out and at the ready.

Makasa said, "Druid."

And now Aram understood. He felt his throat go dry and was suddenly very conscious of trying to swallow. This, as Greydon had taught him, was a kaldorei. A night elf. A druid. A shapeshifter.

As if confirming Aram's unspoken thoughts, the stranger reached up to lower his hood.

"Slowly," Makasa demanded.

"Of course," said the druid, complying. The hood came down, revealing a thin and ancient face with lined indigo skin, long hair the color of ice tucked behind pointed ears, glowing silver eyes that reflected the starlight, and massive brown antlers.

"Ten, twelve points, at least," murmured Makasa. Then at full volume: "You're the stag, aren't you?"

"Guilty, I am afraid." There was a smile audible in the druid's voice to match the visible one on his face.

"You've been watching us." It wasn't a question.

"Guilty, again." He still seemed mildly amused by the interrogation.

"Following us."

"Well, hold on now, young lady. Mostly, I was just heading in the same direction. But keeping an eye on you made the journey more diverting."

"I nearly had you for dinner," Makasa said grimly.

"You nearly tried, yes. No hard feelings."

Aram was too busy staring to say anything. Those glowing silver eyes were disconcerting at first. But within seconds they radiated an infectious calm.

The kaldorei are a sight to behold, surely," Greydon had said. *"Merely laying eyes on one can take the most hardened warrior's breath away. And* that *is something they count on. You may not see it, but you'll feel it. They have . . . an aura. Power. It surrounds and infuses them. It's blasted irresistible. But resist you must. A night elf can be a great friend. Or a terrible foe. I can't say you'll ever meet one in the flesh, son. But if you do, find out which you're facing* before *you lower your guard."*

Aram struggled to follow his father's advice. Then the night elf smiled again and, raising an eyebrow, said, "My name is Thalyss Greyoak. And you are?"

And just like that, words poured forth unbidden from Aram's mouth before he had the thought to form—let alone censor—them. "I'm Aramar Thorne, but you can call me Aram." Makasa scowled at him. He shrugged sheepishly but babbled on: "This is Makasa Flintwill, and this is Murky."

"It is a pleasure to meet you all. And it would be nice to have some company for a time."

"Our party," Makasa growled, "is already larger than originally planned."

"So one more should not matter. Especially one more with a pack full of food he is willing to share."

Makasa and Aram exchanged a telling glance, and Thalyss's eyes twinkled with pleasure.

"The sun is setting, and I have been this way before. I know a good place to make camp for the night. And if you follow me, it will be easier to keep your eyes sharp and your swords leveled at my back." The druid chuckled then and walked with casual impunity, right between Aram and Makasa. Without stopping, he gave a short tug on one end of the nets, and Murky rolled scot-free.

Murky promptly scooped up the nets and scrambled after the night elf, saying, "Mmrgl, mmrgl, *kuldurrree.*"

Aram looked to Makasa. She nodded with some reluctance, and they followed. But Aram saw that her cutlass remained in her hand and at the ready.

She didn't trust the idea that the night elf just happened to be going their way. Makasa's memory was long, but it required no long memory to recall that the pirate captain had a troll, an ogre, and one of the Forsaken under his command. *Why not a druid, as well?*

CHAPTER TWENTY
FRUNDS AROUND
THE CAMPFIRE

They sat around the campfire, while Thalyss prepared a stew of wild carrots and snap peas and potatoes and spices that the night elf had produced by emptying his pack. ("No venison," the druid had said, with a wink at Makasa.) As he stirred the stew, Thalyss spoke of gathering each of the vegetables, carefully and in turn, so that more would grow. "That, of course, is my function as a druid. I do what I can to protect the wild."

Aram was instantly fascinated. "Like the birds and the beasts?"

"Well, my specialty is flora, not fauna. But, yes. We so-called sentient species do an incredible amount of quite insentient violence to the natural order. Druids try to balance that with restoration, recovery, and care."

"Magic," Makasa grumbled darkly.

"When a flower blooms, is that not magical? When a lamb is born to an ewe, are mysteries not revealed? Yes, I am a magic user of a kind. But trust me, my magics are of the natural order—certainly when compared to the forged axe that has so unnaturally cut down nearly every tree in these parts."

Thalyss only had one small stewpot and one large spoon, so they took turns passing the concoction around atop a folded strip of blanket to save their hands (if not always their tongues) from being burnt. When divided by four, the quantity fell short of a feast, but the fare was warm and rich and zesty. Murky seemed quite impressed with the spices, and he poured the remaining contents of the spice vial down his gullet. Instantly, his eyes bugged out—even more than usual. He spat out so much slimy saliva, he nearly put out the fire. Fortunately, the kaldorei seemed prepared for this and whipped the stewpot and its precious contents out of harm's way.

Murky ran to the river and completely submerged his head for several minutes. Finally, he came back, dripping and drooling and apologizing. "Murky mrrrgl, *kuldurrree*. Mrrrgl, mrrrgl, *kuldurrree*."

"Call me Thalyss."

"Dlus."

"Thalyss."

"Dlus . . ."

"No. THAL-yss."

"DUL-uss. Duluss."

"Close enough," Thalyss said.

"Hello, Duluss," Aram said with a smile. "I'm Urum. This is Mrksa."

"Duluss, Urum, Mrksa, n Murky!" Murky said, clapping his hands together and smiling gleefully. "Duluss, Urum, Mrksa, Murky mmmrrglllms!"

"Mrgle, mmmrrglllms," Thalyss said, nodding.

Makasa and Aram both sat up, saying in virtual unison, "You speak murloc?"

"Of course. You do not?"

"No," said Makasa, glowering. Aram just shook his head.

"Oh, it is a wonderful language. True, it can be very difficult to get one's tongue around the subtleties of pronunciation. But well worth the effort. It is so beautifully expressive, would you not agree?"

"It's gibberish," Makasa stated.

Thalyss raised a slim white eyebrow. "As is every language to those who know it not, correct?"

Aram was getting drowsy, but he fought it, intrigued. "What did he say?"

"Hmm?" Thalyss asked.

"Before," Aram replied. "He said our names and something else, and you agreed."

"Oh. Yes. He called us all friends. *Mmmrrglllms*. Friends."

"Mmmrrglllms," Murky parroted. "Furunds."

"Friends," Aram corrected.

"Furunds . . ."

"Friends."

"Frunds. Frunds."

"Close enough."

Murky grinned broadly, and Aram did, too. Thalyss twinkled considerably.

Murky prompted Aram: "Urum, Murky, frunds. *Mmmrrglllms.*"

Aram said, "Aram, Murky, murguhlums."

Murky scrunched up his face. Thalyss said, "You just called the two of you ringworms."

"I did? Say it again, please."

"Mmmrrglllms."

"Mmm-murguhlums."

Murky laughed and shook his head. "Frunds. Frunds. Frunds mmmm."

"He has given up. He says 'frunds' is good enough."

"What'd I say this time?"

"Tasty ringworms."

"Ugh."

"Indeed."

Aram pulled out his sketchbook. Instantly, Makasa said, "You better not be putting me in that blasted book."

Aram said, "I promise I won't sketch you unless you ask me to." But for the first time, he wished she *would* ask him to.

Instead, he swallowed, turned to the night elf, and asked, "Do you mind?"

"Not at all," said Thalyss, striking an intentionally comic noble pose. "Which is my best side?"

Murky came around behind Aram to watch him draw. "Uuaaa," the murloc said, "mmmm mrrrggk."

"What did he say?" Aram asked.

"Good magic," said Thalyss nonchalantly. "He means your drawing."

Aram felt his heart sink. He tried to focus on capturing Thalyss's likeness, but it was suddenly hard to concentrate. He had to get back to redrawing his father. He felt it strongly now, as if Greydon Thorne's life depended on it. *Greydon Thorne, who's probably already dead. That's what Makasa said. He's dead. Except we don't know for sure. And as long as we don't know, then maybe he is alive. And maybe "good magic" can make the difference.*

He ceased drawing the elf midline and flipped back a couple pages to the failed, incomplete memory sketch of his father.

He struggled with it, drawing lines, rubbing them out. It was no use. Drawing from memory was always difficult enough, but he could almost physically feel Greydon's visage withdrawing from his mind, growing distant and indistinct.

He turned back to the drawing of Thalyss, wanting to finish *something*, anything.

And wanting to change the subject of his own mental discussion, he asked, "The other night, Murky tried to tell us a story. But we couldn't understand."

Murky, still behind him, began hopping up and down. This made Makasa uncomfortable for some reason, and she shifted on the dirt, her hand unconsciously straying to her harpoon.

Thalyss asked, "Murky mrrg?"

The little murloc came around to the campfire and gathered up his nets.

Makasa and Aram both reached out to stop him. "Whoa!" "Wait!"

Aram said, "Have him tell the story *without* the nets. We don't need to untangle him again."

Thalyss, as usual, seemed amused. He scratched one pointed ear and said, "Murky mrrg nk mgrrrl."

Murky looked briefly disappointed—but he shrugged it off.

Slowly, he mimed picking up the nets as the druid translated the murloc's narration: "He says he is from a fishing village on the Forgotten Coast. Lived there with an uncle and aunt. Or maybe older cousins . . . ?"

Murky clarified: "Mmmrrgglm, mmmrrggllm."

"Yes, I was right. Uncle and aunt."

They continued. "He left one day to go fishing. But his return was delayed—"

"Let me guess," Makasa said. "He tangled himself in his nets."

"Yes," said Thalyss, "it seems to be a common occurrence with the little fellow."

Makasa shook her head and muttered, "The uselessness of this creature is truly astonishing."

Aram shushed her. He was still drawing Thalyss, glancing

back and forth from the elf to the murloc, who seemed to take no notice of Makasa's contempt and was still performing for his audience.

"When he returned to the village, everyone was gone. His uncle. His aunt. All his friends and family. Gone."

"What happened?" Aram asked. He was no longer drowsy, sitting forward on his knees.

Murky began stomping around the campfire, saying, "RRRgrrrs! RRRgrrrs!"

And half a second before the kaldorei translated, Aram finally understood.

"Ogres," Thalyss and Aram said in unison.

Makasa's scowl vanished. She and Aram exchanged a glance, as both thought of the ogre Throgg, who had cut down so many of their crew before crippling the ship by cutting down *Wavestrider*'s mainmast.

"It was an entire ogre clan. He calls it . . ."

"GRRundee klun RRRgrrrs," Murky repeated, before ranting angrily and rapidly, spittle flying as he spoke.

"I think he means the Gordunni clan of ogres. He says they . . . well. He says something rather impolite about them, actually. But the gist is they have been raiding the coastline for years. Taking murlocs and others. But they had never taken an entire village before."

"What do they do with their captives?" Aram asked.

"Did he find any bodies?" Makasa demanded.

Thalyss and Aram stared at her. The latter knew she wasn't one to mince words, but he thought that was fairly insensitive even for her.

But Murky didn't seem troubled by it; he simply shrugged. "Nk."

He went on, and the druid did, too. "No bodies. No sign of his people at all. The ogres always disappear back into the mountains with their prey. It has been a month since the raid, and Murky has not seen anyone from his village since."

Makasa stood. "How often were these raids?"

Thalyss looked to Murky, who muttered, "Fflflk."

"Fflflk flk?" Thalyss asked, trying to clarify.

"Flk flk."

Thalyss scrunched his brow in thought. He said, "Murlocs do not mark time the way we do. So his answer is, shall we say . . . vague. If I were to guess, I would say the raids came every couple of months."

"Every couple of months along the coast?" asked Makasa.

"Yes."

"Then raiding parties here in the low hills, closer to the ogres' mountains, could come more frequently. We need to maintain a watch."

"He did try to tell us last night," Aram said.

She nodded. "I suppose he did."

Thalyss rose and stretched. "I will take the first watch. I do not mind."

Makasa stared the night elf down. Finally, she said, "No, I'm awake now. You rest."

The druid smiled and shrugged and said to Aram, "I do not believe I have quite earned the trust of your friend."

He had made no attempt to lower his voice. So Aram didn't, either. "Given what we've been through, she has good cause to be cautious."

"And you do not?"

"I do." He looked at Makasa; they nodded at each other. "But I have her to watch my back."

"And do you not watch hers?"

"Yes. But she's much better at it."

"He's learning," Makasa said, which was just about the closest thing to praise he'd ever received from *Wavestrider*'s second mate. "All of you can rest. I have the watch."

Aram pocketed his sketchbook and pencil. Murky curled up by the fire. Thalyss, still smiling, addressed Makasa: "You keep your watch; I shall keep mine. I do not sleep on beautiful nights such as this. In fact, I have not slept on *any* night in the wild for over nine thousand years."

Aram gulped. "Nine . . . thousand . . . years . . ."

"Nine thousand and thirteen, to be precise. There was one drunken night near Skypeak, or else it would easily be ten thousand."

Murky was already snoring, but Aram's eyes widened in stunned amazement as Thalyss began to transform before him and Makasa. Only his antlers and his silver eyes remained the same. He bent fully over as his robes glowed briefly, then vanished, and his arms became forelegs and his hands and feet hooves. His ice-colored hair actually shortened, turning into ice-colored fur, which grew rapidly, progressing down over his entire frame—now covered with strange rune-like markings. Last of all, his face stretched into the snout of a great stag.

With jaws hanging slack, Aram and Makasa watched the beast leap away, following his swift progress under the light of a nearly full moon, until, finally, the stag—the kaldorei— vanished into the dark night.

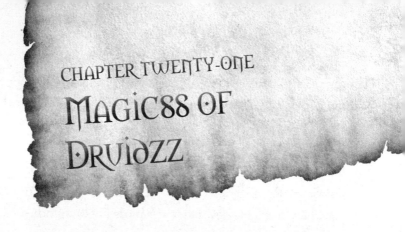

CHAPTER TWENTY-ONE
MAGICSS OF
DRUIDZZ

Makasa roused Aram with considerably more gentleness than she had ever done aboard *Wavestrider*.

She whispered, "Draw your cutlass. Take the watch. It'll be morning in a couple of hours. If the elf comes back before then, wake me. If you see or hear anything—besides that murloc snoring—wake me."

He nodded. She nodded back. "Keep your eyes and ears open," she said. Then, after laying down her harpoon and sword within easy reach on either side of her, she turned her back to the dying fire, laid her head on her shield, and closed her eyes.

As ordered, Aram stood and drew his sword. He flapped his arms about for warmth. Padding softly, he circled the campfire a few hundred times. And he stayed on the alert.

Finally, the first glimmer of light appeared in the east, heralding sunrise. That same sun would already be up in Lakeshire. By now, Robb was feeding the forge, and Ceya was preparing breakfast, maybe sending Soot to wake Robertson and Selya.

Makasa slept on. Aram had never known her to sleep past dawn. He wondered if this slumber was an indication she felt secure under his watch, an indication she was beginning to trust him more. He decided it was more likely an indication she was exhausted.

As he regarded her, something nudged his shoulder from behind. He was so startled, he nearly jumped into the cold firepit. But when he turned to look, it was the stag. The stag with something in his mouth. Aram, sword still out, approached with caution. It was a book. It was—

Aram slapped his back pocket, but his sketchbook wasn't there. The huge blasted beast had approached in what was nearly broad daylight and picked Aram's pocket, while he had stood there, staring at Makasa. The stag reached his head forward. Aram carefully took the sketchbook with his free hand. Then the stag struck an intentionally comic noble pose.

Aram glanced back at Makasa. She had told him to wake her if the elf came back before morning. But strictly speaking, it was *already* morning, and this was the *stag*, not the elf. Plus Makasa was clearly *so* tired . . .

Murky crunching on a fresh carrot finally woke Makasa.

Though Thalyss had reverted to his two-legged form, Aram was putting the finishing touches on his sketch of the stag.

Thalyss

ARAM

Makasa was silently furious, glaring reproachful daggers that clearly spoke, *I trusted you.* He felt ashamed. He *had* betrayed her trust—and just for the artistic satisfaction of drawing the shapeshifter as a buck.

His eyes expressed his regret, but she wasn't ready to forgive him—or herself.

The druid handed Aram a carrot. Then he reached out with one for Makasa. She waved it off. He said, "Be angry if you must, but do not be foolishly stubborn. You need sustenance."

Aram found himself saying, "You need to feed your forge."

She turned her back on him—but took the carrot.

The night elf then reached into his pack. It seemed empty or nearly so. He pulled out one last carrot and snapped off the tip in his mouth. Crunching away, he said, "Where are you headed? I am en route to Gadgetzan, myself."

Aram said, "So are we," before Makasa could stop him.

"Well, then," Thalyss said. "Suppose we make up a party?"

Makasa glowered, but it was hard to take her seriously while she munched on the carrot.

Aram shrugged at her. "Safety in numbers?"

She said nothing, which was as close to an acquiescence as Aram thought they were likely to get.

Murky said, "Murky nk mlggrm mga. Murky mga mmgr mmmm frunds."

Thalyss translated: "He says he has nowhere to go, so he will travel with his good friends."

"Fine," Makasa said coldly. She took another bite.

They broke camp.

Hiking out of the gorge in single file—with Thalyss leading, followed by Murky, Aram, and Makasa—they reached the ridge, which began to turn southeast again.

To confirm this, Aram pulled the compass out from beneath his shirt. Sure enough, their path and the needle were now pointing in the same direction. So either the device was truly sending Aram home—or it was just permanently broken. Aram preferred to believe the former. He tucked it back in under his shirt and looked up. His eyes met Thalyss's, who was looking back over his shoulder, studying the boy. The night elf's tongue snuck out and tapped his upper lip twice. Then Thalyss nodded to himself and turned away.

Dark clouds gathered above them.

And the troll watched them from below.

"Why do we wait?" demanded Ssarbik.

"We wait for confirmation," rumbled Malus.

"You have it, mon," Zathra said, joining them in the clearing. "Da human boy has da compass 'round his neck."

"There," said Ssarbik. "You have your ansswer. What new exxcusse will you uzze to delay ussss?"

Malus ignored the arakkoa. "Who's with him, Zathra? Be specific."

"It be as Throgg said. Dere be da tall dark-skinned human girl from Thorne's ship."

"A good fighter, that one," whispered Valdread cheerfully.

"And the puny murloc? Is he still with them?" asked the ogre, while fastening a pike to his wrist.

"Ya, brudda. Da boy seems particularly fond a da creature." The troll stroked her armor. "Be treatin' him like a pet."

"Interesting," Malus said, stroking his chin.

"And dey be with a night elf, a druid."

"They gather alliezz azz they go!" Ssarbik hissed furiously. "Our possition weakenzz while *you* wasste time!"

Malus still ignored him. "A shifter then?"

"Ya, mon," she confirmed.

"The stag?" asked Throgg, who had earlier taken his own turn observing them.

"Ya, brudda. One and da same."

"And what other magics does this elf possess?" Malus said.

"None dat I seen, but . . ." She let the implications hang.

"Fear not the magicss of druidzz! There izz nothing a night elf may sssummon that I cannot counter! But the compassss . . ."

Finally, Malus turned to the arakkoa. "The compass will be ours, sorcerer. And this is how . . ."

The day waned. For the most part, their path sloped upward, sometimes steeply. Thalyss was very sure of foot, and Murky's webbed, clawed feet seemed to suck onto the rocky terrain and pop free with each step. Makasa also seemed to have no diffi-culties, but Aram was a bit less sound. He nearly stumbled once—a bit too close to the edge of the river gorge, which was now a good hundred feet deep, at least—but Makasa steadied him. Though she hadn't quite forgiven him yet, she was still his big sister and protector. Aram knew those things weren't mutu-ally exclusive.

Thalyss had an actual canteen, and he shared its contents with the others. Makasa seemed reluctant. Aram wondered if her hesitancy was because she feared the druid had put something in the water. But he ultimately came to the conclu-sion that Makasa simply didn't like being beholden to, well, anyone—especially not a stranger.

For his part, however, Aram was glad for Thalyss's company. Murky's, too, for that matter. Both were considerably more talk-ative than Makasa and made the long walk less of a chore. Of course, Aram knew the conversation was another source of irri-tation for Makasa. More than once, she had told them to hold it down, concerned they were making themselves targets for any nearby marauding ogre clans. But they were already in plain sight, walking along the ridgeline. If the Gordunni ogres were searching for targets, the four travelers weren't exactly hard to find. It was probably for this reason that Makasa had given up trying to silence her companions, but that had done little to quell her annoyance.

Thalyss did most of the talking, either on his own initiative or by translating for a similarly chatty Murky. Thalyss pointed out lichens and moss and elucidated which were healthful and which were mildly or thoroughly poisonous. His sharp gray eyes picked out raptors at some distance. He spoke of their nesting and hunting habits. Aram thought that Charnas of Gadgetzan would enjoy conversing with Thalyss. For that matter, so would Greydon Thorne. Like Aram's father, the night elf was interested in everything and everyone. He even attempted to get Makasa to talk, to tell her story. He met with no success at all, but that hardly damaged his cheerful mien.

With Aram, the night elf had better luck. Aram talked of Lakeshire and the forge, of his brother and sister and dog, of his mother and stepfather. As much as possible, he avoided speaking of Greydon or the ship, of the attack and their reason for being stranded as they were in Feralas. But Thalyss didn't press those points, and seemed perfectly satisfied hearing about the flora and fauna surrounding Lake Everstill or the fish Murky's uncle netted along the Forgotten Coast.

It occurred to Aram that despite the quantity of verbiage constantly emerging from the kaldorei's mouth, Thalyss actually revealed almost nothing about himself. If Aram were inclined to suspicion as Makasa was . . .

Almost for her sake, he asked, "What is your business in Gadgetzan?"

"There is a druid tender there, an old friend, part of the Cenarion Circle. I need to consult with her on . . . druidic matters. Oh, and I have a gift for her, as well. Just a little thing. But I think she will be quite pleased."

"You sound like you're going courting," Aram said.

Thalyss laughed. "Oh, she is a few centuries too young for me, I would wager. Though I would not mind . . ." He seemed to get lost in such thoughts for a moment—and Aram briefly found himself thinking of the lost Duan Phen—but the night elf soon laughed himself out of his musings. He said, "And what awaits you and Makasa in Gadgetzan, my young friend?"

"Hopefully, a ship to the Eastern Kingdoms. A ship home."

Thalyss turned back to look at Makasa and asked, "Do you make your home in the east, too?"

She said nothing, at first. For some reason, Aram thought it likely that the night elf already *knew* she was from Booty Bay in the Eastern Kingdoms.

Finally, Makasa said, "My home is aboard *Wavestrider*. Once the boy is safe, I will return to it."

Thalyss raised an eyebrow. "Even if she is at the bottom of the sea?"

"Even if," she said without hesitation.

Aram looked back at her. She met his glance. "Even if," she repeated quietly.

Thalyss stopped, so Murky stopped, and Aram, who was still looking back over his shoulder at Makasa, tripped over the murloc, landing painfully, shoulder against rock.

Murky said, "Urum mmmr?"

"I'm fine," Aram said, chagrined. The others watched him lurch to his feet, rubbing his shoulder.

Thalyss said, "There is a switchback trail here back down to the river." He held out a hand. It was starting to drizzle. "There is even some cover below, a ledge, which could come in handy with a storm brewing."

"And if the river floods?" asked Makasa.

"Oh, well, in that case . . . we would all drown. Except Murky, I suppose. But we are almost out of water. And there is no cover up here at all. Not from rain . . . or ogres."

Makasa lowered her head in defeat. She was losing control, had lost command of their travels. She couldn't fault the night elf's logic, but Aram knew she didn't like depending on it.

They all followed Thalyss down the trail.

It was treacherous. The more so, as the rain began to make the rocky path slick. Aram's shoulder ached, as did his feet, his calves, and even his head. If and when he did get back to Lakeshire, he'd sleep for a fortnight.

Finally, they reached the bottom and made camp against the wall of the gorge, beneath the ledge of rock Thalyss had promised. There was no wood for a fire. And no food. But at least the river enabled them to slake their thirst.

After drinking his fill, Murky pulled out his nets and said, "Murky mgrrrl mmm flllurlok."

Thalyss said, "He is offering to use his nets to fish for our supper."

"*No!*" Makasa and Aram said at once. Murky's shoulders sank.

Makasa hefted her harpoon. "I'll try to hunt. Though given that the ogres have all but left this place a barren wasteland, I don't hold out much hope."

"That is quite unnecessary," Thalyss said. "I will procure our meal."

Aram tilted his head to regard the night elf. "You don't mean to say you still have supplies in your pack after last night."

"No, no, it is quite empty. Even my spices were spent," he said with a glance at Murky.

Murky sank a bit more and muttered, "Mrrrgll."

"No worries, little frund. I can find us all the food we might need."

Makasa eyed the old druid. "What part of 'barren wasteland' did you not understand?"

The kaldorei laughed. "Care to make a wager on who brings home dinner?"

"I don't gamble," she replied flatly.

He laughed again. "Of course not."

So Makasa departed upriver to hunt, and Thalyss downriver to gather, leaving Murky and Aram alone. Aram said, "I suppose it would help if we looked for firewood. You go upstream; I'll go downstream."

Murky nodded enthusiastically, happy to be of some service. They split up.

Aram headed downriver. The light rain had stopped for the moment. As the minutes passed, he expected to catch up to Thalyss pulling fungus off a rock. Instead, he spotted the night elf sitting cross-legged in front of a patch of damp soil.

Aram started to speak, but something held him back. He didn't approach. He watched.

The druid reached a hand into his pack and pulled out a small brown leather pouch. He carefully poured . . . something . . . out of the pouch and into his open palm. Then he tilted his hand over the soil. Aram realized the pouch had been full of seeds, as Thalyss pushed one after another into the dirt with a finger and then covered the small holes with soil.

The druid reached into an inner pocket of his robe and drew out another leather pouch, this one dyed purple. From it, he drew out something wrapped in oilskin. He carefully unwrapped it, revealing what appeared to Aram to be an enormous acorn, big as the night elf's fist.

The druid waved the acorn over the planted seeds, while chanting quietly in a language Aram couldn't understand.

Within seconds, shoots popped out from the soil.

And within minutes, Thalyss had harvested a large assortment of good-size yams and turnips, senggin root and carrots. Even multiple handfuls of windblossom berries. Aram watched the night elf carefully rewrap the giant acorn, then put it back in its purple pouch and in his pocket.

Then the boy doubled back to camp before he could be noticed.

What goes on in the mind of a murloc?

He had been told in no uncertain terms not to go fishing with his nets, and it's not as if he didn't understand why. He knew he had a tendency to get tangled in them. All right, fine: hopelessly tangled in them. This wasn't some new discovery of Urum and Mrksa's, either. His uncle Murrgly often complained of Murky being more trouble than he was worth. It was why Murky fished alone, rather than with his uncle and the other flllurlokkrs. It was why Murky alone wasn't taken when the RRRgrrrs raided.

So perhaps the little creature thought he had something to prove.

Or perhaps it was the rumbling in his tummy, and the fact

that Mrksa had said that neither she nor Duluss was likely to find meat or vegetable.

Yes, Urum had sent him to find firewood. But he had as yet found none, and might he not also net some driftwood along with the fish that would warm his tummy and theirs?

He owed them for the food they had already shared. He owed them for his very life. And then, of course, as his gurgling stomach continued to remind him, he owed himself a meal. By murloc standards, he had barely eaten over the last few weeks. He was quite, quite hungry.

He would be careful this time. Very careful. He would not get tangled. He would do as Uncle Murrgly had taught him: he would anchor himself carefully and maintain a good grip; he'd swing the nets out over the river, let them fall across the water, let the weights drag the bottom edge down, and let the flow expand the nets' reach. He'd wait, wait, wait. Then he would slowly draw them back, maintaining his footing with suction and claw against the pull of the river. He would then pour out his catch onto the rocks. He would do all this, he was sure.

It was raining in earnest now, but the cold downpour didn't bother him. He found a likely spot on the shore where he could brace himself against a sturdy stone. He slowly played out his nets. He swung them back and forth, back and forth, preparing to let them fly. He released his nets!

But his thumb-claw caught an edge. The large stone stopped him from following the nets' momentum into the water, but without the ability to spread forward, the nets chose to swing back around on Murky. He saw them coming and, eyes wide, threw up a hand to stop them. But the hand somehow managed to go right through a square empty space in the webbing. The balance of the net whipped around him like a cocoon.

He stifled a mournful cry. He didn't want the others—especially Mrksa, who might come back this way anytime—to find him like this, to have to set him free yet again, especially after they had told him not to fish. No, this time he must free himself. He leaned back against the rock and tried to push the strands of net up over his head. That didn't work. He then tried to push them down so he could step out of the mess. That didn't work, either. Frustrated, he struggled every which way he could, but that only made the situation worse.

And worst of all . . . he wasn't alone.

Aram was the first back to camp. He had collected a few pieces of damp driftwood off the shore, but he hadn't searched too hard. He wanted to look well ensconced by the time Thalyss returned.

And Thalyss returned next, leaning on his stick, his pack full of his newly harvested crop. The rain had picked up, and Thalyss used a bit of simple druidic magic—simple according to him, anyway—to spark a small fire beneath the rocky ledge with Aram's damp wood. He stuck the yams in the coals, took out a small knife, and began to cut the other vegetables into his stewpot.

Aram watched all this, and Thalyss watched him watching. "Are you not curious?" the night elf asked.

" 'Bout what?"

"Where I found our feast!"

"Oh, well . . . I just assumed you druids know where to look."

The druid looked slightly disappointed, losing his smile for perhaps the first time since Aram had met him, but he said, "That we do, my boy. That we do."

Makasa came then, with no meat but more wood.

She saw Thalyss's vegetables and demanded, "Where did all that come from?"

Thalyss's smile returned as he said, "Druids just know where to look."

Makasa shook her head, dropped her small pile of wood near the fire, and moved in under the ledge on the other side of Aram. "Where's the murloc?" she asked.

"I sent him to gather wood," he said. "He went upriver. You didn't pass him on the way back?"

"No," she said, trying to remember if there was a spot where she might have missed him.

Aram more or less read her mind. "You don't think . . . you don't think he's *in* the river, do you?"

All three of them contemplated the likelihood of this and found it not implausible.

Aram said, "Do we give him a few more minutes or go look for him now?"

The storm punctuated the question with an ominous rumble of thunder.

All three of them stood as one—sighing as one, as well.

Aram smelled a whiff of jasmine on the breeze, just before a fourth voice whispered, "Sit back down, my friends."

Aram knew that voice even before he spotted the Whisper-Man silhouetted by a flash of lightning. Instantly, Makasa was on the attack.

She lunged with her harpoon; the Whisper-Man dodged, but she was prepared, and as he reached to draw his own black sword, her cutlass sliced his arm off at the elbow.

This seemed to catch him off guard, though it didn't seem to bother him much. His remaining hand drew out a black shale dagger, and he sliced at her backhanded. She was forced to retreat, but Aram was there to take her place, swinging his cutlass, forcing the undead swordsman to parry with his dagger, and leaving him open to Makasa's harpoon, which stabbed into his gullet.

"Whisper now," she dared him, but he emitted no sound.

But silence did not indicate surrender. He wrenched himself sideways, yanking the hilt of the harpoon from a surprised Makasa's grip. He stabbed his dagger into his own left thigh for safekeeping and tore the harpoon free of his neck. He flipped it and was prepared to throw, when a booming voice backed by thunder shouted, *"MOVE!"*

Instinctively, Makasa and Aram cleared a path, turning in time to see Thalyss rush forward while rapidly transforming into a mighty ice-colored, rune-marked, silver-eyed *bear*! The beast slammed into the Whisper-Man, who practically shattered into pieces against the granite side of the ravine. Here was a leg, there was another. His head lolled off his torso, only held in place by the pocket of his hood. One forearm still lay where Makasa had cut it off.

"Is he dead?" Aram asked. "Can he die that way?"

The bear shook his great head.

Makasa said, "We should burn him." Cautiously, she approached the meager fire, while the other two remained on alert to see what would happen next.

And what happened next was the sound of choking. Choking that segued into hoarse laughter, adding a chilling touch to an already chilling scene.

His remaining hand reached up to right his head, to lock it back into place with an audible snap, followed by a disgusting squelching noise. The laughter stopped, replaced by the now too familiar sound of his voice. Raising his hand slowly, he pointed at Makasa and whispered, "I told Malus you could fight. I saw your skill on the boat." The pointing finger moved toward Aram. "You didn't do badly, either, young squire. Strife has improved your instincts." Then the Whisper-Man lowered his hand back down to his side and lolled his head toward the bear. "But I must say, night elf, you were the true surprise tonight. I've killed many a druid over the years, and I've never seen one who could shift quite so fast. You caught me completely off guard. And that's no easy feat."

"Why do you follow us, pirate?" demanded Makasa. "What could we possibly have left that you still want?"

But Aram had other concerns. "Where's my . . . my captain?"

"Your father, you mean? I'm afraid you'll never see him again in this world, my boy."

Immediately, he wished he hadn't asked the question. *If I hadn't asked, I wouldn't know the answer. And as long as I didn't know, there was a chance . . .* He realized all eyes were on him. He was afraid he'd cry in front of the enemy, but Aram's anger held back any tears. He said, "I'm not your boy."

"No, of course not. And I can understand why I'm not a welcome sight. But the truth is I didn't come here to fight you. Any of you."

"Just to kill us," Makasa said.

"No, not that, either. You'll recall I didn't even have my sword out when you attacked me. And if I wanted you dead, I'd have hardly announced myself before striking."

Aram smelled the Whisper-Man's jasmine water—mixed with the stench of death—and thought the undead killer couldn't help but announce himself. But Aram glanced at Makasa, who was running the battle back through her mind, confirming the truth of the Forsaken's words.

The Whisper-Man continued. "In addition, if a fight to the death was the plan, I wouldn't have kept my friend Throgg waiting in the wings. You can come out now, Throgg."

Makasa, Aram, and the bear whipped around. Throgg was crossing the river. His pike-hand caught the glint of another bolt of lightning, which was instantly followed by a crack of thunder that practically seemed to thrum the ogre's name.

When he reached shore, the Whisper-Man spoke again. "That's close enough, Throgg. We don't want to initiate another conflict. As I said, that's not why we came. And it would be seriously counterproductive."

Makasa turned back to him and said, "What. Do. You. Want?"

"To make introductions. I am Baron Reigol Valdread. Or at least I was, once upon a time. My companion, as I mentioned, is Throgg. We work for Captain Malus. We know from the *Wavestrider*'s manifest that you are Makasa Flintwill and Aramar Thorne. But perhaps you would be so good as to identify your night elf friend."

There was silence.

"Well, perhaps not," whispered Valdread. "That's fine. In any case, my message is not for him, but for you, Squire Thorne."

Aram glanced from the Whisper-Man to Makasa to Thalyss to Throgg and back. "What message?" he asked finally.

"Captain Malus wanted me to tell you that he does not seek your life. He wants one thing and one thing only: the compass."

"Compass?" Aram asked. "What compass?"

"Protect this compass at all costs," his father had said.

"The one you wear around your neck. The one you received from your father. Please, now, let's not play games. We've been watching you. We know you have it."

"All right, fine. I have it," Aram said. "But it doesn't work. The needle doesn't even point north."

"Then parting with it will not be a hardship."

"He's not inclined," Makasa stated grimly, "to give you or your captain anything. Ogre or no ogre."

Throgg growled behind her, and thunder rumbled behind him, as if nature itself had sided with the Hidden.

Valdread was reaching for a leg and seemed—or at least pretended—not to have heard her. "Hm? Oh. No, we didn't think you'd *want* to cooperate. And that's eminently understandable. But we do have an inducement."

Makasa crouched, ready for another fight.

"No, no, not violence, young lady. Must you always jump to that conclusion?" He laughed then, still a very unpleasant sound. "Well, I suppose that's understandable, as well. In any case, we offer young Aramar a simple trade. The compass for the murloc."

"What murloc?" Makasa said before Aram could speak.

"More games? Really? Again, my companions have been watching you. I'll admit to some surprise that a murloc, of all things, is of any value to you. But to each his own. What say you, squire? Which do you value more? The compass or the creature? You have my word that if you hand over our prize, the murloc will be set free and none of you will be harmed."

"You think I'd trust your word?" Aram spat.

"I haven't lied to you yet, have I? In any case, I'm not sure what choice you have, if you want your pet back."

"He's not a pet! He's—"

"I meant no disrespect. And I don't mean to put you on the spot. You have until sunrise to decide. But let me be clear. The only way you'll ever see the murloc again is by turning over the compass. If you don't, it dies. And that won't stop us from coming after you, either. In the end, Malus will have that compass. So be smart, young squire. And this can all end come the dawn."

It was an exit line, but Valdread still couldn't quite reach his leg. He drummed his fingers in frustration against his chest. Finally, he called out, "Throgg, help me gather up my parts!"

Throgg started forward. Makasa, Aram, and the bear stayed on the alert, but they cleared a path as the ogre attempted to pick up Valdread's loose arm and two legs. But three limbs were too many for a one-handed ogre, and he kept dropping one or another.

Valdread whispered, "Just give me one of them. Any of them!"

Throgg threw him an arm, which slapped the Whisper-Man across the face, knocking off his hood, revealing his pale skull-like head with a now dislocated jaw. He quickly snapped the jaw back into place, and then, scowling, reattached the arm with a click of bones and further unearthly squelching.

The scent of jasmine wafted strongly, and Aram felt his gorge rise. He managed to swallow it back down, but he thought he'd never be able to bear even a hint of jasmine again.

The ogre, meanwhile, had managed to spear both of Valdread's legs on the tip of his pike-hand. He clomped over to the undead swordsman and pushed both legs off the pike into what there was of the Whisper-Man's lap. Valdread spent some time reattaching them, clicking the bones in place and allowing what passed for his skin to squelch back together, all while biting his thin lip between his teeth in concentration. Then, he pulled his hood back over his head and stood with surprising ease. Almost as an afterthought, he removed the shale dagger from his left thigh and resheathed it. Finally, he was prepared to depart.

Makasa said, "You are resilient, Baron. But also fragile. One of these nights, you may find—"

"Yes, yes," Reigol Valdread said with a hint of impatience. "In the end, I'm a dead man." He and Throgg walked right past them, but he paused to speak again. "We'll leave you to your decision. But, please, young squire . . . make it the right one."

And then they were gone, leaving Aram, Makasa, and the bear Thalyss standing in the rain.

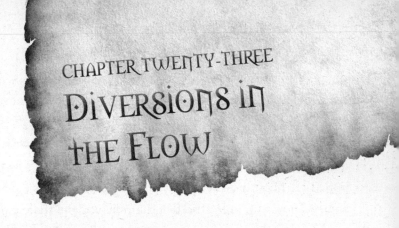

CHAPTER TWENTY-THREE
DIVERSIONS IN THE FLOW

The three of them were back beneath the ledge and out of the rain. Lightning still lit the sky on occasion, but the thunder came only after a great delay. The storm was moving on.

Thalyss, having shifted back into his elven form, asked, "What is this compass? What is its significance?"

It was a question Makasa wanted an answer for as well. She had seen the compass many times, of course, around Aram's neck and, before that, around her captain's. But she'd never thought much about it until now. She favored Aram with a penetrating look, one that caused him to turn away.

With a reluctance he couldn't quite understand, Aram pulled the compass out from under his shirt and showed it to the other two.

On this cloudy night, there was no sun or constellation to compare it to, but both Makasa and Thalyss instantly saw the needle did not point north.

"This is the prize?" said the druid with no little confusion. "The prize for which these pirates, who are clearly *not* pirates, killed your captain and crew?"

"It's not even working," Makasa said darkly. "It's pointing . . . southeast?"

"Yeah, I know," Aram said.

They were all silent. Thalyss's tongue tapped against his upper lip thoughtfully, but he and Makasa were stumped. Aram had more information, but again felt a bizarre disinclination to speak.

Ultimately, though, he knew he had no choice. "Greydon— my father—gave it to me." He turned to Makasa. "During the pirate attack, just before he ordered us into the dinghy. He told me to protect it at all costs."

"Then that settles it," said Makasa immediately and firmly. "We must not hand it over. Had it been worthless, I wouldn't give it to the murderers of our crew. But now, there's no question."

"But Murky?" Aram had no more desire to give up the compass than Makasa. *But what other choice do we have?*

"I am sorry about the murloc," Second Mate Flintwill replied. "But he means nothing to us when compared to following the final orders of Captain Thorne."

Aram shook his head. "Those may have been his final orders, but they don't match up with his *many* lessons. Lessons of loyalty to his crew, his onboard family. Makasa, *you know this.*"

"I do. But Murky is not crew. Not family."

"Isn't he, though?" Aram asked. "Are the four of us not a crew on this voyage across Feralas?"

"No! A crewman has worth. Serves a purpose. What has this murloc done to prove himself worthy? Given us one fish, caught by accident?"

"He's done nothing to prove himself worthy," Aram agreed. "But everything to prove himself loyal. Besides, this isn't *about* proof. What did I ever do aboard *Wavestrider* to prove my worth—beyond being our captain's son?"

He could see he had scored a point. She had spent too many months believing Aram to be as worthless as she now regarded Murky. She grumbled, "It's only been a few days. It's not the same at all. We are no crew here."

"Murky signed on with us as surely as if he'd penned his name on a manifest."

"I doubt he can write his name, *Urum.*"

"Stop it," Aram said, getting angry. "I know you better than that."

"You don't know me."

"I don't know your story, but I know your heart, sister. Don't pretend otherwise."

The word *sister* worked its magic on her. She stopped arguing.

He didn't. "We don't rescue shipmates because they've proven their worth. We rescue them to prove our own." It sounded like something Greydon would say—though Aram had never exactly heard Greydon say it.

Just then, Thalyss held out his hand. "May I see it, Aram? May I hold it?"

Aram, his head still swirling from his argument with Makasa, looked at him uncomprehendingly.

"The compass," Thalyss said.

Aram felt that same hesitancy.

The kaldorei said, "I may be able to discern some sense of its purpose, its value to your father and to his slayers."

"I think its purpose is to point my way home, to Lakeshire. My father told me as much when he gave it to me."

The night elf frowned. "*Any* compass—any map, for that matter—could help get you home." He still held out his hand.

Aram glanced at Makasa, but she was looking inward. So he relented and lifted the chain off his neck, offering it to Thalyss.

The druid held the compass in the palm of his left hand. He felt the weight of it. He closed his eyes. He held his right hand, palm down, a few inches above it. He chanted something brief in Darnassian and felt a power—weak but definitely present—magnetizing the compass in some anomalous manner.

He opened his eyes and spoke. "The needle is made of crystal. But not the crystal of the deep earth. It is a shard of pure starlight from the heavens, imbued with the celestial spark."

Aram said, "What does that mean?"

"Simply put, it means the crystal needle is not of this world. There *is* an enchantment of some kind upon it. Unfortunately, this is beyond my expertise. My powers favor the flora of the clean earth, its plants and trees. I can discover nothing else of this device."

He handed the compass back to Aram, who quickly hung the chain back around his neck and tucked it under his shirt. Aram's thoughts were a jumble. Thalyss was right. A working compass and the maps from the dinghy would have done just as much to point him homeward as this enchanted thing.

But then what was his father thinking?

If the compass held more secrets, Greydon knew them. He must. How many times had his father hinted there was more to their journey than met the eye? (Even his mother had hinted as much the day she sent him from Lakeshire!) At the end, Greydon Thorne had regretted being out of time, but there had been six months *to tell Aram the truth! Captain Thorne could make time for daily lessons in trivia and humiliation, but not for the essential reason he had brought Aram on the voyage in the first place?!*

What kind of father brings his son aboard ship, knowing there would be danger from those seeking the compass? What kind of father gives that compass to his son and adopted daughter, knowing that danger would follow wherever they went? If the compass must be kept from the hands of this Malus, why had he not simply thrown it into the sea?!

*   *   *

Like Aram, the other two were lost in their own thoughts. Thalyss emerged first. He said, "I cannot tell you more of the compass, but I can tell you this. I believe it is why I was drawn to you both in the first place."

Makasa raised her eyes to Thalyss like two daggers. "I thought you were traveling to Gadgetzan."

"And so I was. I did not speak false. Nor did I reveal all."

"Reveal it now," she demanded.

He nodded and spoke. "You know what I am: a druid, at one with this world, in synch with its energies. Some nights past, I felt a presence, a detour in my own road. If I have calculated correctly, I believe that must have been the night you two made landfall. It drew me forward, drew me to you both, like—well, like the needle of a working compass. From the moment I first laid eyes on you both, I felt a kinship. To be perfectly honest, the feeling was so intense, I did not quite trust it. I watched you for a time, to see how you lived off the land. Then I saw you rescue Murky, observed how you behaved toward the poor little creature, and I knew our encounter was destiny."

"There's no such thing," Makasa growled.

"There is, young warrior. There is a harmony to nature, a way and a flow. Like the path of a river, like the path through the soil that a stem takes to find the sun. Do you think it is any different for beings such as we four travelers?"

She didn't respond.

He continued. "I am not talking of guarantees. A river may be dammed. A stem may be chewed away by aphids or grasshoppers. And a traveler may be diverted in any number of ways. But the flow exists, and we are without a doubt a part of its whole."

Aram mused on flows for a time. He was still angry with Greydon, but it was not an anger he could easily sustain when he remembered what the Whisper-Man had said: *I'm afraid you'll never see him again in this world . . .*

Greydon Thorne was dead. His father was dead. This wasn't about obeying the man's final orders as a captain. This was about honoring—or at least attempting to honor—his final wishes as a father.

Makasa said stubbornly, "We're not giving them the compass."

"Maybe not," Aram said. "But one way or another, we have to rescue Murky."

It's a shame they never got the chance.

They came up with a decent plan a good hour before dawn and broke camp, though they left the fire burning under the ledge so that anyone watching from a distance would still believe they were waiting for Malus and his crew. Makasa and Thalyss might not be quite the trackers Zathra was, and they could find no trace whatsoever of Valdread's footsteps, but the ogre was not being half so careful. Throgg's was an easy trail to follow.

Silently as possible, they moved through the gorge, upriver. Thalyss heard something first and signaled the others to hide behind some rocks. Seconds later, a huge form—the ogre—emerged in silhouette, not five yards ahead of them. They scanned about for the Whisper-Man or the troll or Malus. Then Aram glanced back at the ogre as he turned. He managed to swallow his gasp. *This ogre had two hands!*

Then a second ogre joined the first. And then a third. *How many ogres did Malus have?!*

The three ogres murmured to one another, too quietly for Aram or Makasa to make out. But Thalyss's pointed ears were sharper, and he clearly didn't like what he was hearing. He signaled their need to get out of there.

Easier signaled than done. Thalyss pointed to a slim crevice between two large stones and led the way. Aram followed, and Makasa, her harpoon and cutlass at the ready, took up the rear.

But choosing the crevice turned out to be a significant tactical error. Thalyss emerged from between the rocks to find a fourth ogre standing with his broad back to the gap. The night elf had moved silently and had not yet been discovered, but this was no way out. He signaled Aram to turn around. The boy complied and signaled Makasa to do the same.

Unfortunately, by this time, the sky was clearing and the light of a full moon glistened off Makasa's sword as she turned. It caught the eye of one of the ogres, and roaring, he charged at Makasa Flintwill. She strode forward to meet that charge, ducked under the swing of the brute's massive club, and slashed him from belly button to breastbone with her sword. But the other two ogres were upon her.

"Run!" she called to Aram as she threw her harpoon between the eyes of the second ogre—but her newly declared brother wasn't about to leave her behind, even assuming there was anywhere to go. He drew his sword but wasn't sure what to do with it.

Makasa unleashed her iron chain, swinging it in tight circles to keep the third ogre at bay. Thalyss whispered to Aram to move. The boy was blocking the night elf from emerging from the crevice, which was too tight to allow him to shapeshift into either bear or stag. Suddenly, the two stones Thalyss stood between were pulled asunder from behind by the broad-backed ogre. Thalyss tried to turn to face this new threat, but the ogre's club came down on the back of the night elf's head, and antlers or no antlers, the druid fell unconscious at "Broadback's" feet. The ogre put two pinkie fingers in his mouth and whistled, loud and shrill.

Aram turned, but Broadback slapped the cutlass from the boy's hand and grabbed him up, tucking him under one massive arm. Aram called out, but Makasa was still trying to keep her own opponent at bay. With some effort, the boy managed to draw the hunting knife from his belt and stab the ogre in the ribs. But Broadback simply shifted Aram to his other arm, pulled the knife out, and tossed it into the nearby river.

Seeing she had no choice, Makasa changed tack, intentionally allowing the chain to slacken as if her arm were tired, luring the ogre in. The instant he took a step forward, she swung the chain upward, shattering the monster's jaw. He roared in pain and dropped to his knees. She stepped forward and quickly ended his life.

That just left Broadback, who stood over an unconscious Thalyss and had a struggling Aram tucked under one arm. With his free hand, the ogre scooped up Aram's cutlass. Without a word or a grunt, Broadback held it against Aram's neck, forcing the boy to become still.

Broadback and Makasa faced each other grimly. Neither made a sound. But within seconds, heavy footsteps approached from upriver and down, summoned by Broadback's whistle. Ogres, more than Aram could count from his current, rather limited vantage, came to a stop on either side of the standoff.

Makasa quickly did her own math. She sheathed her bloody cutlass and let her chain hang limp. Broadback chuckled, guttural and dark. Then Makasa reached for the harpoon that still stuck out of the second ogre. Ogres on both sides took a threatening step forward. Broadback stopped chuckling. She pulled her harpoon free and launched herself backward.

She fell into the river with a splash and went limp, allowing the current, swift from the recent rains, to carry her downstream. A few of the ogres threw spears. Aram couldn't see, but he heard no cry and had to hope the ogres had missed their target.

He did not for one moment feel abandoned. He knew in his soul Makasa would never leave him to die. She had done what she had to do to escape and fight another day. His sister would come for him, attempt a rescue. Of this, he had no doubt at all.

In the meantime, Aram's job was to stay alive. He tried to speak, but no sound came out. But that was unacceptable. He couldn't allow himself to fall silent every time he was in crisis—not if crises continued to come upon him so fast and furious. He cleared his throat and—trying to keep his voice from cracking—said, "Fine. You caught me. Bring me to Malus. We'll make our trade."

Broadback lifted Aram up so they could look each other in the eye. The ogre leaned in. His rank breath filled Aram's nostrils. His single horn came close to grazing Aram's forehead. Aram swallowed hard and repeated, "Bring me to Malus."

Broadback snorted and threw the boy over his shoulder as if he were a sack of flour—and not a particularly full sack, at that.

"Bring me to Malus! The Whisper—*Valdread* promised we'd be safe if we agreed to Malus's terms."

Broadback finally spoke; rather dismissively he said, "I know no Malus, no Valdar'd. We bring you to Gordok, king of the Dire Maul Gordunni." He stepped away from Thalyss and pointed him out to another ogre. "You and night elf will please Gordok well. He tired of watching murlocs die. He seek fresher sport."

Finally, Aram understood. These were not Malus's ogres. These were of the marauding clan that had raided Murky's village, taken his uncle, his aunt, and everyone he knew. Hanging behind Broadback, Aram could just see another ogre heft the unconscious Thalyss onto his shoulder before the march began.

Within minutes they were out of the gorge and still climbing. Within the hour they were already heading northeast into the mountains. Aram had no idea where Makasa was now, how close she was or how far. And though he still had the compass tucked under his shirt, he knew that with each step the ogres took, Murky's chances of rescue—and survival—receded farther into the distance . . .

PART THREE:

ABOVE SKYPEAK

CHAPTER TWENTY-FOUR
FEARS OF A BURLAP SACK

Aram spent the first miles draped over Broadback's shoulder. It was uncomfortable and humiliating, but he'd be blasted if he was going to cooperate with his own abduction. *Let the ogre tire himself out carrying me!*

But step after jarring step, mile after tortuous mile, it gradually became clear Broadback wasn't likely to tire soon. By the time Thalyss regained consciousness and asked—rather politely, Aram thought—to be put down to walk on his own, Aram was ready to add his voice to that particular chorus.

Without stopping, Broadback addressed them both: "Slaves try to run, slaves travel rest of way in sack. Slaves go too slow, slaves travel rest of way in sack. Slaves talk at all, slaves travel rest of way in sack. Understood?"

Thalyss said, "Understood."

Aram said, "Yeah."

Both were unceremoniously dumped on their rear ends on the stony ground. One good shove from Broadback made it instantly clear they could rub their backsides *as* they marched, not before.

So, they marched—in the center of a diamond-shaped phalanx of six ogres, including Broadback directly behind them. There was no way Aram could attempt escape, even if he was willing to risk *the sack*, which hung limply over the shoulder of one of the ogres he followed. The large burlap sack might have been currently empty, but the threat of it clearly was not. The pace they maintained was brutal, unmercifully based on the longer stride of the large ogres heading up the relatively steep incline. But slowing had earned him another rough shove from Broadback, so breathing hard, he made very sure he matched their gait.

They passed ruins to the south. Aram's eyes widened over broken towers, broken columns, and semicollapsed sections of palaces—or perhaps temples—grander than any intact structure he had ever seen in his life. Even as he marched between ogres in clearly dire circumstances, he found himself wishing he had his freedom, not simply to run but to explore these fallen edifices. He racked his brain to access his father's lessons in order to identify the decaying buildings passing on his right. He thought maybe they were the ruins of Isildien. He assumed the night elf would know, but there was no way to confirm his guess without speaking, and no way to speak without winding up in a burlap sack.

The kaldorei, meanwhile, lowered his head to mourn. It was not the first time—or even the hundredth time—he had seen Isildien in the ten millennia since the city had been destroyed. But every time was just as painful as the first. Ten thousand years ago, Isildien had been nothing short of glorious. And now it was reduced to this fractured shadow of itself. And the worst part, he knew, was that the night elves had brought this fate upon themselves by abusing the very arcane powers they had believed were their birthright. It was why he, like many of his people, now shunned the arcane and used only the druidic magic of nature. It was balanced. It was safe. And it was his penance.

Thalyss looked up, and he and Aram exchanged glances. It suddenly occurred to Aram that the druid no longer had his staff to rest upon—the ogres had left it behind by the river—yet it didn't seem to trouble the kaldorei. Aram wondered if the druid ever really needed it at all. He also wondered if Thalyss, who offered Aram a sympathetic smile, considered shapeshifting his way out of their captivity. Aram briefly fantasized grabbing hold of an antler and swinging himself up onto the great stag's back as the transformation caught the ogres off guard, allowing their hostages to make a break for it. But many of the ogres had spears, and there was no cover in sight. The fantasy ended unpleasantly as Aram pictured himself in the sack while the ogres enjoyed venison for supper.

He ran a similar scenario with Thalyss's bear form—and it ended with similar results. He wondered what other animals the night elf might be capable of, but no creature he could think of—shy of a dragon—seemed to promise success.

He wondered about Makasa. He knew with absolute certainty she would come for him, and he tried to calculate when she might make her move. As he marched, he counted the ogres in the company. In addition to Broadback and the other five surrounding Aram and Thalyss, numerous glances over his shoulder revealed seven more ogres taking up the rear. Thirteen ogres in the cold light of dawn seemed too many even for the mighty Flintwill to chance an assault. She was a warrior—the three ogres she had dispatched before sunrise proved that—but she was also smart enough to wait for her moment. This would not be the time.

And at this time, Aram's heart was full and troubled. Yes, Makasa would come. She'd come for him, for her brother, the last brother she had on this earth. He knew this, and he knew that meant she had not risked attempting to rescue poor Murky.

Sunrise had come and gone, and Malus did not have the compass. By now, the funny little murloc was dead. Aram bit his lip and wiped his eyes. Surrounded by ogres, he couldn't afford to shed any overt tears. But in his heart, he lit a candle for Murky and hoped the murloc's gods would treat him well.

*   *   *

Sunrise had found Malus, Ssarbik, Valdread, and Throgg standing over the cold firepit beneath the ledge.

"Sssatissfied?" the arakkoa complained. "You and your gamezz! Why would you think the boy would ever trade the prizze for a lowly murloc? Were you *afraid* to take the compasss by forcce, or are you jusst that big of a fool?"

Malus moved so suddenly, Ssarbik was caught completely off guard. The big man grabbed the sorcerer by the throat and lifted; Ssarbik's feet quickly cleared the ground. "Try to chant your way out of this," Malus said.

Ssarbik choked and struggled in his captain's grip.

"I don't care whom you serve, bird-man. Forget your place again, and I *will* wring your neck like a chicken's." He opened his hand, and the arakkoa dropped to the ground, gasping for breath, wheezing through his beak. Ssarbik shot Malus a murderous look, but Malus ignored it.

Baron Valdread chuckled audibly. Throgg looked away. He was secretly pleased, but not so secretly frightened of the sorcerer's magic; he didn't want to give Ssarbik reason to take revenge later.

Murky noticed few of these details. He was still hanging off the ogre's shoulder, wrapped in his own nets and his own thoughts.

He saw that his friends were gone, that they had left him with his abductors. He realized sadly that he wasn't too surprised. He had only just met the *kuldurrree*, and Mrksa had stated more than once that she wanted to leave Murky behind. But he had thought Urum would try to help, had hoped that maybe his new friend would not abandon him. And it broke his heart just a bit to learn he was wrong.

When Malus sighed and said to Throgg, "Kill the murloc," a small piece of Murky thought his death now would be a mercy. He had lost his family, his village, and now his new friends. There was no place for him in this world . . .

Just then Zathra returned. Malus turned to her. "Did you find their trail?"

"In a way," she said, smiling grimly and pausing for effect.

Malus was in no mood for guessing games. "Well, out with it."

"Dey be ambushed not far from here. Ogres." She glanced at Throgg. "Some branch a da Gordunni clan."

Throgg harrumphed loudly.

Malus mused on this revelation. "I know of the Gordunni. Their king is Gordok. Actually, that's what they call all their kings. Not that it matters." He returned his focus to the troll, saying, "What did you find?"

"Da human female killed tree a dem ogres. Deir bodies be left behind, and I can tell by da wounds."

"Can you track them?"

"Ogre tracks be clear ta see. Be leadin' up into da mountains toward Isildien. But dere be no tracks for da elf or da humans. No bodies, eider. So dey be taken and carried off."

"Carried off, alive or dead?" asked Malus.

"Dere be no human blood dere, and only a speck a elf blood. So unless da ogres strangled dem, dey probably alive."

Throgg said, "Ogres not take dead humans or dead elf along."

"Not even to eat?" whispered an amused Valdread.

Throgg considered this and shrugged. He said, "Elf-meat taste horrible. But stag-meat and bear-meat good. Human-meat stringy. But stringy good sometimes. If Throgg in mood." He started to drool.

Valdread encouraged him. "How would you prepare the boy? Would you use spices?"

Throgg started to answer. "Cook with blood in carcass," he said.

Zathra shook her head in disgust. "You insane, brudda," she said. "You gotta drain da boy first. Dey be hardly any meat, so you be wantin' ta strip what dere be off da bones. Maybe make jerky outta him."

Throgg shrugged again. "Still better to take alive and eat fresh."

"Foolzzzz! What of the compassss?!" gasped an exasperated Ssarbik, each syllable painfully tearing up his still sore throat.

"Still wid da boy, I be bettin'," said the troll. "No reason ta tink it be a any interest ta da Gordunni."

Throgg added, "Ogres can't eat compass."

Valdread, who was enjoying the conversation immensely, cocked his head and said, "Then Thorne's 'cabin boy' may have been ready to accept your bargain, Captain."

Malus nodded, lost in thought. Contrary to Ssarbik's frustrated assumptions, Malus had not forgotten the compass for one second. The *need* for it filled his every waking thought—and a good portion of his dreams, as well. He had to have it. And not as a prize or gift to the arakkoa's master. No, he had his own designs, his own purposes. For in the end, he was determined to finish what he had started fourteen years ago. And to accomplish that, the compass was absolutely *essential*.

Throgg said, "Throgg hungry now. Does Throgg still kill murloc? Can Throgg eat murloc? Murlocs taste like chicken."

Malus shook his head. "No, don't kill him."

Throgg looked disappointed.

A sympathetic Malus patted the ogre rather gently on his good arm, explaining, "Not yet. He might still be of use. It seems we find ourselves in the odd position of having to mount a rescue mission for Aramar Thorne."

"Resscue?!" There was outrage in the arakkoa's hissing. But when Malus glanced at him, Ssarbik lowered his head submissively and said no more.

Murky, who just barely understood the gist of the exchange, found himself torn. On the one hand, thoughts of a merciful end no longer seemed appealing, especially since feeding an ogre was not exactly his idea of an appetizing way to go. So he was glad his own death had now been postponed. Moreover, he was thrilled Urum and his new friends hadn't actually abandoned him. But he was also horrified to learn the GRRundee had taken Urum, Mrksa, and Duluss. Uncle Murrgly and Aunt Murrl had been taken and never seen again. And though he knew his current abductors were hardly benevolent, he was practically giddy over the fact they were planning to give chase.

He called out, "Murky mrrugl!"

But none of them understood he was offering to help in any small way he could, so they ignored him.

Following Zathra's lead, the Hidden proceeded up into the mountains in pursuit of the ogres, the captives, and their prize.

CHAPTER TWENTY-FIVE
CHILDREN OF THE THORNE

Night fell, and the trail leveled off some. The ogres and their captives kept up their march for another hour or two until the moons were high and the travelers had reached a line of trees. The creatures made a crude camp, chopping down an entire pine to build a bonfire. They roasted a whole pig, which one of their number had pulled from another burlap sack.

Aram and Thalyss were pushed to their knees and bound with thick ropes. In fact, the ropes were so thick, they couldn't be tightly secured around Aram's slim wrists, and the boy quickly realized he could slip out of them at any time, which might come in handy if Makasa made an appearance.

And Makasa considered it.

The river had not been overly kind. It had carried her away

from the ogres' spears, but it had also slammed her against a number of rocks and torn Lord Bloodhorn's rawhide pack from around her waist with what remained of their supplies. In the end, she had also been forced to choose between her iron chain and her harpoon; she couldn't hold on to both without drowning. And this time, she wasn't able to throw the harpoon for some future retrieval. She let it go.

Minutes later, she managed to achieve the shore, battered, bruised, and bleeding. She paused to catch her breath. In that moment—while fighting a sudden wave of exhaustion—she actually considered ditching the troublesome cabin boy. She told herself she wanted to, that the only reason she couldn't was because of the life debt she still owed his fallen father. But the lie wouldn't take, wouldn't hold. Aram was her brother now; she knew that. There had been no possibility of saving Adashe, Akashinga, or Amahle from the Horde. But saving the life of Aramar Thorne might still be within her power. Exhaustion could wait.

She doubled back. The ogres—save the three dead ones— were already gone, and so were Aram and Thalyss. But their trail wasn't hard to follow. They were moving swiftly. It was a challenge for Makasa to catch up. But free of companions, Makasa could maintain an extremely brisk pace. A few hours after sunrise, she had spotted the raiding party up ahead.

Now the challenge was not being seen. There was very little cover at this elevation. Fortunately, the Gordunni weren't expecting pursuit; they rarely looked back. So Makasa was able to gain a bit more ground, to get close enough to spot Aram and Thalyss between the ogres. She saw the boy struggle to keep up, and saw the broad-backed ogre shove him forward. She thought she'd like to kill that ogre.

Aram and Thalyss maintained their silence as they watched the ogres fight over the best parts of the pig. It never occurred to either of them to ask for some. Instead, Aram fed himself on memories. Even the least pleasant served to carry him away, offering some small measure of freedom . . .

They rode in silence. Aram and this man who had returned to claim his rights as Aram's father. Rights that Greydon Thorne had voluntarily relinquished. He offered no explanation, no apology. And every step of the horses took them farther away from Aram's home and true family in Lakeshire.

They stopped at an inn and ate in silence. They slept side by side in silence. The next morning they rode off again in silence.

But each one's silence was of a different flavor. Aram's was bitter. He resented being forced to leave his family and Lakeshire against his will, and though his mother and Robb had been complicit in the decision, Aram was determined to punish Greydon for it . . . probably for the entire next year.

Greydon's silence was different. It was the silence of indecision. It was a silence of struggle. He didn't know what to say or when to say it. He didn't know how to break through his son's righteous anger—the more so because Greydon knew it was righteous. What right did he have to come back into Aram's life now? What right did he have to make demands of the boy he had abandoned?

So, in the end, it wasn't the father but the captain who broke the silence. He said, "You'll like Wavestrider. *She's a fine ship."*

Aram turned his head slowly and gave his father a look of such contempt it nearly shut the man up for good. But he braved the boy's ire. "She has a fine crew," he said next. "However mad you are at me, remember that they don't deserve your anger or contempt. Nor will they put up with it."

Aram looked down. He had to admit it was sound advice, even if he didn't care for the source. Besides, he soon found a way to ignore the source. Hadn't Ceya told him to open his heart to strangers? Hadn't Robb told him to feed his fire? They had already given Greydon Thorne's advice in so many words.

Thus, when they arrived at port, Aram allowed himself to be impressed by the Wavestrider. *She was old, true. A bit beat-up, with a hull that had been patched over and over. But the artist in Aramar recognized her graceful lines, her elegant design. She was beautiful, he thought, even if she was under his father's command.*

A girl descended the gangway and approached, and Aram decided right then and there that he would offer her his friendship openly. She was tall and imposing and a few years older than he was. She had black skin and short black hair, and she was armed with a cutlass and carrying a harpoon.

Greydon said, "Aramar Thorne, this is Second Mate Makasa Flintwill. She'll show you the ropes aboard ship."

Aram stuck out his hand and said, "I'm sure we'll be great friends."

She looked at him as if she found the notion extremely unlikely. She said, "We're not friends. I'm an officer. You're a cabin boy. Do everything I tell you, and maybe *we'll get along well enough."*

He had rolled his eyes then.

Instantly, she grabbed him by his shirtfront, pulled him in close—nose to nose—and said, "Don't roll your eyes at me, boy. Don't roll your eyes in my sight."

Shaken, Aram had glanced over at his father. But his captain seemed more amused than concerned and nodded his approval to Makasa.

She nodded back, released Aram, and turned on her heel, striding back toward the gangway. Without looking back, she said, "Follow me. Keep up."

He raced after her.

Now he waited for her.

When the ogres stopped to make camp, Makasa knew the bright light from their bonfire would make the surrounding darkness that much darker. It allowed her to close in and consider her options.

Thirteen ogres. She still had her cutlass and shield and chain and a hatchet. But she felt the loss of the harpoon acutely, as if— like the Whisper-Man—a length of her arm had been removed, which in a way it had. Her unwavering confidence wavered.

Thirteen ogres were just too many. She knew she could slip up silently and kill two or three before the others were aware of her, but that still left at least ten to fight, which was at least seven more than she could handle at once. And worse, the broad-backed ogre knew her weakness. While the others kept her at bay, he could threaten—even kill—Aram.

On the other hand, the situation would hardly improve once the creatures reached their destination. She was facing thirteen now. How many would she face when they rejoined their clan? Fifty? One hundred? Twice that many? Five times? Still, she knew that in a village—no matter how primitive—there would be places to hide and more distractions in play for Aram's jailors. Possibilities might arise.

But on the third hand, she would stay at the ready. Who knows? Ogres weren't known for their brains or caution. Perhaps all thirteen would sate themselves and fall asleep. If she could permanently silence eight or nine before an alert was sounded, that would be an entirely different story—especially if one of those silenced was the broad-backed ogre.

So Makasa waited in darkness, not twenty yards from Aram, longing—despite the dire situation *and* her usual discipline— for roast pig.

The ogres completely devoured the beast, bones and all. There was literally nothing left, and nothing offered, of course, to either Aram or Thalyss.

Broadback tied one end of the rope that bound them to his

own wrist and settled back against a rock. He shouted something guttural to three of the ogres, clearly placing them on watch. Then he closed his eyes. Within a couple minutes, he was snoring loudly. A few other ogres slept as well, but more than the three on guard duty stayed awake, grunting at each other, shouting, guffawing, and snorting. The cacophony, all put together, was considerable enough to allow Aram and Thalyss to whisper to each other without drawing attention.

"Where is Makasa?" Thalyss asked first.

Aram jerked his head toward the darkness. "Out there, somewhere. She's waiting for the right time."

Thalyss nodded, never questioning or doubting Aram's certainty on this point. "And Murky?" he whispered.

Aram shook his head. There wasn't much hope in that corner.

Thalyss nodded again, though more sadly. "Do you still have the compass?"

"Yes." Aram glanced around to make sure none of the Gordunni was watching. Then, with little effort, he slipped a hand free and reached under his shirt.

The night elf offered a surprised smile at Aram's dexterity—and then his surprise doubled as they both looked at the compass. The crystal needle on the compass—after so many days of consistently pointing southeast—was now pointing to the *northeast*! *And it was glowing!*

Thalyss swallowed hard, tapped his upper lip with his tongue, and whispered, "Has it ever done that before?"

Aram, too stunned to speak, shook his head—then quickly tucked the compass back under his shirt, lest its glow catch other eyes. He tried to put what little he knew of the compass into some context that would or could explain this. But no explanation emerged. He offered Thalyss a questioning look.

The druid could only shrug. He said, "Try to get some sleep. I will keep an eye out for Makasa."

Aram slipped his hand back between the loops of rope and whispered, "There's no way I could ever sleep."

"You would be surprised. Try."

Aram rolled his eyes then, something he hadn't done in weeks. He felt instantly guilty and wondered if Makasa was close enough in the darkness to have seen it.

"Try," Thalyss repeated.

So Aram closed his eyes, thinking, *There's just no way . . .*

They paraded past him, one after another.

Matriarch Cackle said, "Good magic," and held up a sliver of crystal.

Baron Reigol Valdread, the Whisper-Man, whispered, "Good magic," and held up a sliver of crystal.

Ceya Northbrooke Thorne Glade said, "Good magic," and held up a sliver of crystal.

The ship's lookout, Duan Phen, said, "Good magic," and held up a sliver of crystal.

Robb Glade said, "Good magic," and held up a sliver of crystal.

Throgg the ogre said, "Good magic," and held up a sliver of crystal.

Robertson Glade said, "Good magic," and held up a sliver of crystal.

Selya Glade said, "Good magic," and held up a sliver of crystal.

Makasa Flintwill said, "Good magic," and held up a sliver of crystal.

Thalyss said, "Good magic," and held up a sliver of crystal.

First Mate Durgan One-God said, "Good magic," and held up a sliver of crystal.

Even Murky said, "Good magic," in clear and understandable Common, and held up a sliver of crystal.

Third Mate Silent Joe Barker said nothing, but held up a sliver of crystal.

Captain Greydon Thorne said, "Good magic," and held up a sliver of crystal.

They circled Aram, surrounded him. Each one—and more— holding up his or her sliver of crystal. The crystals began to glow. The glow moved to the center, above Aram's head. The Light became blinding. The Voice of the Light said, "Aram, Aram, use this good magic to save me . . ."

Shaken, Aram turned away and hid his head . . .

Aram opened his eyes abruptly, feeling decidedly like a failure for having turned away from the Light. Thalyss was watching him intently. Under the night elf's gaze, the dream itself receded quickly, but that feeling of defeat and unfulfilled promise remained. He looked around the camp. It was quieter now. Plenty of snoring, but no laughter or shouting. The three ogres were still on watch, and four more sat around the fire, feeding its flames with more wood. It felt as if he had dozed off for only a few minutes, but the first glimmer of dawn was visible on the horizon.

The druid's eyes were clearly asking the boy if he was all right.

Aram whispered, "I'm fine. You can sleep now, if you want."

There was a rough jerk on the rope, and Aram felt a slap across the back of his head. Aram and Thalyss looked over at Broadback. The ogre's eyes were still closed, but he muttered, "No talking or the sack."

With dawn approaching, Makasa was already putting some distance between herself and the Gordunni, so that she wouldn't be spotted. But she was yet close enough to see Aram abused again and to tell herself she'd *definitely* like to kill that broadbacked ogre.

CHAPTER TWENTY-SIX
·DiRE MAUL

Come morning, Broadback's ogres and their captives continued their trek northward. By late afternoon, they were marching uphill along a ridge. The path was narrow; the ogres now had to travel single file, yet this offered no opportunity for Thalyss and Aram's escape. On either side, the trail was surrounded by massive thickets of wooden spikes—"thorns" unlike any Aram had ever seen before. It was now clear where all the region's trees had gone. The spikes came in sizes ranging from a foot long to ten. Some were only as thick as his twelve-year-old wrist; others, he noted, were the diameter of an ogre's not insubstantial waistline. And each and every one was sharpened to a dangerous point.

Soon, the ridge widened—allowing two ogres to walk abreast in what had become a corridor between two high walls of the spikes. In addition, tall wooden guard posts—each manned by a single ogre—loomed above the trail at intervals. Aram and Thalyss exchanged a glance. Neither saw how Makasa could follow.

Half an hour later, they passed two more guard posts flanking a massive wood-and-iron gate. Without slowing or speaking, Broadback signaled with a wave, and the gate opened. The raiding party passed through and emerged in twilight above a small valley surrounded by still more spikes. Colossal ruins were everywhere. What Aram had seen of Isildien from a distance was dwarfed by what he now beheld at close range: huge stones, shattered columns, grand edifices, the construction of which all but defied his considerable imagination.

Despite their predicament, it was a breathtaking sight, and Aram—momentarily forgetting the injunction to remain silent—whispered an awestruck, "Where are we?"

Instead of punishing the boy for speaking, Broadback seemed pleased by Aram's wonder, stating with simple pride, "This Dire Maul."

Aram wondered how many other humans had seen this place. *Or lived to tell the tale.* He wished then he could halt their march and pull out his sketchbook. In fact, his hand involuntarily reached toward his back pocket before he stopped himself.

Thalyss saw this and shook his head sadly. In Dire Maul, he saw something quite different from what Broadback or even Aram saw. What Thalyss witnessed was night elf glory brought

low, majesty lost to ruin, with idiot ogres squatting everywhere and wild hyenas skittering about the shadows. He stifled a mournful sigh.

They descended into the high valley.

The Gordunni ogres were spread out across the valley of Dire Maul among stone edifices, most adapted from ancient ruins, others more recently and crudely constructed. Off to the left, Aram spotted a large dome—easily twenty feet high—seemingly made entirely of thorns. (Not wooden spikes—but actual thorns, growing from massive thornbushes surrounding the base of the dome.) There were ogres everywhere. Trained now by his encounters with the gnolls, tauren, centaur, and quilboar, Aram saw the grand variation, adults and children, males and females. The smallest child was still as tall as Aram—and twice as wide. They passed one large male, sleeping and snoring across a good twelve feet of broken stone. Mostly, the ogres' coloring ranged from a blushing peach to a deep burgundy red, though he saw one seven-foot female with skin of ashy blue. Most had two prominent lower tusks and a single horn centered on his or her forehead. But some had two horns, and one had *two heads*! All moved aside to allow Broadback's party to pass as they approached what had once certainly been a great stone temple to some long-forgotten—or at least long-ignored—god.

They walked up a pitted stone ramp and through an ominously cracked stone arch guarded by two eight-foot-tall ogres armed with fearsome axes. Huge bushes of weeds shot up through missing pavement stones. Thorny vines climbed up the walls.

The prisoners and their captors entered the temple—or whatever it was now—to find more axe-wielding ogres and a few bold and drooling hyenas watching their silent procession. They turned right down a long corridor where a good portion of the roof had caved in. A path had been cleared beneath the open sky, but most of the fallen stones had been left just where they lay. Aram and Thalyss saw a huge hole in one wall leading out to open air. Each exchanged a quick glance to make sure the other had taken note of a possible escape route for later. But Broadback took note, too, and warned them off such thoughts with a low growl. Unfortunately, he wasn't quite as stupid as he looked.

They approached a massive but makeshift wooden door, manned by an entire troop of ogres. Broadback nodded to an immense one-eyed hunchbacked ogre, who signaled to his fellows. They started cranking on a great wheel, and the wooden door rose noisily.

During the journey, there had been little need for pushing and shoving the prisoners after the first few minutes of their captivity, but now, as they entered the temple's central chamber, Broadback seemed more inclined to demonstrate Aram and Thalyss's lowly status, first by shoving them forward and then by forcing them to their knees before Gordok, the ogre king.

Gordok was immense, as wide as Broadback and—though

seated on a throne carved out of an ancient altar—clearly taller than Throgg. He had a single white horn on his forehead and another directly behind it atop his bald head, plus so many piercings everywhere that though Aram tried several times to tally them all up, he always lost count. He ate walnuts out of a large quilboar skull held aloft by an ogre girl—small by ogre standards, yet still taller than Aram. Declaring she stood too far away, the king slapped her—for she was clearly not too far away to be punished—and reached into the skull for a few nuts. After shattering them in his thick fist, he shoved meat and shell alike into a huge maw that revealed serrated teeth, each sharpened to a point.

Broadback stood behind his two prisoners and slammed a fist against his chest in greeting. He waited, while Gordok slowly chewed with his mouth open, looking down his broad, flat nose (pierced with a thick gold nose ring) at Aram and Thalyss, as bits of nut and shell dropped into his thick blue-black beard from between his pierced lips. The king regarded captor and captives alike with something akin to contempt—or maybe just boredom.

Finally, Gordok nodded and said, "Wordok." Aram soon realized it was Broadback's actual name.

"Wordok," the king repeated. "Gordok not happy. Deese slaves not last. Not last minutes."

"Eh, no," acknowledged Wordok sadly. Then, catching himself, he put a better face on himself and his haul. "But boy killed Kerskull. And elf change to great bear. So, fun, yeah?"

I killed Kerskull? Aram and Thalyss exchanged a quick glance. Broadback/Wordok was certainly exaggerating their qualifications. The ogre knew Aram hadn't killed anyone, while Thalyss had been knocked unconscious before getting a chance to shift.

Gordok considered this new information as he chewed. Despite the serrated teeth, Aram thought there was something cowlike about the way Gordok masticated.

Finally, the king said, "Kerskull dead?"

"Yeah. Bordok and Kronk, too."

"Wordok kill dem." It seemed less of an accusation than a correction.

"No," Wordok assured his master. Then, doubling down on his lies: "Boy kill Kerskull. Bear kill Bordok and Kronk."

Gordok still seemed unconvinced. He stared down at Aram. "Boy puny. Not kill Kerskull."

Wordok pulled Aram's cutlass from his belt. "Boy used this. Kerskull's blood still there."

Aram and Gordok both squinted at the weapon. Sure enough there was a bit of blood on it, and Aram realized that as Wordok had taken out the weapon, he had wiped the flat of the blade against the small knife wound in his side that Aram had given him. *Well*, Aram thought, *at least it's true I drew the blood on that sword.*

"I killed him," Aram said, hoping he'd earn more respect than punishment for killing one of the king's clan. At any rate, his fib earned him a quick smile and nod from Wordok.

Gordok continued to squint at the blade. Then he abruptly turned to Thalyss. "Elf kill Bordok and Kronk?"

Thalyss actually yawned, then said dismissively, "Were those their names?"

"Show me bear," the king demanded.

"Only at night," the night elf replied calmly.

Gordok grunted. He slapped the ogre girl, took some more nuts, and then looked up at the ceiling for thirty or forty seconds as he contemplated and chewed.

Wordok ventured, "Better than murlocs . . ."

Gordok laughed. "Yeah! Sick o' dem murlocs for sure!"

"So, fun, yeah?"

"*Gordok* say if dey fun." But Gordok glanced at the girl, who seemed to regard Wordok's two prizes with interest. He took another look at them himself and nodded in a way that almost resembled approval. Clearly disposed now to keep a *bit* more of an open mind, he shrugged and said, "Toss dem in pit."

They were dragged from the temple and marched downhill in the general direction of the dome of thorns. From this angle, Aram could see it was situated about twenty or thirty yards from an empty pen surrounded by a wooden fence. Beside the pen was a large amphitheater with sandstone seats and a ringed arena, all carved right into the hillside. The sun was sinking now, and the way the afternoon light reflected off the stone floor of the arena made it appear blood red.

Focused as he was on the amphitheater and what it might portend, Aram almost didn't see his new lodging until he was literally right on top of it: a large, deep pit with smooth stone walls, again streaked with red. It was probably just the light, he thought. But he grew less certain. The low sun didn't reach down to the bottom of the dark pit, but a single torch below illuminated a number of shadowy figures creeping across its depths.

Wordok grunted at a pit guard, and in response a thick rope ladder was released and allowed to unroll down to the floor of the crater. Wordok pointed at the ladder, and Aram voluntarily descended, followed by Thalyss.

Achieving the bottom, it took Aram some time for his eyes to adjust in the dim torchlight. Before he could see clearly, he heard a sniffing sound. He looked behind him and saw two glowing eyes staring at him from a slim, low fissure that had been dug into the wall of the pit. Aram stumbled back a step or two away from the small crevice, and the sniffing was replaced by a low growl. Suddenly, the glowing eyes leapt forward and a dark form tackled Aram to the ground.

A terrified Aram, struggling in vain to throw off his attacker, saw the flash of teeth, which snapped shut just short of his nose. Then, almost as quickly as the attack began, it ended. Thalyss was there, wrenching Aram's opponent off and tossing whatever it was aside. The thing rolled into the torchlight, and Aram saw it was a yellow, spotted gnoll, a small, starved, and skinny male, little more than a pup, which meant it was about Aram's height when hunched over, but twice as broad in the shoulders.

Aram was breathing heavily, trying to fight the urge to run back to the ladder and beg to be pulled back up. Then, in a flash, he thought of his father and the matriarch, and though a second earlier he had been desperate to be free of the creature, he now launched himself at the gnoll with gusto, shocking Thalyss, the gnoll, and himself.

"Aram, stop! What are you doing?" shouted the night elf, as the two young "warriors" rolled about in the dirt. Aram elbowed his opponent in the gut and managed to shut his mouth once with an uppercut to the jaw. But in return, Aram felt the gnoll's claws rake painfully across his back before the creature lifted him clear off his feet and threw him hard against the pit wall.

Aram crumpled to the muddy floor in a bruised and bleeding heap. The hunched form of the gnoll loomed over Aram, panting and seething.

Then Aramar Thorne threw his head back and laughed. The sound echoed off the sides of the pit. The gnoll bristled at being mocked; his lips parted to emit another low growl. Aramar stood and approached the gnoll. Aram slowly raised his hand; the gnoll flinched, and Aram slapped him hard on the shoulder, laughing again. The gnoll's lips curled then, and he laughed his loud, raucous hyena-laugh and slapped Aram with considerable force on his bleeding back.

Aram swallowed back the pain and spoke. "I am Aramar Thorne of Lakeshire." He nodded toward the night elf. "This is the druid Thalyss."

The gnoll sniffed at Aram and then Thalyss. Apparently,

their scents met with his approval, and he began bobbing up and down happily like a dog in hope of a treat. He pounded his chest with a thick paw and said, "Hackle of the Woodpaw gnolls."

"I hope we can all be friends, Hackle," Aram said. "I suppose we'll need friends down here."

At the repetition of the word *friends*, Hackle's expression suddenly turned surly. He dropped down on all fours, and circling wide, slunk past Aram, returning to his fissure. As he crawled inside it, he grumbled, "No point making friends with those Hackle soon have to kill."

CHAPTER TWENTY-SEVEN
Good Magic

With a few scattered herbs taken from his pockets, the druid tended to Aram's back. Aram didn't know if the kaldorei was using magic or the simple skills common to any village healer or apothecary, but either way, the treatment soothed his torn skin.

Thalyss glanced over at Hackle, or at all they could see of Hackle: his two glowing eyes staring back at them from the fissure he had dug for himself in the side of the pit.

"How did you know to do that?" the night elf asked.

"My father taught me."

"A valuable lesson. A wise man."

"Sometimes," Aram said. He thought his voice sounded grudging and quickly changed the subject. "Thanks. That feels a lot better."

"Well, the bleeding has stopped. The scratches did not go deep. But there is not much I can do for this shirt." It was shredded in strips and sticky with blood in back.

Aram shrugged. He still had his mother's dirty sweater and his father's old coat tied around his waist, but it was too hot to wear either down in the pit, and he didn't think he'd much care for the feeling of wool rubbing against his open wounds or leather sticking to them. He reached behind him and pulled the shirt away from his back. But something tugged the shirt forward . . .

It was the compass! It jerked slightly underneath his shirt. Thalyss saw it, too. Aram pulled it out and checked it. The sliver-like crystal needle still glowed faintly, but now it pointed to the east, and the whole compass was gently tugging in that direction, too. Aram looked around quickly to see if anyone else was watching and saw the gnoll's eyes upon him. "Stop it," he muttered with desperate frustration—and the compass instantly ceased to move. He and the night elf exchanged another surprised glance as Aram tucked the compass back under what remained of his shirt.

"Odder and odder," said the kaldorei, and he tapped his upper lip with his tongue.

"Disturbing, I'd call it." It was an understatement. What lay to the east that was important enough for the compass to literally try to drag him in that direction? *Gadgetzan and Lakeshire were to the southeast anyway!* No. There was more going on here than his simple desire to return to hearth and home.

After a considered and considerable pause, the night elf offered his own theories. "Perhaps the magic of that crystal is not sending you some*place* but rather to find some*one* or some*thing*. Perhaps that someone or something was on the move, still east of us but heading north as we did. And perhaps you are closer now than you have been yet."

Aram's mouth hung open. He wanted to question the kaldorei further. But other concerns forced such thoughts from his mind. He said, "We have bigger problems at the moment."

"Oh, you think so?" the elf said with a wry smile. "Do you think Makasa can even get past the barricades of spikes or the gate or the ogres—let alone find a way to help us escape from this pit?"

"I think Makasa can do almost anything," Aram said and meant it. "But we need to be ready. We need to find a way to make her job easier."

"Then let us educate ourselves, shall we?"

They crossed the pit together and introduced themselves to their fellow captives. There weren't many, just an old one-legged tauren and about a dozen murlocs.

While Thalyss spoke with the murlocs, Aram sat down beside the tauren, who called himself Woolbeard, a name that so suited his appearance, Aram had to stop himself from facetiously commenting that if it was the tauren's birth name, it was amazingly prophetic. He was soon glad he had held his tongue. "Woolbeard" was a name given to the tauren by the ogres as a sign of contempt. Aram asked his real name, but the old tauren just shook his head, saying, "Woolbeard's the name I'll die with. Might as well accept it."

Woolbeard, long ago broken by his slavery to the ogres, soon spelled out their current predicament. It was pretty much what Aram had pieced together, though it didn't particularly please him to find his suspicions confirmed. Gordok amused himself nightly by pitting his slaves against each other as gladiators in his arena. Moreover, the ogre king was tired of watching murlocs fight, so the odds were good that the first combatants of the evening would be drawn from among Woolbeard, Hackle, Thalyss, and Aram.

Aram asked the obvious question: "What if we refuse to fight?"

Woolbeard sidestepped it. "Boy, you do what you like. But if you're paired with me, I'll split your skull for you."

Aram smiled, consciously choosing to keep their discussion light. "You think you can catch me?"

Woolbeard waved the concern away. "Eh, eventually. They keep a wooden leg for me topside, and I get around pretty good. You probably think you're too fast for me. But the murlocs are too fast for me—and too slippery, too. Except they tire, and I don't. Or Gordok gets impatient and has one of his warders shove the murloc toward me. It'll be the same with you, boy. You'll tire or get shoved my way, and I'll split your skull." Then, as an afterthought, he said, "Nothing personal, of course."

"Oh, of course."

The old tauren took a long look at Aram and frowned. "Understand, it's over for us. I've tried escaping. They cut off my leg. I've tried not fighting. They beat me near to death. All that's left is to do what they say and hope for a quick end."

He fell silent.

Thalyss approached with two of the murlocs. Even before the night elf spoke, Aram thought they looked like Murky. But then again, all the murlocs looked like Murky. "Aram, this is Murrgly and Murrl. Murky's uncle and aunt. The other murlocs are also from Murky's village."

Aram swallowed hard. He wasn't sure how to tell them that their nephew was almost definitely dead—and that it was almost definitely Aram's own fault.

The druid seemed to sense Aram's dilemma and said, "I told them Murky was captured by another raiding party, and that we wanted to help him but were captured before we had the chance."

The larger of the two murlocs—to be honest, Aram wasn't sure if it was the uncle or aunt—said, "Mmmmrgl nk mrrrgll. Murrgly Murrl mrrrgle Murky mlgggrr flk."

Aram turned to Thalyss, who listened, struggling to understand. "Hmmm. I believe Aunt Murrl here says not to feel too bad. The truth is they both had assumed Murky was already dead."

Uncle Murrgly pawed the ground and said, "Murky nk fll-lurlokkr. Mrrrgle Murky mlgggrrr flk."

Thalyss translated. "Murky is no fisherman. My impression is they thought he would have starved to death by now."

Aunt Murrl placed a gentle hand on Aram's shoulder. "Mmrgl mrrugl Murky."

"She is thanking you for trying to help him."

Aram met her gaze and said, "I wish we could have done more."

She nodded back at him, and they all fell silent. Aram knew he didn't want to fight any of these creatures, and certainly not for the amusement of ogres. But both Hackle and Woolbeard had made it perfectly clear that an alliance was unlikely. It would take more magic than the druid had in his pockets to change that.

But what about the magic Aram had in his *pockets?*

He pulled out his sketchbook and pencil.

With all his heart, he wished his father were there to pose for him. His father and Makasa. He longed to hear her say, "You better not be putting me in that blasted book." But neither Greydon nor Makasa was likely to make an appearance, so instead, he started by showing the book to the murlocs.

Aunt Murrl practically cooed over Aram's sketches of Murky, and even gruff Uncle Murrgly squinted back a tear.

He sketched them both together, then made rough drawings of the rest of the murlocs as well. By the time he was done, he no longer had any difficulty distinguishing male murlocs from female, old from young, etc. The females were slightly larger than the males. The younger murlocs had bigger eyes and were a brighter green, only growing darker with age. Even their language was beginning to reach him. He heard *mmmm mrrrggk* over and over, and knew he was on the right track.

After that, Aram sat down with Woolbeard, showing him the sketches of the tauren he had drawn at Flayers' Point. Woolbeard seemed impressed, and when Aram turned the page to Bloodhorn, Woolbeard actually whistled. He said, "I like the look of her. She have a name?"

"Lady Bloodhorn," Aram said.

"A lady? Never heard a tauren called a lady before."

"That's what my father called her. They were trading partners."

"*Were?*"

"My father's dead."

Woolbeard grunted his condolences, then said, "My own wife died ten years ago." He tapped Bloodhorn's portrait. "Wouldn't mind meeting a fine lady like this one."

"If we ever get out of here, I could introduce you both."

For a brief moment, Woolbeard had forgotten where he was. But now the tauren looked down his snout at Aram and shook his head. "That's not likely, boy." But he said it with more kindness and less of a tone of doomed inevitability than before. (In any case, he didn't repeat the threat to split Aram's skull for him.) It was clear Aram's acquaintance with Lady Bloodhorn had raised his stock with the old tauren. When Aram asked permission to sketch him, Woolbeard shook his head. "Not sure I want *this* version of me captured in your book."

"What's your real name? I could try to capture him."

He said nothing for a long time. Then he muttered something too low for Aram to hear. Aram waited patiently. Finally, Woolbeard shook his head and said, "You survive the night, and maybe I'll try to remember my true name."

"And in the meantime?"

"In the meantime, I'll try to remember what I used to look like, and you can try to put that memory in your book."

Minutes later, with the drawing complete, Woolbeard nodded his approval, saying, "Boy, I haven't looked that good in years. If you do get out of here, you show this to that Lady Bloodhorn of yours. It'll cast my spell on her good."

"No doubt," Aram said, pleased that in the time it took to execute the sketch, his chances of escape seemed to have improved considerably in the tauren's mind.

Thalyss watched all this with bemused amazement. "You are a natural," he said. "You and that book, anyway. You can reach most anyone with that, can you not?"

"We'll see," Aram said. He turned to face the fissure and began sketching. Over the past hour, he had snuck the occasional glance at Hackle and always found the gnoll's glowing eyes upon him. And, still, all Aram could see were those eyes, so he mostly drew Hackle from memory, occasionally turning the pages back to the gnoll brute to augment his recollection.

Woolbeard

ARAM

And he took his time with it, too, weaving his spell on the young gnoll.

That sorcery began to do its work. A curious Hackle emerged slowly from the fissure, allowing Aram to improve his drawing with more and more of its subject in view. He captured the patterns of the gnoll's dark spots against his fur, including the spot around his light blue left eye, which contrasted starkly with his dark brown right eye. He captured the leather skullcap Hackle wore and the single incisor that stuck out even when the gnoll's mouth was closed.

At last, the gnoll began to warily circle, sometimes on all fours, sometimes upright. But gradually, with each pass, he drew closer and closer to Aram.

Finally, Aram felt he was done. He put his pencil down and beckoned Hackle. At first, the gnoll pretended not to notice. He quickly sat down where he was and rapidly scratched the back of his neck with his foot in much the way Soot was wont to do. But when the scratching stopped and Hackle glanced back over, Aram's eyes were still upon him. Aram beckoned again.

So in the end, Hackle approached. Aram showed him the sketch and watched Hackle smile. Aram flipped back through the leaves to reveal the drawing of the small gnoll pup, which Aram had sketched a lifetime ago. He could hear Hackle's swift intake of breath. Aram turned the leaf back, and Hackle lingered over the drawing of the Grimtail brute.

Aram said, "In a year or two, you'll look much like him."

Hackle

ARAM

Hackle grinned broadly. Then his expression fell, and he shook his head. "Hackle runt of litter. Too small for a Woodpaw brute."

"It's not always about size," Aram told him. "It's about who's the fiercest warrior."

Hackle smiled again. "Hackle plenty fierce," he said, straightening his back.

Aram flipped the leaf. "This is Cackle. Matriarch of the Grimtail clan."

The young gnoll stabbed a finger at the sketch, confirming. "Cackle?"

"Yes."

"Hackle is Hackle!"

"I know."

The young gnoll giggled then, and the giggle soon expanded into peals of laughter punctuated by him repeating over and over, "Hackle, Cackle! Hackle, Cackle! Hackle, Cackle!" The coincidence of the rhyme seemed to supply the gnoll with an endless source of glee. It took him an easy five minutes to settle back down and left him panting loudly. He grinned at the sketchbook and then at Aram.

"Good magic?" Aram prompted.

Hackle nodded. "Good magic!"

"Maybe we can be friends then."

Hackle kept nodding unconsciously. But shortly his mind and his memory caught up to his current warm feelings toward Aram. He stepped back abruptly. "No," he growled. "Ogres want fight. Ogres want victory. Hackle warrior. Prove in arena. Prove every time!" Then he muttered, "Show them they wrong."

Aram struggled to make the gnoll understand. "The ogres keep Hackle as a slave. Why does Hackle care what ogres think?"

Hackle shook his head. "Not ogres. Gnolls! *Woodpaw* think Hackle not warrior. Not worthy. Drive Hackle away! Ogres catch Hackle! Think he die in arena first night! But Hackle show ogres, show gnolls! Show them all they wrong!"

"Hackle is a warrior!"

"Yes!"

"But that doesn't mean he has to fight everyone, friend and foe alike. It doesn't mean he has to fight tonight."

Then, directly across from them, the rope ladder unrolled down the wall of the pit. And from above, Wordok's voice bellowed, "All climb! All climb now!"

CHAPTER TWENTY-EIGHT
WHERE THERE'S A FLINTWILL, THERE'S A WAY

Makasa carefully made her way through the jungle of wooden spikes. It was treacherously slow going; nevertheless, she couldn't resist a grim smile. To creatures as large as ogres, the dense thickets of oversize stakes must have seemed impenetrable. And without a doubt, they were intimidating; every single spike was sharp enough to impale. But when Makasa Flintwill had looked at them more closely, it had immediately become clear that if you weren't as wide as an ogre, there was considerable . . . wiggle room.

It was an intricate dance. She basically advanced stake by stake, sliding around one, ducking under another, oozing and undulating between each spike. She had removed her shield to give her greater flexibility and to use it to force aside the occasional stake impeding her progress. She kept the hatchet handy, too, for when one couldn't be avoided and required removal. But mostly, she relied on herself. She had excellent muscle control and a good eye, and even in the rapidly fading light, she rarely miscalculated. Still, every few minutes, the point of a spike would snag on her clothes or catch at the iron chain wrapped around her chest or slip between her leg and her sword, lifting the cutlass up awkwardly, requiring Makasa to extricate herself with delicate finesse.

And then there were the cuts. On her left cheek. On her right thigh and knee. On both ankles. All over both arms. The cuts were shallow but stinging and left drops of blood behind. There were moments when she actually wished she were more like Aram—smaller, shorter, slimmer—but these moments were fleeting. She valued her size and strength and knew she'd need both for what was to come.

She had avoided the main ridge—its guard posts, gate, and sentries—though the steep slope below the crest had made the stake-dance that much more challenging. This maneuvering had taken her most of the day, but by sunset, she had come over the top to descend through these "thorns" into the Dire Maul valley. By nightfall, she had reached the edge of the final thicket of spikes and scoped out the ruins before her. Feeling triumphant, Makasa became briefly careless, scratching herself against a long slim spike, carving a long shallow cut into her forehead. Like the other cuts, this one stung and, worse, dripped blood into both eyes. She blinked several times and carefully raised an arm to wipe the blood away. Then, in a rare moment of pure spite, she used her shield to force the offending thorn upward until it snapped off at the base. It fell at her feet. She stared at it in the moonlight, and a thought occurred. Keeping to the shadows, she emerged from the thicket, carrying the long thin stake like a spear—*or like a harpoon*. With her shield once again strapped to her back, her free hand quietly drew out her cutlass, and she silently proceeded from shadow to shadow into the heart of the ogre clan's territory.

She was initially surprised to find nearly every structure empty. She peeked into a hut and could see signs of recent habitation. But there were no ogres in sight, not in the hut, not anywhere.

A helpful cloud concealed the White Lady, the larger of Azeroth's two moons. The second moon, the Blue Child, was but an azure sliver that night and gave off just enough of a glow to aid Makasa, without putting her at much risk.

But there were lights up ahead: multiple torches converging near a large dome of *actual thorns*. She thought the dome might be some kind of prison, which meant the prisoners might be on display there. It was as sound a hypothesis as any. She didn't dare take a direct route but silently and stealthily made her way by fits and starts through the ruins toward the dome.

But the torches, the ogres, weren't actually converging on the dome. Her heart sank as she saw where they *were* headed: a large amphitheater being used as a gladiatorial arena. From the shadows, she first heard and then spotted the broad-backed ogre acting as master of ceremonies, playing to the crowd at

times, but mostly to what could only be the king of the clan.
Enthroned on a massive stone chair, this was the biggest ogre
Makasa had *ever* seen. His servant, a rather small ogre girl,
made him look bigger still, and he slapped her periodically to
prove his dominance. Yet it wasn't the king who gave Makasa
pause. It was Aram (dragged out with the night elf, a crippled
tauren, a young gnoll, and a dozen or so murlocs) being placed
into a holding pen, a *slave pen*, in plain view of all the ogres in
the arena. Makasa had confidence she could kill *any* ogre—
probably even one as large as this nasty-looking king. But she
couldn't kill *a hundred* ogres. Once again, she'd have to watch
and wait.

An ogre handed a thick wooden peg leg to Woolbeard, who
carefully strapped it on to his knee stump and then tested it by
lurching about the pen with surprising speed.

Meanwhile, Wordok was proclaiming loudly to the assem-
bled throng, "Fun match tonight! Old tauren skull-splitter fight
elf can change to great bear!"

Aram watched Thalyss shake his head and chuckle. Somehow,
the night elf was still amused by their predicament—or at least
by some of its details. With another chuckle, he leaned toward
Aram and whispered, "What do you suppose would happen
to Wordok if, instead of a bear, I changed into a feathered
moonkin?"

Aram found himself shrugging, though for the life of him,
he couldn't figure out why he or Thalyss should care about

Wordok's likelihood of survival when their own seemed so much in question. Also, Aram had never seen a "moonkin" and was suddenly dying to know what one looked like.

"But first," Wordok shouted, while holding up Aram's cutlass, "we see little killer of Kerskull fight gnoll pup!"

A few yards away, Hackle began to growl. Aram heard him grumble, "Hackle no pup . . ." before shooting a murderous look Aram's way.

Aram swallowed hard and tried to take a deep, calming breath. He was looking everywhere for Makasa, but he couldn't see her, couldn't be sure that she was anywhere near—or that there was anything she could do even if she were.

The holding pen was opened, and Hackle strode out. Aram didn't move at first, but a warder with a long spear poked him in the rear and his still-smarting back until the boy complied and entered the ring.

Once the crowd got a good look at him, they began hooting their disdain. Aram couldn't make out most of it, but he did hear, "That flea kill Kerskull?!" and "Kerskull worthless!" plus a handful of other remarks disparaging Aram, Kerskull, or both.

Wordok approached and handed Aram his bloodstained cutlass. For a brief moment, the boy fantasized about stabbing the ogre and making his escape during the resulting confusion. But he knew it would never work.

Another ogre handed Hackle an ironwood war club accented with three or four iron nails. Aram couldn't help wondering if

Greydon Thorne had purveyed the weapon that was about to kill his son. But he shook the thought away.

With no ceremony, Wordok and the other warders promptly abandoned the ring. The arena grew silent.

Watching from the shadows, hidden behind an ancient stone megalith that stuck out at an angle from the turf between the amphitheater and the pit, Makasa debated internally whether to intervene. She was *prepared* to intervene—even at the cost of her own freedom or life. But her preference was to wait. If Aram could survive the contest, she felt considerably more optimistic about rescuing him from whatever cell they stuck him in—*after* the bulk of the ogre population had gone to sleep. And Aram surviving didn't seem impossible.

The murlocs are probably from Murky's village, and they have survived the arena for some weeks. If they can survive that long, can't Aram survive one night? After all, he managed to survive the attack on Wavestrider. *Plus, that gnoll he's supposed to fight is a real runt of a thing.*

But she realized she was trying to talk herself into expecting an outcome that most of Aram's history wouldn't support. So she waited—but remained at the ready, knowing that one way or another, she *would* save her brother.

CHAPTER TWENTY-NINE
THE ARENA

The two young gladiators faced each other. Aram, frankly, was terrified. He felt his knees go weak, and the only thing that was preventing his teeth from chattering was the fact that his jaw seemed to have locked. He didn't want to kill the gnoll, but he *really* didn't want to die, and—despite the months of his father's training aboard *Wavestrider*—recent events had more than demonstrated that his fighting abilities in a life-or-death struggle were insufficient. He held his sword off to the side, forced his jaw to unclench, swallowed, and whispered, "I don't want to fight you."

"Aram fight or Hackle kill Aram," the gnoll said quietly, looking unhappy. Then he shook his head and corrected himself: "Hackle kill Aram anyway. But better Aram die fighting."

"But if we both *refuse* to fight—"

Now Hackle shouted, "Hackle never refuse fight!"

And, finally, from his throne, Gordok shouted impatiently, "Fight NOW!"

The gnoll rushed wildly at Aram, swinging his club. The whole crowd instantly roared its approval. It wasn't a precision attack, and Aram was able to duck and roll out of the way. He wished for a different weapon. Something he could hit Hackle with, maybe stun him without killing him. But those kinds of thoughts were quickly pushed from his mind, as Hackle swung his club back around and the tip of one nail snagged on Aram's shirt, tearing it open just below where the compass hung on its chain and nearly slicing open his belly at the same time.

Aram leapt back; the gangly gnoll advanced on him, swinging—or rather, overswinging—his club wildly. This time it didn't even come close. Aram thought he saw a pleading look in Hackle's eyes. In any case, he knew the gnoll didn't really want to hurt him. He just needed to give Hackle a reason, an excuse not to fight.

Hackle continued to swing his club in long sweeping arcs that forced Aram back but never really came close enough to inflict any damage. At first, this show thrilled the ogres, who cheered on the gnoll more with every swing. But the swings led to no impact, no blood, no carnage, and the crowd began to turn, hissing and taunting both combatants. From Aram they got no reaction, but Hackle seemed to feel every shouted slight like a blow brought down on his shoulders. Somehow, the ogres could sense this and turned against him completely. Worst of all, they began to laugh at him and his wildly ineffective swings.

He couldn't abide it and tightened up his game. He advanced more quickly; the swings of his club came shorter and faster and with more specific intent.

Aram was forced to deflect a swing with his sword, and the jolt rattled him all the way back to his shoulder socket. He hesitated to parry again, afraid the cutlass would be shattered into fragments by the force of Hackle's blows. Again he wished for a different weapon, this time not out of any desire to be merciful, but because this was not his sword, not the sword his father had given him the day he first boarded *Wavestrider*. That weapon had been torn from his grip and left inside the chest of the Whisper-Man. The cutlass he held now had been pried from the grip of a dead pirate, and Aram superstitiously questioned its loyalty.

From her vantage, Makasa watched as all of Greydon Thorne's lessons seemed to abandon his son. The boy wasn't even trying to use his sword; he was simply dodging the gnoll's war club, which came closer to braining Aram with every swing.

She glanced over at Thalyss, who was watching intently from inside the holding pen, hoping the druid would intervene so she wouldn't have to. But the night elf suddenly started to smile. *What had he seen?*

She looked back at Aram. He was running. Running away from the gnoll at top speed.

*   *   *

The crowd, which had fallen silent when Hackle had stepped up his attacks, began to laugh again. Belatedly, Hackle gave chase. Aram ran all the way around the ring, and Hackle loped after him, his embarrassment increasing with every step and his fury rising in concert.

Aram wasn't trying to escape the gnoll so much as buy himself some time to think, to come up with a strategy, a plan—or one halfway decent notion of what to do next. Then, on his second time around the ring, a wild idea entered his head. It wasn't much, but it was all he had, so he immediately attempted its execution.

He stumbled, rolling over in the dirt. In order not to overrun him, Hackle stopped short. Aram looked up. Their eyes met. Again, Hackle looked miserable. But he raised his war club over his head and was prepared to bring it down to crush Aram's.

Just as the club began its descent, Aram—who had already pulled his oilskin-wrapped sketchbook out of his back pocket—whipped the book forward, holding it up in front of him like a talisman, shouting, "Beware my magic!"

Hackle hesitated, his club frozen midswing. The crowd gasped audibly. Aram quickly scampered to his feet. He unwrapped the book and held it out, keeping it between himself and the gnoll.

From his throne, a confused Gordok shouted at Wordok, "Boy have magic book?!"

An equally confused Wordok took all this in, shrugged to himself, and shouted back, "That how Kerskull die! Fun, yeah?!"

Gordok considered this, then nodded sagely. All this seemed to impress the other spectators, and they remained silent, eager to see what would happen next.

Aram kept his eyes locked on Hackle's. He spoke directly to the gnoll, while simultaneously attempting to put on a show for the audience. "You know this is good magic, don't you?!" he shouted, knowing his words would mean one thing to Hackle and something entirely different to the crowd.

Hackle nodded, still holding his club in the air.

"You don't want to hurt me and risk the magic, do you?!"

Hackle shook his head.

But from the crowd, a one-eyed ogre shouted, "Puny gnoll afraid of book!"

Each word struck Hackle like a slap across the face. A low growl began emanating from his throat. He advanced.

But Aram was ready for this. He had already opened the book to its last sketched page, the page with Hackle's picture. Turning his back to the crowd, Aram showed the likeness to the gnoll—and only the gnoll. "Take another step, and I rip this out. That's *bad* magic. Trust me, Hackle, you don't want the bad magic. You want the good magic."

Hackle nodded dumbly. Aram advanced a few steps. Hackle backed away just as many.

Aram shouted, "Then lower your war club! We were not meant to be enemies, you and I!"

The club slowly sank.

Makasa could not believe her eyes or her ears. *It was working!* She could hear the ogres whispering that Aram was casting a spell on the gnoll with his magic book.

And in a way, he was.

Taking his biggest risk yet, Aram tossed his sword across the ring and called out, "Throw away that club! You must not use it against the good magic!"

And Hackle, almost smiling, complied with Aram's command. The club thunked into the dirt a few inches from Aram's cutlass.

The ogres were all now silent as the grave. But Gordok was still confused and not a little frustrated. He looked around at his fellow ogres. He stared at Aram and the book. He shot a look at Wordok, who was grinning stupidly at all the "fun." Finally, he slammed his fist down with so much force, it *shattered* the stone armrest of his throne. "Use magic!" he commanded. "Kill gnoll wid magic book!"

Aram tried not to visibly cringe, but he briefly glanced away from Hackle, breaking the "spell."

"Kill gnoll wid magic book!" Gordok shouted again.

Hackle turned a contemptuous look toward the ogre king and shouted back, "Not that kind of magic! Not that kind of book!"

Gordok and Ogre Girl

"WHAT?!" roared Gordok, rising to his feet. *"WHAT?!"*

He turned again to Wordok, who shrugged sheepishly at his king. A growling Gordok resumed his seat and smacked his right fist into the palm of his left hand with enough force to shatter twenty stone armrests. He shouted down at Hackle, *"DEN KILL BOY!"*

Aram looked at Hackle. Hackle looked at Aram. Then both of them made a mad dash for their weapons.

Hackle was faster but at the end slowed down so as not to overrun his club. Aram didn't slow, didn't go for his sword. Instead, he leapt, using his momentum to slam into the gnoll, tackling him and rolling with him beyond both club and cutlass. The pain in his back reminded Aram he was still at a disadvantage against Hackle's natural weapons, so before the gnoll could strike with tooth or claw, Aram brought both his legs under him and, with all the strength he could muster, kicked the gnoll away.

The stunned crowd finally snapped out of its collective stupor and cheered the action. This briefly distracted Hackle—but not Aram. In a flash, he was on his feet; he scooped up his cutlass, kicked away the club, and—before the gnoll could rise—had the tip of his sword pressed against Hackle's throat.

Makasa could almost read Aram's mind. *Can I do this?* he was thinking. *Can I take this poor creature's life?*

Kill him, she urged with all her heart. But deep down, she knew—despaired—that such an act was not her brother's way.

*   *   *

The crowd again was hushed. Many of the ogres were smiling. To them it had been an entertaining—if unorthodox—show.

Gordok was less enthralled. In fact, he looked completely disgusted. He shook his head and said with a dismissive wave, "Fine. Boy kill gnoll."

"No."

Instantly, Gordok was back on his feet and bellowing, *"NO?! NO?!"*

Aram smiled triumphantly—thinking he might as well take his triumphs where he could find them—and said, "This gnoll is not my enemy. I will not harm him." Of course, he still kept the blade to Hackle's throat, just in case.

Hackle groaned loudly as the entire crowd began to shout down their scorn. He looked up at Aram with pleading eyes. "Please," he growled despairingly, "kill Hackle. End Hackle's shame."

Aram continued to work his magic. "No. You are brave and honorable and my friend. I cannot—will not—kill a Woodpaw gnoll who gives his all as you have, a Woodpaw gnoll who has proven his skill as you have! I will not kill a Woodpaw gnoll with the true heart of a warrior as you have!"

Hackle growled again, but this growl was a growl of pride. Their eyes met. There was indeed magic between them.

Nor were they the only ones affected. In the pen, Thalyss smiled, quite impressed. And Woolbeard . . . Aram's words reached something deep inside the old tauren, something long forgotten. He found that he was slumped over the fence and raised himself up to his full height.

Farther off, Makasa shook her head. Aram was simply . . . unbelievable. But the piece of him she found most incredible was the piece that reminded her most of Greydon Thorne. She wouldn't smile. He wasn't out of danger yet. But for once, not smiling took some real effort.

Hackle whispered resignedly, "Aram should kill Hackle. Worse for both if Aram don't."

Aram frowned and shook his head minutely, whispering, "Don't forget the good magic. Luck is on our side tonight . . ." He trailed off, realizing he had dropped his sketchbook while tackling Hackle. He looked around and spotted it lying in the dirt about ten feet away. He felt terribly anxious to pick it back up and stow it safely in his back pocket. His sword point drifted an inch or two away from Hackle's throat.

Hackle saw an opportunity to jump his opponent—but was far past mustering up the will to kill this human. Instead, he muttered, "Worse for both then."

Aram turned back to Hackle and again shook his head.

Throughout this brief exchange, Gordok seethed. Then a smile crept over his face. He sat down once more. Calmly, he asked, "Boy won't kill gnoll?"

"No," Aram repeated, disturbed by Gordok's change of demeanor. Suddenly, the ogre king seemed strangely sanguine about this turn of events.

Gordok smiled and offered up a warning. "Slaves who won't kill slaves must face Ol' One-Eye."

The ogres erupted with their largest cheer yet!

Aram mustered up his courage and shouted his defiance for all to hear: *"FINE! SEND OLD ONE-EYE!"* Then he looked down and whispered to Hackle, *"Who's Old One-Eye?"*

CHAPTER THIRTY
OLD ONE-EYE

Gordok's grin seemed to stretch across his entire face. "Summon One-Eye," he said with barely suppressed glee.

A potbellied ogre standing near Broadback lifted a massive ram's horn up to his lips, puffed out his cheeks to a degree Aram would not have thought possible, and blew! The sound of the horn echoed across the entire valley of Dire Maul and beyond.

Almost immediately, the horn was answered by a thundering roar that Aram imagined could be heard in Flayers' Point—if not in Lakeshire.

In the silence that followed, Aram's sword arm went slack, falling away completely from the gnoll's throat. Hackle didn't budge; he only groaned mournfully.

Aram glanced Hackle's way and—seeing the gnoll was disinclined to rise, let alone attack again—raced across the ring to retrieve his sketchbook. He had just rewrapped and stowed it in his back pocket, when from behind him, he heard the sound of wings. He turned around, and his jaw went slack. This was no common bird of Azeroth. He stood paralyzed, terrified.

From the holding pen, Thalyss called out a warning. *"Wyvern!"*

It had the face of a wolf, the mane of a lion, the tail of a scorpion, and giant, giant bat wings. And it was approaching fast. After flapping once to get more height, it tucked its wings and dove straight down toward the amphitheater and the ring.

Aram glanced back toward Hackle; he still lay prone on the ground, resigned and waiting for death. Aram sprinted back over to him and yanked the gnoll to his feet, pulling him away seconds before the wyvern's rear claws stabbed down into the dirt where Hackle had lain.

The crowd roared. There was no longer any question as to whom they would root for now. They cheered the wyvern on, urging it to *"SQUASH THE GNOLL!"* or *"EAT THE BOY!"* and suchlike.

Aram was trying very hard not to roll up into a little ball. He had never seen a wyvern before but had heard they were about as big as a horse. This one was easily three times that size. Its stinger with its two venom sacs arched upward on the wyvern's long ridged tail, preparing to strike. It swung back and forth hypnotically. Aram couldn't tear his eyes away. He thought, *Now I* am *going to die . . .*

Still he had managed to keep his sword arm up and his other arm around the gnoll, practically supporting Hackle's entire body weight. The gnoll's head hung down in defeat. He muttered, "Hackle told Aram. Better to kill Hackle . . ."

This snapped Aram out of his stupor. "C'mon!" he shouted. "Hackle never refuse fight!"

Hackle's eyes met Aram's; then he grinned; then he laughed; then he shoved Aram with all his strength, sending him flying halfway across the ring—and thus saving him from a strike from the stinger.

Aram rolled to a stop, somehow managing to hold on to his cutlass. Rising up on one knee, Aram saw the wyvern turn its head all the way to the left to find him. There was something familiar about the gesture. Something that reminded him of a Lakeshire tomcat that was always skulking around the forge. He had sketched that cat. It only had . . . *Of course! Old* One-Eye! The wyvern's left eye-socket was empty!

As the beast slowly turned its bulk to face its prey, Aram stood; his two eyes found Hackle, still grinning as he picked up his war club.

"It's One-Eye!" Aram shouted.

"Hackle know!"

"No, listen, he has only *one* eye!"

"*She* has only one eye!" shouted Thalyss from the pen.

Aram shot the night elf a look. "Really?! Now?!"

The druid shrugged. "You wanted to be wrong?!"

"Fine! *She!* She only has one eye!"

But Hackle understood. The beast had a blind spot, one that Hackle and Aram could exploit. Together.

And that's when it happened. Makasa watched from behind the megalith—still ready, if necessary, to make her presence known and felt. And though she was not a woman to be easily impressed, she was *mightily* impressed by what she now beheld: without another word or thought, the boy and the pup had become partners, a team.

One-Eye lunged toward Aram—but was pulled up short as Hackle grabbed hold of her tail.

The crowd gasped.

The wyvern turned her good right eye toward the gnoll, lifted her tail—gnoll and all—and slammed the whole package down hard against the ground. But before she could sting the stunned Hackle, Aram was at the beast, slashing his cutlass across the wyvern's shoulder.

She roared in pain—as the ogres roared their disapproval— but One-Eye had to turn again to locate the boy.

And so it went. Aram and Hackle had little chance of actually finishing off the wyvern, but they were doing a decent job of keeping her distracted enough to prevent her from actually finishing off either of them. One would attack her, then the other.

Gordok was finally enjoying the show. He liked that the slaves were putting up a respectable fight at last. Usually, Ol' One-Eye made short work and a quick meal of anyone she was summoned to dispatch. Still, the ogre king had little fear of an unpleasant outcome. The damage they were doing to the wyvern was minimal relative to her size. This game of theirs couldn't last. He knew his creature would win in the end; he knew the rebellious slaves would die horribly.

Makasa knew it, too. And she thought this might just be her moment. If she went in now and killed the monster fast by driving her stake-harpoon through the beast's heart, the resulting chaos would give her and the boy a chance to escape on the back of Thalyss's stag form. She moved out a bit from behind the megalith, trying to catch the druid's attention without attracting anyone else's.

But Thalyss's attentions were focused elsewhere. His back to Makasa, he was crouching before Uncle Murrgly, speaking to him in the murloc tongue. The druid knew wyverns and ogres had no history as allies. *So why was Old One-Eye serving Gordok?*

In response, Murrgly pointed to the nearby dome of thorns . . .

Meanwhile, as One-Eye turned to swipe at Aram with her claws, Hackle swung his club against her soft and sensitive venom sac just below the beast's stinger.

The wyvern let out a blood-curdling scream that sounded almost human. She leapt upward and flapped her wings as she turned in midair to pounce upon the gnoll. Aram found himself beneath her and stabbed upward with his sword. The monster was too high—or the boy was too short—for the wyvern to feel more than a slight pricking, but feel it she did. Wings flapping to keep her aloft and hovering, she rotated her body perpendicular to the ground. Her jaws snapped at Aram, barely missing. The wyvern's huge head was wheeling upward again, but without thinking, Aram reached out and grabbed hold of One-Eye's beard, which dragged him up and off his feet.

Outraged at this stowaway pulling down with all his weight on her chin hairs, One-Eye tossed her head back. Aram was sent flying—and landed on the back of her head, facing rearward, with her stinger-tipped tail swaying before him between her flapping wings. If she tried to sting him now, he could leap off and hope she'd sting herself instead. He had no idea if she could be poisoned with her own venom, but that was his current plan.

But the stinger didn't strike. Instead, she tried to shake him off, so he grabbed a fistful of her mane with his free hand and held on for dear life.

The crowd at this point was on its feet—even Gordok. The sight of the boy atop the wyvern was unprecedented and thrilling. Every time the great beast shook her head, they expected Aram to be sent flying. A few ogres were even holding out their hands to catch him—though what they planned to do with him once caught wasn't so clear.

Hackle, Thalyss, Woolbeard, and the murlocs were rapt, too, staring up at Aram and One-Eye with slackened jaws.

Makasa was so surprised, she briefly found herself standing out in the open for anyone to see. She quickly rectified that error, but her thoughts were still crashing about wildly in her head. She wasn't quite sure how to save Aram from this particular unforeseeable predicament and prayed he had some idea that might save himself.

Aram's only idea was to try to cut off the monster's head, but he couldn't figure out how to angle his sword—even assuming he could summon up the force. Yet in studying the problem— while still desperately holding on as the wyvern tried to buck him off—he spotted something beneath her mane. With his sword-hand, he pushed hair aside and saw that it was . . . *a collar of thorns*, biting into Old One-Eye's neck!

His hand came away sticky with the creature's blood, and he realized she must be in near-constant pain. Instantly, she wasn't a monster anymore. Details about the wyvern flooded the boy's brain, observations Aram the portrait artist hadn't been able to focus on because Aram the would-be warrior was too busy trying to stay alive. Her muzzle was gray. She was old and tired, thin and covered with scars. She had a ragged energy, slow in general with only short bursts of speed. The thought flashed across the boy's mind that like him, she might be nothing more than a slave to the arena. Suddenly, he didn't want to hurt her.

Then again, he didn't want to be killed by her, either. *But maybe . . .* He slipped his cutlass flat between the collar and her neck, twisted the blade up, and yanked with all his might, smiling to himself and thinking, *It takes a Thorne to remove a thorn!*

The collar snapped apart, and then, as One-Eye shook her head to remove Aram, it dropped off the wyvern's neck and landed with a thud in the dirt.

Only two creatures, besides Aram, truly understood what that meant: One-Eye abruptly alighted, and Gordok roared his displeasure!

Aram slipped off the wyvern, on her left side just to be safe. The massive beast turned her head to watch with her right eye as he backed away, his sword pointed toward the ground to minimize any sense of threat. Hackle, unsure what had changed, but recognizing that *something* had, moved cautiously to join Aram.

The crowd, including Thalyss and the other prisoners, remained silent. Makasa forced herself to stay behind the megalith. There was no doubt that One-Eye now seemed considerably less inclined to eviscerate and eat Aram than she had been just a few seconds ago.

One-Eye approached slowly. Aram, in a grand gesture, threw his sword away.

Hackle said, "Boy, what are—"

"Shhhh." Aram held out his arms, hands open, palms up.

The wyvern took another step, huffing and puffing. Her tail still weaved back and forth above her, prepared to strike. But

Aram took a step forward, and the wyvern . . . sniffed at him. Her tail sank and thudded softly in the dirt.

During this display, Gordok had burned and seethed in silence. Finally, he snapped out, "One-Eye!" She ignored him. Furiously, he called louder, *"ONE-EYE!"*

Slowly she turned her good eye toward the ogre. His arm jutted out suddenly, pointing toward the dome of thorns—pointing toward the true source of his power over the beast.

"KILL! KILL NOW!"

Old One-Eye lowered her head submissively. She turned again to look at her prospective prey. Then with some reluctance—or so it seemed to Aram—her tail rose again to threaten the boy and the gnoll.

And just at that moment, a horn sounded.

All eyes turned toward the potbellied ogre. But he pointed to the horn resting on a nearby stone and said, "Not me!"

The horn sounded again, and now everyone understood that the sound came from the gate to Dire Maul . . .

CHAPTER THIRTY-ONE
Hidden in Plain Sight

The Hidden had opted not to hide.

Zathra had tracked the phalanx of ogres. Soon enough, she spotted clear signs that the human female was pursuing the ogres as well.

"So she got away," whispered Valdread. "Impressive."

"You are too eazzily impresssed, Forssaken one," hissed Ssarbik. "Esscaping ogrezz requirezz no great ssskill."

Throgg frowned, but said nothing.

Malus said, "March on."

They marched a league and were rewarded when the boy's tracks and the night elf's suddenly appeared among the ogres'.

"Well, they're not dead, at least," Malus said coldly.

"Might be dead by now," Zathra corrected. "We still be tree hours behind."

"Then go faster," Malus said. "The boy will keep the compass safe and hidden as long as he's alive to do so. Once he's dead, it could wind up anywhere." *And without it*, he thought, *I'll never be certain it's over. And if it's never over, then I did what I did for nothing.*

Zathra picked up the pace—until Ssarbik himself begged for "resspite." Malus was tempted (and grimly threatened) to leave the arakkoa behind. But as night was falling, thus limiting Zathra's abilities, Malus ultimately settled for sending Skitter ahead.

Before dawn, they were on the move and on the trail. Ssarbik continued to complain of "exxhausstion," so Malus had Throgg put the murloc down in order to carry Ssarbik on his shoulders instead. As Valdread extricated Murky from his nets, Malus threatened the murloc with death if he didn't keep up, but the creature quickly wrapped his nets around his waist and followed—with no little enthusiasm—at a rapid pace just behind the troll, who took point.

They finally caught up with Skitter at the ridge of wooden stakes. Zathra communicated with her pet, then confirmed the scorpid's information by observing the various tracks herself.

"Da ogres took da boy and da elf straight along dis ridge. Skitter be sayin' dere be guard posts furda along."

"What of Flintwill? The young woman?" asked the baron.

"Her tracks disappear into dis here." She pointed at the thicket of spikes.

Ssarbik scoffed. "Thozze? Imposssible!"

Valdread smiled beneath his hood. "As I said, she's quite impressive."

"Keep your jaw attached," Malus growled.

Zathra agreed. "No one wants ta be seein' da undead drool."

Valdread nodded to acknowledge her point. "Yes, drooling makes us corpses look particularly mindless. On the other hand, you charmers could, I'm sure, pull off the look without losing any further sign of intelligence."

Throgg was trying to reach for the machete attachment in his quiver, but the arakkoa was in the way, and he grabbed Ssarbik's neck by accident.

"Let go! Let go!" squealed the bird-creature.

"Sorry," said the ogre nervously. "But Throgg can cut through small spikes. Pull up big ones."

Malus shook his head. "We'd be spotted. So we might as well make our lives easier and proceed the fast and direct route."

And thus, the Hidden had chosen not to hide.

The first few guard posts were passed with hardly any incident. That is to say, Zathra's crossbows dispatched their sentries silently.

But the fourth sentry was particularly alert and rather handy with the quantity of spears at his disposal. The greater range of his first throw kept Malus's troop back, but before the ogre could blow a warning on his horn, Ssarbik began to chant. "We are the Hidden, the voyagerzz of Shadow. We ssserve and will conquer. What we conquer will Burn. Burn azz the masster willzz. Burn for the Hidden. Burn. Burn."

Shadow flames of indigo and dark purple began to engulf the guard post, which was rapidly set ablaze. The sentry was forced to leap to safety but in his panic jumped the wrong way, into the forest of wooden stakes. They left him there, a gruesome but ineffective scarecrow. Within minutes, the carrion birds flew down to keep him company.

And so it went until they arrived at the gate. There, they were spotted, and a horn was sounded twice. The gate was barred against them. On either side of it, the sentries in the guard towers rained down multiple thick spears and thin javelins that kept the Hidden at bay.

So Zathra sent her armored pet into the thicket of spikes. Unseen, Skitter crossed to one of the guard towers and, still unseen, scurried up to the top to sting its sentry. Within seconds, the ogre was gasping for breath and violently thrashing about before collapsing dead.

An unhappy Throgg scrunched up his face at the waste of ogre lives but said nothing.

Malus nodded to Valdread, who brashly raced forward and began climbing up the other guard post. He was rewarded by being turned into a virtual pincushion of javelins, which hardly slowed him down. The ogre sentry seemed to find this astounding and so kept throwing until the bitter end. Thus the baron had his sword out and the ogre's head off in no time at all.

Zathra had followed Skitter up the first tower and was soon firing both her crossbows down on the ogres manning the other side of the gate.

This provided cover for Valdread, who began by climbing down the ladder but got impatient and jumped the rest of the way. His right leg snapped off on impact but landed within reach. Ogres watched dumbfounded as he reattached it, and they kept those expressions permanently once the baron was mobile and had set to work with his sword.

Malus, who had followed Valdread, soon climbed down as well. While Zathra and Valdread kept the last few sentries busy, their captain opened the gate. Throgg came barreling through, closely followed by the murloc, which actually gave Malus and the others pause.

Valdread tilted his head as he yanked a javelin from his shoulder and said what Malus was thinking. "Strange little creature. He could have taken this opportunity to run the other way and escape us all: Hidden and ogres alike. Instead, he follows Throgg right into the thick of things."

Malus nodded. Of course, the amphibian wasn't fighting—mostly, he was simply trying not to get killed. *Still*, Malus wondered, *why hasn't he run . . . ?*

Malus's musings were interrupted by Ssarbik, who sauntered through the gate last, *after* Throgg had brained the final ogre sentry with his mace-hand. The arakkoa shot a contemptuous glance at Malus and hissed, "You jusst ssstand here? I don't sssuppozze it occurred to you to *lead* the charge?"

Malus casually backhanded Ssarbik and started down the hill into Dire Maul. An amused Valdread helped the bird-creature back to his feet, saying, "You really never learn.

Honestly, I can't thank you enough for providing so much entertainment." Zathra laughed openly, and Throgg hid his smile by scratching at his forehead horn with his mace.

"Keep up!" Malus demanded.

They all followed.

"Arkus, to da gate! Kill intruders!" Gordok shouted. "Wordok, get slaves back in pen!" The king then called for his armor and weapons, slapping the young ogre girl when he decided she was responding too slowly.

A large armored ogre with a spherical head—Arkus, presumably—led a contingent of ogre warriors uphill toward the gate.

Ignoring Old One-Eye completely, Wordok and three other armed warders raced toward Aram and Hackle. The latter seemed ready for a fight, but Aram glanced back over his shoulder and saw that the two warders guarding the holding pen were prepared to launch their spears at the backs of the boy and the gnoll. Aram put a hand on Hackle's arm, whispering, "Not now. But soon. I promise."

Almost against his will, Hackle lowered his war club.

Wordok quickly relieved Hackle of his weapon, and then after scooping up Aram's sword, dumped both into a nearby barrel. The other warders ushered Aram and Hackle back into the pen with Thalyss, Woolbeard, Murrgly, Murrl, and the other murlocs.

Woolbeard hobbled over and rubbed Aram on the head. "My boy, that was truly something!"

The old tauren then shouted a few words in Taur-ahe. One-Eye turned her head and growled back in response.

"She can understand you?" Aram said, stunned.

"Well, of course she can, boy. Did you think she was a dumb animal?"

"Then why does she stay? She's not chained."

"I believe I can answer that." It was Thalyss. He approached Aram and drew him away from the others. "Makasa is here," he whispered.

"She is?! Where?!"

The druid hushed him. "She is hiding behind that standing stone over there. She has been trying to catch my eye."

Aram snuck a look but couldn't see her. "Trying?"

"There have been a few times when she nearly came running to your rescue—and only needed to be sure of my cooperation. But she would have gotten herself killed, and you were busy making friends anyway."

"Is *that* what I was doing?"

Thalyss laughed loudly. "What would you call it?" He didn't wait for an answer. "Listen, there is something inside that dome of thorns over there. It is what keeps One-Eye subservient to Gordok. In fact, at this point, I would guess it is the *only* thing keeping her subservient. Certainly the thorny collar you removed did not hold her here. I think that was placed on her neck as a reminder of what the ogres do hold in that dome."

"Which is . . . what?"

Thalyss told him. Aram nodded, struggling to absorb all this new information. Then something seemed to click into place for him, and he waved the rest of the prisoners over. Every single one obeyed his summons without protest or question.

"Listen," he said. "Are you ready to leave this place . . . ?"

By now, the ogre king was almost completely strapped into his armor. Five ogre females stood nearby with his weapons. It took two of them to bear his double-bladed battleaxe and two more to carry his morningstar. The fifth—the young girl—held a curved dagger almost as long as a short sword. Gordok beckoned her forward—but immediately shoved her back roughly, as the sounds of battle reached his ears.

He smiled broadly. "Sound like Gordok won't need weapons. Arkus doing job."

Something round went soaring out of the darkness over Gordok's head and landed with a bounce or two in the ring, before rolling to a stop in front of Old One-Eye.

Over by the holding pen, Wordok couldn't see what it was. "What's that?" he called out. Gordok didn't answer. No one who could see it clearly did.

The wyvern squinted down at it with her one good eye. Suddenly, her stinger lashed out and punctured the sphere. She held it aloft on her tail for all to see.

It was Arkus's head.

CHAPTER THIRTY-TWO
HiGH StAKES

The not-so Hidden emerged into the torchlight, stopping at the top of the amphitheater to size up the situation. Malus had been fairly confident, even against an entire clan of ogres, but the huge wyvern—able to attack from the sky with tooth, claw, and venomous stinger—gave him pause. Still, the boy was in a slave pen, looking not *too* worse for wear. Odds were good he still had the compass. The Hidden's leader quickly began to formulate a plan.

But one of the largest ogres spoke first. "Gordok, king of Dire Maul Gordunni, demand to know why intruders come here to die."

Malus eyed the heavily armored Gordok and instantly had his strategy mapped out.

"We come for the boy," he said, pointing toward Aram. "He is all we require. Isn't that right, boy?"

Aram knew what that meant. Captain Malus had a hand on Murky's shoulder. Murky, who was alive and grinning, foolishly happy to see Aram, Thalyss, and his aunt and uncle.

And the truth was, Aram was foolishly happy to see Murky. Murky, who would be dead if Malus didn't get the compass. After all the losses Aram had suffered, Murky's survival meant all of Azeroth in that moment. Aram smiled at the murloc and said, "Yes. I'm all you require."

But Gordok had his own requirements. He pointed uphill toward the gate. "Intruders raid Gordok's lands!" He pointed at Arkus's head, still piked atop One-Eye's stinger. "Intruders kill Gordok's warriors!" He pointed at Aram. "Now, intruders demand Gordok's slaves?"

"Yes," Malus said.

"What intruder called?" Gordok growled.

"Malus."

"There's your problem, right there," Aram shouted out. "Being named Malice. No wonder you turned out rotten."

At this, Malus actually chuckled. He said, "You are much like your father, Aramar Thorne. Like the man he *was,* before I brought him down."

In the slave pen, Aram felt the blood rising in his cheeks.

Behind the megalith, so did Makasa. But both held their places and their tongues.

For his part, Gordok didn't care for being left out of the conversation and ignored; he expected and commanded all attentions to be paid to him. The fact that his wyvern was within shouting distance and his ogres had now completely encircled Malus's party demanded nothing less. He called out, "Malus ready to die now?"

"No one else need die if you give me the boy."

Gordok made a great show of counting the Hidden. (He counted Murky, but did not count Skitter, who was back in place as Zathra's armor.) "One, two, dree, four, five, six need die. Den Gordok kill and eat boy, for boy is Gordok's to kill, Gordok's to eat. Boy is not for Malus." He raised an arm, knowing that when he brought it down again, the strangers would die.

But Malus had his strategy ready. "Then I challenge you, Gordok. Intruders have breached your gate. They have killed your warriors. You have failed as king of the Dire Maul Gordunni. The orcs have a rite known as mak'gora, a challenge of single combat. I believe ogres keep this tradition, as well. So I, Malus, challenge you, Gordok, to single combat. I challenge you for command."

"Little Malus man challenge great Gordok?!"

"Yes. Will you deny the rite of challenge? Do you fear to face me?"

"Man cannot challenge Gordok! Only ogre can challenge Gordok!"

Malus looked to Throgg, who looked back, confused. Frustrated by the ogre's brainlessness, Malus shouted pointedly, "Then an *ogre* will call for the challenge!"

Throgg finally caught on. He took a step forward and bellowed, "Throgg of Shattered Hand challenge Gordok of Dire Maul Gordunni!"

Now, every ogre within earshot reacted; the amphitheater was abuzz with whispers.

For the first time, Gordok's voice betrayed some hint of concern. "Shattered Hand is orc clan, not ogre clan."

Throgg smiled and raised his bloody mace-hand with pride. "Throgg ogre. But Throgg Shattered Hand."

Malus smiled, too. Gordok was trapped. If he denied the challenge, he'd instantly lose face with his entire clan, even—or especially—if he ordered Malus's entire party slaughtered. The ogre king had no choice but to accept the challenge. In which case, Malus liked his odds.

One-Eye yawned loudly and, lying down, rested her head on her front paws. She flicked Arkus's head off her tail. It bounced through the arena and landed at the feet of the potbellied ogre. He nervously kicked it out of the way.

This generated laughter from Hackle and Woolbeard. The laughter became contagious, and the murloc prisoners joined in. So did Murky, Throgg, and Valdread. Malus didn't see what was so funny, but what he did see was that Gordok was embarrassed, so he forced his own laughter and eyed Zathra and Ssarbik until both joined in uncomfortably. Thalyss and Aram made a similar analysis and began laughing, too. The laughter swept through the entire amphitheater, until everyone was laughing except Gordok, Makasa, and One-Eye herself.

"Enough!" Gordok thundered. "Challenge accepted! Gordok fight Shattered Hand ogre! Gordok kill Shattered Hand ogre!"

Throgg started forward, but Malus held up an arm, declaiming, "Throgg chooses Malus to fight as his champion!"

Aram watched Throgg's face fall.

Now, it was Gordok's turn to laugh. "This true? Great Drogg of Shattered Hand not fight?! Little Malus man fight for Drogg?!"

Throgg turned to face Malus. "Throgg fight for Throgg," he whispered.

Malus thought Throgg could probably beat Gordok, but the odds were still too close to even for his tastes. Malus preferred to rely on himself. In part, because he trusted his own arm, his own sword, his own skill more than those of any other creature, living or dead, in Azeroth or Outland. But in part, it was because he knew that if by some twist of fate he did lose, he wouldn't have to worry about the consequences; he'd finally be free of any consequences. And that was just fine with him, too. Calmly and firmly, he said, "Malus fight for Throgg. Tell him."

Throgg inhaled deeply. His brow furrowed. But he abruptly turned to Gordok and shouted, "Malus fight for Throgg!" Then he quickly added, "Malus fight because Gordok not worthy of Throgg!"

A furious Gordok roared something unintelligible. Then he shouted, "Gordok kill little Malus man! Then Gordok kill Drogg! Then Gordok kill and eat boy!"

Aram smiled bitterly. *At least he hadn't been forgotten.*

Within minutes it was all arranged. One-Eye had been shooed from the ring, and was now seated on the side of the holding pen closest to the dome of thorns.

Murky had been handed over to Valdread, who stood at the back of the amphitheater with Throgg, Zathra, Skitter, and a complaining Ssarbik. "Thiss cccircuss sham izz unneccesssary! We don't care about the boy! We jusst want the compassss!"

Valdread eyed him with amusement. "And you have an alternate plan to achieve the compass, I assume?"

This shut the arakkoa up.

In the pen, Uncle Murrgly was trying to calm Aunt Murrl, who was crying happy tears over Murky's survival. He tried to tell his wife that her idiot nephew would most certainly be dead soon, but the foolish female wouldn't listen to reason. (And secretly, this gave Murrgly hope.)

Woolbeard limped over to Aram and whispered, "Well, boy, so much for your plan."

"Nothing's changed," Aram whispered back.

Hackle cackled loudly and slapped Aram on the back, knocking the air from the boy's lungs.

Meanwhile, Thalyss had finally made eye contact with Makasa. Wordlessly, with nothing but a few subtle hand gestures, he communicated that she should wait for his signal, and he pointed toward the section of the pen flanked by One-Eye as her angle of approach. She tried to balk at this, but he was insistent, and she acquiesced.

Gordok was in the ring, effortlessly hefting his two-handed battleaxe in one hand and the handle of his morningstar in the other. His long curved dagger was tucked into his belt. He faced Malus, who hadn't even unsheathed his sword.

"Winner gets the clan and the boy," Malus said.

"Winner keep clan and eat boy," Gordok corrected. He was supremely confident now. Throgg might have been a problem. Gordok had heard things about the Shattered Hand. But this foolish little Malus man could never be a serious opponent. Gordok was eager for blood, and his only worry was that the fight might not last long enough for him to work up an appetite. He had fed on two whole boars before coming to the arena. It would be an embarrassment if he were still too full to finish eating the entire boy before the night was over.

"As long as the stakes are clear," Malus said calmly.

Wordok and his warders, including a handful with spears, still guarded the holding pen. Three concentric circles of ogre warriors surrounded Throgg and the others. The rest of the Dire Maul Gordunni clan was quite literally on the edge of their seats, as Gordok signaled the potbellied ogre, who puffed out his cheeks and blew a clarion call, signaling the start of the mak'gora.

CHAPTER THIRTY-THREE
THE CHALLENGE

With a flourish, Malus unsheathed his broadsword but, otherwise, wasn't there to give the ogres a show. Gordok had longer arms, a longer weapon, and once he began swinging his morningstar in circles, an *extremely* long reach. So Malus was content to slowly back away, to maintain his distance, to wait for his moment. He counted on the ogre king's impatience, and his strategy was soon rewarded.

Gordok quickly wearied of pursuing the human round the ring. He remembered the crowd laughing at the gnoll for chasing the boy and had no desire to become anyone's object of scorn. With his left hand, he swung the morningstar to drive Malus to the edge of the arena, then rushed him.

Malus was ready. His sword deflected the morningstar downward and to Gordok's right. Its spiked iron ball slammed into the dirt, putting the chain across the ogre's body, restricting his forward momentum, and allowing Malus to easily lean away from what was designed to be Gordok's quick attempt to use his battleaxe to end the contest by beheading his opponent.

With both of Gordok's arms fully extended and awkwardly crossed over each other, Malus had a clear opening to slash upward with his sword. The tip of Malus's blade caught the ogre just above his armor, severing the strap on Gordok's helm and slicing a thin red line along the side of his neck. Malus had drawn first blood, and the crowd of ogres was instantly on its feet with a roar. They weren't exactly rooting for the human— but they *always* rooted for blood.

The "little Malus man"—who was easily six and a half feet tall and no maypole—leapt forward, slamming his entire fifteen stone right into Gordok's chest and gut. The ogre stumbled back—only a few steps—but Malus landed both feet on the morningstar's chain, and its handle was yanked from the king's hand. In addition, Gordok's loose helm slipped down over his eyes. In the two seconds it took him to snag it off his head and throw it away, Malus was practically behind him, stabbing his sword into the ogre's unarmored rear left thigh.

Here, however, Malus miscalculated. He had thought the wound would be enough to force the ogre down to one knee. He didn't think it possible a creature that big could support so much weight on an injured limb.

But Gordok had not become king by surrendering to injury or pain. The curved dagger was out, and while Malus was still expecting the ogre to buckle, it found a new home between two of Malus's ribs.

Furious with himself for being careless and overconfident, he spun away, pulling the slippery blood-soaked dagger free of Gordok's hand. Malus left the knife sticking out of his side. For the time being, it would stanch any greater flow of blood. As for the pain . . . well, Malus hadn't become leader of the Hidden by surrendering to such a thing, either.

Despite the error, the ogre was now down to one weapon; the leader of the Hidden *still* liked his odds.

What *Aram* liked was that the battle had completely captured everyone's attention, especially that of Wordok and the other warders guarding the slave pen, not to mention the Whisper-Man and the rest of Malus's crew. Even that strange bird-creature was staring at the contest and licking his beak at the sight of blood.

Aram tapped Hackle and Woolbeard on their shoulders. They closed ranks as Aram and Thalyss slipped away to the back of the pen.

Thalyss signaled, and Aram was thrilled to see Makasa for the first time, as she emerged from behind the megalith and quickly skirted the distance to the pen, using the wyvern's bulk for cover.

Old One-Eye spotted Makasa immediately, but Thalyss whispered something in Taur-ahe: a promise. The great beast turned her head full around to eye the night elf. Her gaze then turned to Aram, who nodded, taking the promise on as his own. The wyvern's rear left paw reached up to scratch at her neck—still free of its thorn collar—and then she nodded back at Aram and turned to face the battle again, as if Makasa weren't there.

Seconds later, Makasa was there. "Now's our time," she whispered. "Climb over."

They did. Aram dropped down quietly right before her. For half a second, she almost smiled at the sight of him—but covered quickly. Aram made no attempt to hide his own grin, so she gave him an annoyed little slap on the cheek, saying, "This is serious. We have to move. With any luck, we'll be long gone by the time they're done killing each other."

Aram nodded but said, "We can't leave quite yet. Not without the other prisoners and not without Murky."

Makasa had spent the last two days and nights alone with only one single overriding thought to keep her company: She would rescue Aram (and maybe Thalyss if it wasn't *too* inconvenient). Now, she was instantly at her wit's end. She shook her head and growled, "Someday, boy, you'll have to learn you *cannot* save everyone!"

"Maybe," Aram stated, "but not today."

Makasa looked about ready to knock the kid out and carry him off unconscious, but before she could, a smiling Thalyss whispered, "Follow me."

And before an exasperated Makasa could say another word, the elf and the boy had taken off, and all she could do was race after them toward the dome of thorns.

*   *   *

Malus and Gordok's battle had come down to a swordfight (even if Gordok was using an axe). Swing and parry. Lunge and deflect. Gordok was favoring his right leg, and Malus still had a dagger sticking out of his side, but neither seemed much perturbed by his condition. Gordok was stronger, but Malus wasn't weak. Malus was swifter, but Gordok wasn't slow. Gordok had the longer reach, but Malus was the more talented swordsman. And so on. They were quite evenly matched. Much more evenly matched than either had thought when the contest began. Their faces were grim masks of concentration. This was work.

Murky had seen Urum and Duluss slip away, but he no longer feared their leaving without him. He wanted to be ready. He wanted to help. So slowly and silently, he began letting his nets unfold onto the ground in front of himself and the undead Forsaken, who at the moment was completely focused on and quite amused by the conflict in the ring.

Standing behind the dome—out of sight of the amphitheater— the druid studied this latest thorny problem up close. Multiple bushes of sharp, spiky thorns rose up out of the ground. They twisted and entwined about each other, creating a solid curved dome of thorns too thick for even a wyvern to tear apart. After reaching into his robes, Thalyss removed the large acorn from its purple pouch and oilskin wrap. Then he waved it near the roots of the thorns, chanting quietly.

Aram and Makasa watched as the thorns in the immediate vicinity receded slowly. Too slowly for Thalyss's tastes. "This is taking too long. Plants are meant to grow, not shrink." He began rooting around in his pockets.

Makasa asked, "What are we doing?"

"Gaining a valuable ally," Aram explained without explaining much else.

"*A ha!*" Thalyss said—a bit too loudly, but they looked around and no one seemed to be coming after them. The night elf pulled another acorn—small by comparison, but normal size actually—from another pocket. "This should do the trick. Stand back."

He shoved the second acorn into the soil between two thornbushes and covered it over with a bit of dirt. He stepped back to join Aram and Makasa—then seemed to change his mind and knelt once more in order to *spit* on the soil-covered acorn. He grinned at the others and whispered, "A little moisture never hurts." Then he stepped back again, held out the first acorn, and began to chant.

The main thing Malus had going for him was his patience—or in any case, Gordok's lack thereof. Malus had no one to impress, whereas Gordok couldn't be seen taking too long to dispatch one lowly human. Each combatant was waiting for his opportunity, but Gordok couldn't afford to be too picky, and Malus knew it. So he set about creating an opportunity Gordok couldn't refuse.

Malus had his sword in his left hand. Gordok had his battleaxe in his right. Malus lunged to Gordok's left, leaving the human's back exposed by his intentionally overextended thrust. It was the moment Gordok had been waiting for—the moment Malus had created for the ogre.

Gordok raised his right arm high to bring his axe down hard and fast to slice Malus completely in two.

But Malus simply dropped his sword from his left hand into his right and stabbed upward. Malus's sword plunged deep into the Gordunni king's side, arresting the ogre's swing. As Gordok grimaced in pain, Malus yanked the curved dagger out of his own torso and slashed the blade across the ogre's neck. Only a tiny bit of blood oozed from Malus's wound, but Gordok's throat was another story.

Mortally wounded by his own dagger, the ogre was dying but not yet dead. The battleaxe slipped from his hand, but his fist swung up, catching Malus on the chin and sending him flying.

Gordok staggered after, desperate to kill his killer before time and his lifeblood all ran out.

Though Malus had been rocked by the blow, he had held on to both his sword and Gordok's dagger. He didn't quite have time to stand up, but as soon as Gordok got close, he stabbed the two blades down through Gordok's feet and into the ground, pinning the dying king in place.

The crowd was silent as Malus rolled away from Gordok's powerful but impotent grasp. Malus stood, ran across the arena, scooped up the handle to the morningstar, and turned to face the ogre king's back. Swinging the heavy morningstar tore at the wound in Malus's side, but he ignored the pain. When he'd worked up the proper momentum, he advanced. Gordok stood with his back to Malus, trying to free his feet, trying to turn his head. But every effort made at this point was too little, too late. Malus swung the morningstar around one last time, making lethal contact with Gordok's skull. It was over. The king of the Dire Maul Gordunni was dead.

Still, for a good ten seconds, his body remained standing. The entire amphitheater was hushed, waiting. Then the ogre's left leg collapsed beneath him, and Gordok came crashing down into the dirt, making a sound like distant thunder heard through a blanket.

Malus was breathing hard, but slowly a dangerous smile bloomed on his face. He turned to face the crowd, declaring, "The challenger has triumphed! The boy is mine!"

It was only then that all eyes turned toward the pen and found the boy wanting. Valdread started forward, but Murky quickly lifted the nets up as high as he could, which was quite high enough to completely entangle the baron and even snap off his brittle right leg at the knee. Ssarbik, Throgg, and Zathra stared. Throgg even laughed.

After pulling the nets down over the fallen Valdread's head, Murky ran off—and for once managed to escape without hopelessly tangling himself. He hated to leave his nets behind—he could hear his uncle shouting, "Nk! Nk! Murky mmrrgggleee mrrugggl mgrrrrl nk mmmurlok!"—but he would sacrifice even his prized (and pretty much only) possession to help his frund Urum.

Zathra and Throgg started after Murky, until Malus, holding his side, heaved out, *"FORGET THE MURLOC! FIND THE BOY!!"*

And just at that moment, a *giant oak tree* grew—or rather, exploded—right out of the ground, ripping the dome of thorns to absolute shreds!

Everyone froze in place. Where the dome had been there was now just the great oak and the *THREE WYVERN CUBS* who had been trapped inside!

One-Eye was up on her feet and roaring. The cubs—small compared to their mother but each as big as a bear—answered her call and immediately took to the air, flying east into the distance.

Grinning broadly, as he watched the astounding cubs fly away, Aram stepped out from behind the oak tree, flanked by Thalyss and Makasa, who had her stake-harpoon in one hand and her cutlass in the other.

A smiling Thalyss was carefully rewrapping his acorn and returning it to its purple pouch. He spoke to the mama wyvern in Taur-ahe.

One-Eye turned her head toward the boy and nodded.

Thalyss said, "She has agreed to help us—to help you, Aramar—in recompense for services rendered."

Aram whispered to Makasa, "We're halfway home." Then he pointed at the slave pen and shouted, "Free the prisoners!"

With little effort the wyvern smashed down one side of the pen. Before the dust had cleared, Hackle—laughing maniacally—was leading the murlocs out.

Woolbeard took up the rear, shouting, "Boy, you've done it!"

Up until this point, the ogres had all been leaderless and rudderless, unsure what to do. But Wordok knew he needed to hold on to his prisoners, and he sprung into action to recapture them, barking orders to his fellow warders. The closest two rushed the prisoners, but the old tauren—energized and inspired by Aram's survival and success—lurched forward and clocked their heads together. He didn't exactly "split their skulls for them," but both dropped, for the moment dazed. Woolbeard laughed triumphantly.

Malus, still holding the morningstar, was crossing the arena, making a beeline for Aram, who was about thirty yards away. But Gordok's honor guard, who had descended from the stands to marvel at their king's corpse, intercepted him. He proceeded to make short work of them—but it cost him precious time.

Wordok's shouting reached the ears of the ogre warriors guarding Ssarbik, Throgg, Zathra, Skitter, and the still-entangled Valdread, who was busy cutting through the cursed nets with his black shale dagger. The Hidden were soon surrounded on all sides by three rows of spears.

Ssarbik began to chant then, but a spear was thrust under his beak, poking into his sensitive throat, and he fell silent.

Valdread sighed and said, "Would someone hand me my leg?"

For the record, no one did.

Wordok's warders were racing across what remained of the pen, only to come face-to-face with One-Eye. She bit off the head of the first warder, impaled the second on her stinger, while one swipe of her claws reduced the third to shreds and tatters.

The two warders with spears let loose their shafts, which distracted One-Eye enough to allow Wordok past her. But though the spears found their target in her side, they did little real damage to the huge wyvern, and soon she had dispatched both hurlers.

Having finished off the honor guard, Malus saw—as usual—that he'd have to do everything for himself. After dropping the morningstar and pulling his sword out of the dead Gordok's foot, he rushed forward.

Wordok easily caught up to the limping Woolbeard and smacked him out of the way. Dazed and knocked off balance, the tauren fell and struggled to rise.

With his two massive mitts, Wordok grabbed for murlocs left and right and tossed them back over his shoulders—both to get them out of his way and in the hope that they would soon be recaptured, back in the pen or the pit. But when he grabbed Uncle Murrgly and Aunt Murrl, Murky literally skittered up the ogre's back, locked his legs around Wordok's neck, and used his hands to completely cover Wordok's eyes.

The ogre dropped Murrgly and Murrl to grab at Murky, but the murloc was slippery enough and stretchy enough that it took Wordok a couple of moments to pry the creature loose. Soon, however, he had both of Murky's ankles in one fist and both of the murloc's wrists in the other. He began pulling them in separate directions. Murky screamed, and Wordok instantly stopped pulling.

Murky, a bit surprised, looked down. Wordok, even more surprised, looked down, too. There was a wooden stake sticking out of his chest. They both looked up. Murky yelled, *"Mrksa!"* Wordok said nothing. He simply collapsed to his knees, inadvertently dropping Murky on his head.

The little murloc didn't seem to mind. He popped right back up and ran to Makasa and gave her a big slimy hug. She tried to tug him off, because she could see that the broad-backed ogre wasn't quite dead yet.

Wordok of the Dire Maul Gordunni staggered back to his feet. He reached blindly for the war club hooked to his belt, but his hands couldn't quite find it. So he pulled the bloody stake from his chest and rushed forward, while Makasa was still trying to extricate herself from the happy grateful murloc clinging to her arms.

Fortunately, Hackle appeared. He simply tripped the wounded ogre, and Wordok went down on his face. Hackle took up the ogre's own war club and ended him with one blow. Makasa nodded to the gnoll in what passed with her for gratitude. He nodded back. Murky finally let go of Makasa, though it was somewhat unclear whether or not he ever realized what kind of danger he and Makasa had been in.

Malus, meanwhile, drew nigh. Hackle turned with his club, but Makasa stepped in front of the gnoll, swinging her chain to keep Malus at bay; she had seen him fight aboard *Wavestrider* and wasn't about to take any chances.

Neither was Aram. He yelled out, *"One-Eye!!"*

Malus barely turned in time to parry the wyvern's striking stinger. Put on the defensive, Malus was forced back by One-Eye, away from Aram and the others.

From the moment Malus had arrived on the scene and spotted the wyvern, this had been the one battle he hadn't wanted to fight and the main reason he had challenged Gordok to single combat. So much for his plans.

Like Aram, Malus tried to take advantage of the beast's visual limitation, but he didn't have a Hackle—or even a Throgg—to create distractions for him. (Surrounded by ogres, the rest of the Hidden made no move to come to their master's aid.) Malus lunged for the wyvern's throat—after all, it had worked on Gordok—but one of the giant beast's paws smashed him hard through the thick wooden fence of the slave pen. Stunned by the blow, he collapsed in a heap among the shattered timbers.

*   *   *

Most of the ogres in the amphitheater remained in their seats, watching the action by the pen as if it were further entertainment being presented on a slightly less visibly convenient stage. A few others—those not guarding the Hidden—began to slowly leave their seats to stand over Gordok's corpse. None were making any attempt to join the battle. With their leader dead, they seemed at a collective loss as to what to do next.

Still, Hackle and Makasa stayed on the alert in case the crowd decided to rush them. Makasa called out, "Aram, whatever we're doing, we'd better get to it!"

But Aram and Thalyss were busy helping Woolbeard to his feet, and Murky was trapped midembrace by his aunt and uncle. The three murlocs babbled rapidly in their native tongue. The gist of their exchange was that even Uncle Murrgly was proud of his nephew. Murky might not be much of a flllurlokkr—in fact, he was a disaster in that area of expertise—but there was no doubting his bravery. Aunt Murrl slobbered all over him, still somewhat shocked that he was alive.

The small crowd of former prisoners gathered together. Aram said to Woolbeard, "There won't be any sentries left at the gate. Take the murlocs; lead them home. I don't think anyone's going to follow."

"Why tell me? You can show us the way. You're our leader, after all!"

Aram stared at the old tauren with genuine surprise. "Me?"

"Who else?" said Woolbeard and Thalyss in perfect unison.

"Well, uh . . . I'm not going that way."

"Murky nk mga fllm. Murky mga Urum!"

Thalyss translated: "Murky says he goes wherever Aram goes."

Hackle called back over his shoulder, "Hackle go with Aram, too!"

Makasa gritted her teeth, not exactly gladdened by yet another increase to their party. But both Murky and the gnoll had shown her something this day, and in any case, this was no time to argue. "*Whoever's* going, it's time we go!"

Murky quickly reassured his aunt and uncle that he was doing the right thing, that his place was now by Urum's side. Their general admiration for Urum helped smooth this over, though Uncle Murrgly felt morally bound to ask if his nephew was sure Urum *wanted* Murky by his side. With confidence, Murky assured his uncle that he and Urum were great frunds.

After Duluss had translated, Urum chimed in a confirmation: "Murky's on my crew!"

Murrgly liked seeing this new confidence in the little mmmurlok and gave his blessing. Aunt Murrl gave her blessing and much slobber.

They left Murky and joined the other murlocs heading up the hill.

Woolbeard started after them. But before he'd gone five yards, he stopped, turned, and called out, "Aramar Thorne of Lakeshire!"

Aram turned.

"I am Wuul Breezerider of the Mulgore shu'halo!"

Aram shouted back, "An honor to finally meet you!"

"No, boy! It's been *my* honor to meet *you*." Then Wuul Breezerider turned to limp after the murlocs.

Almost immediately, these escapees were intercepted by the young ogre girl who'd been Gordok's servant. The old tauren brandished a war club and made it clear he was prepared "to split her skull for her." But she simply requested to be allowed to go with them. Having seen the treatment she received under the ogre king, Breezerider and the murlocs quickly welcomed her into their number. In fact, she proved immediately useful, putting an arm around the old tauren's shoulder and helping him climb the hill.

More ogres, meanwhile, were starting to leave their seats. Old One-Eye roared and most of them sat right back down. Thalyss then spoke to the wyvern in Taur-ahe, making all the formal and proper requests for permission to climb up onto her back. The wyvern grunted a response, and the night elf waved the others forward. Aram climbed up first, straddling One-Eye just behind her neck. Thalyss got on behind him. Then Murky and Hackle. It was only now that Makasa understood how they'd be departing. She didn't relish the idea, but again this was no time to argue. She jumped on behind Hackle.

The wyvern extended her wings and launched herself up into the sky. The whole band glanced back over their shoulders as they left the ground, the Hidden, the Gordunni, and Dire Maul behind.

Malus was shaking the wool out of his head and only just pulling himself up to his feet. He looked up just in time to see Aram flying away on the back of the wyvern and shouted, *"STOP THE BOY!!"*

Zathra clicked her tongue twice. The scorpid leapt from the troll's chest onto the face of the ogre who had been pointing a spear at her mistress, allowing Zathra to raise her crossbows. She aimed and fired at Aram. With a little luck, he'd fall more or less at Malus's feet with the compass still on him.

But the night elf's sharp eyes caught all this. The druid pushed Aram down and took the two crossbow bolts meant for the boy in the center of his back.

CHAPTER THIRTY-FOUR
FINAL NESTING PLACE

One-Eye flew them all up into the sky, out of range of cross-bows, the Hidden, and the Gordunni, on an easterly heading. Aram, confused over why the night elf had suddenly pushed him down, popped right back up. Turning to look behind him, Aram found Thalyss smiling benignly. Murky was shouting something, but Thalyss shushed him. "Look about you," said the druid. "You will not get many chances like this."

Nodding, Aram glanced over One-Eye's head and marveled in absolute wonder at the view laid out before him. The two moons of Azeroth shone down on Feralas below. The view was astounding. The land beneath, which had seemed a wasteland from a boy's-eye view, was a paradise of potential from above. Stones and stumps, interesting in and of themselves from this vantage, soon gave way to treetops divided into discrete sections by stripes of sparkling water reflecting moonlight. The vista went on forever, and Aram imagined he could see all of Kalimdor from atop the wyvern's back. He imagined that maybe, with just a little more height, he could see all the way to Lakeshire. And on top of it all, there was the soaring. This amazing sensation of flight, of speeding over the landscape without attention to terrain or obstacle. It reminded him of something . . . *something* . . .

Aram shook off the vague memory and turned to smile back at Thalyss—just in time to see the druid slump over silently. Only then did Aram see the crossbow bolts in the kaldorei's back! He called out, "Thalyss!" The night elf started to slide off the wyvern, but Aram and Murky held their friend in place.

Makasa, whose view of the night elf was largely blocked by both Hackle and Murky, shouted, "Aram, what is it? What's wrong?"

"It's Thalyss! He's been shot! Two arrows in the back!"

"Is he alive?!"

Aram leaned down over Thalyss's face. He could just barely hear the night elf breathing—wheezing, really—with great difficulty. Aram turned to call back to Makasa, "He's alive. But I don't know what to do! Do I pull the arrows out?!"

"No!" Makasa warned. "Not yet! They may be all that's keeping him alive. I can't reach him. Can't see from here. We need to land!"

Aram shouted, "One-Eye, land! Find somewhere safe to land!"

If One-Eye took any notice, she gave no indication. She just kept flapping her wings at a horrifyingly moderate pace as she followed the flight path of her three cubs, whom Aram could just make out in the far distance.

"She won't land!" Aram yelled, panicked. "I don't know how to make her land!"

"Then try to keep him comfortable 'til she does! Try to keep him conscious!"

Aram tried to rouse Thalyss. The night elf grumbled as Aram might have grumbled aboard *Wavestrider* when Makasa was trying to rouse him. After some shaking, Thalyss opened his eyes and said again, "Look about you, Aramar Thorne."

"I've looked! Listen, you're hurt. Can you tell One-Eye to land?!"

"I could tell her. But she is hardly likely to comply. She will want to join her cubs in their nest. Until we arrive, we might as well enjoy the ride and the view."

But Aram had had his fill of the view. He kept his focus on the kaldorei. Talked to him, worried him, urging Hackle and Murky to do the same, until the night elf would respond with some pleasantry that seemed to take no special notice of his condition.

Thalyss began to shiver. Belatedly, Aram realized it was cold up in the heights of the sky. His father's coat was tied around his waist, and he quickly removed it and laid it over the night elf, who whispered, "Usually have my own fur coat to keep me warm. Thank you."

An hour passed. Then another. And another. Thalyss, still breathing, closed his eyes, and nothing Aram could say or shout generated any response whatsoever. Off and on, Aram made another appeal to the wyvern, who continued to ignore him and fly on, approaching one of the highest peaks from above. Then, abruptly and without any kind of warning, she tucked her wings and dove down steeply. Aram had one hand grasping her mane and another holding tight to Thalyss. Murky did the same, whispering, "Duluss, Duluss, nk mlgggrr, Duluss . . ."

The wyvern turned sharply, leaving her passengers nearly perpendicular to the ground. Thalyss started to slip again, but Hackle reached over Murky to help secure the night elf.

Makasa wanted to help but couldn't reach.

One-Eye extended her wings again, riding a powerful updraft skyward into the rocky terrain overlooking Thousand Needles.

Then suddenly, she pulled up short and landed—more gently than Aram would have imagined possible—on what was clearly her nearly inaccessible rocky nest, where the three wyvern cubs were already waiting and grooming one another.

One-Eye turned back and growled to indicate her impatience.

Aram, Murky, and Hackle slid off her back, supporting Thalyss. Makasa was already beneath them, waiting to take the elf in her arms. She laid the old druid down on his side upon a flat slab of stone and began looking at his wounds. The bolts were deep in his back. Makasa knew they had barbed heads; she didn't dare try to remove them.

The night elf coughed.

"He's alive!" Aram quickly knelt beside his head.

"I am forced to disagree," Thalyss whispered with a smile. "I am pretty well finished, Aram."

"No. We can—"

"You cannot." The elf coughed again. Bloody spittle dribbled from between his teeth. His breathing was shallow and ragged, and the smile faded from his lips—though not from his voice, which still sounded vaguely amused. "Makasa tried to tell you . . . You cannot save everyone, my friend . . . It is a lesson you are slow to learn . . . and perhaps . . . that is just as well . . ."

"Don't talk. Save your strength."

"For what? Besides . . . when have you known me . . . not to talk?"

"You kept your mouth shut when we were marching with the ogres."

"Well . . . I am not much . . . for burlap sacks . . ." He gasped for air, then raised a hand and pointed past Makasa. "Look at that . . ."

As one, they all turned—Aram, Makasa, Murky, and Hackle—to see One-Eye's reunion with her cubs. She had her poisonous tail wrapped around one, rubbed her sharp-fanged muzzle against another, and hugged—practically cradled—the third in her talon-clawed paw and wing.

The druid said, "You see that, Aram . . . You did that . . ."

"*We* did that," Aram replied.

"Maybe we did at that . . . Lift me up . . . I want to see where we are. I want to know where I am going to end."

With Makasa and Hackle's help, Aram raised Thalyss up. All five of them looked about for the first time since landing. Spread out beyond and below, Aram could see the great Thousand Needles canyon, flooded by the Cataclysm, with its tall, narrow flat-topped spires emerging from the water. Some of these spires were so large, there seemed to be entire towns built upon them.

"Ah." Thalyss sighed. "We are atop . . . Skypeak. I had a memorable night near here . . . once upon nine thousand years ago. Well . . . it would have been memorable except . . . for the drinking." He tried to laugh but barely managed another cough.

Aram turned to look back down into Thalyss's eyes. The silver had gone gray, reflecting no light. They were clouded, blind, perhaps seeing that long-ago night—but certainly not seeing the boy in front of him.

"Aram," he said, each breath an effort now. "This is important. *You* . . . have a . . . a talent for . . . for bringing people together with . . . your magic . . ."

"Your magic!" Aram said, grasping at straws. "The acorn! It brings life!"

"Yes . . . please . . . get it for me . . ."

Quickly and nervously, Aram reached into the druid's robes, found the inner pocket, and removed the purple pouch. He fumbled to open it, but the night elf's hand closed over Aram's and the pouch.

"Listen . . ." His voice was very faint. "You have to promise me . . ."

"But—"

"Listen!" he said, now with some urgency. "You are traveling . . . to Gadgetzan . . . to catch that ship home . . . There is a druid tender . . . another night elf . . . in the city . . . Her name is . . ." He swallowed and coughed up more blood. Aram wiped off his friend's mouth with a corner of his sleeve. "Her name is Faeyrine . . . Faeyrine Springsong . . . Promise me you will bring her the pouch . . . the seed . . ."

"I promise, but—"

"I am not a plant, Aram," Thalyss said gently. "There is . . . no magic in the seed . . . for me. You *must* take it . . . to Springsong." He turned his head then, resting his blind eyes on Murky as if he could clearly see the murloc before him. "You will help him . . . do this for me?"

"Mrgle, mrgle. Murky mrrugl Urum, Duluss. Murky mrrugl."

Thalyss smiled again. "That is . . . good . . . my murloc . . . frund . . . But I thought . . . I was looking at . . ."

Makasa said, "We will deliver the pouch. You have all our words and may consider it done."

"Thank you . . . dear friends . . . You see . . . there *is* a . . . destiny to things . . . A way . . . a flow . . . The compass . . . It drew my path . . . to join with yours . . ."

"Sorry, sorry," Aram said—though what he might be apologizing for was unclear.

"I have . . . no regrets . . . I see it now . . . Your path is a wide road . . . It will draw in many souls . . . I am . . . honored to be among . . . the first . . . Guard that compass well . . ." His tongue tapped his upper lip one last time.

"I will. I promise."

"Oh, and one . . . more thing . . . The seed . . . Do not . . . let it . . . get . . . wet . . ."

And then he was gone.

"Gordok is dead! Long live Gordok!" Malus's pronouncement brought only a prolonged silence from the Dire Maul Gordunni filling the amphitheater.

Finally, an immense hunchbacked ogre named Kor'lok—one of the young warriors who had been holding a spear in Throgg's face—turned toward Malus. Kor'lok, born with a single central eye in his brow, had been told his entire life that this rare feature marked him for greatness, like the ogre lords of yore. Often, he had dreamt of challenging Gordok for clan supremacy. He was certain he could kill the old king. But he feared that Wordok or Arkus or both would challenge him in turn, and that—exhausted from the first battle—he might fall. But now all three obstacles were corpses. All that remained was this human. And, yes, the little creature had skill. But now *he* was weary and bleeding from a prior challenge. Now—without a doubt—it was Kor'lok's turn to rule.

He took a step forward and shouted down at Malus, "Who Gordok? You?!"

Malus raised his sword and shouted back, "I killed Gordok! Now, I *am* Gordok of the Dire Maul Gordunni!"

Kor'lok scoffed. "Human not Gordok! Only ogre Gordok!"

"Do you challenge me?" Malus smiled, though perhaps Kor'lok was too far away to see.

Kor'lok raised his spear. "Kor'lok challenge! Yes!"

"*Whom* do you challenge?!"

"Little Malus man!"

"Why would Kor'lok challenge Malus, if Malus is not Gordok of the Dire Maul Gordunni?!"

This stumped Kor'lok briefly. His brow furrowed; his single eye squinted as he tried to work this puzzle out. Eventually, he said, "Little Malus man can be Gordok 'til Kor'lok kill little Malus man!"

"So Malus is Gordok now?!"

"Now! Yes! Soon! Dead!"

"Do all the Dire Maul Gordunni agree that Malus is Gordok?!"

At first, no one spoke. Then Kor'lok shouted out, "Agree! Agree!"

A somewhat halfhearted chorus of voices rose to confirm Malus's current—though theoretically temporary—status. In any case, no one challenged the notion.

Malus raised his sword again, and the arena fell silent. He shouted, "Then Malus is Gordok! I am Gordok! And Gordok accepts Kor'lok's challenge!"

Kor'lok grinned, quite pleased with himself. He raised both his arms in triumph—expecting a cheer—and was extremely disappointed when none was forthcoming. But that would change once he became the new Gordok.

He took another step forward but stopped when the current little Gordok raised his sword yet again, repeating, "I am Gordok! And Gordok accepts Kor'lok's challenge!! And Gordok chooses Throgg to fight for Gordok!"

Kor'lok's brow furrowed again. This was not part of his plan. Still, this unexpected twist wouldn't trouble him for long—as Throgg immediately stepped forward and impaled young Kor'lok from behind on his sword-hand.

Kor'lok, destined for greatness, collapsed dead in the aisle of the amphitheater.

Malus raised his sword and said, "Who else challenges Gordok?"

There was general silence. He scanned the arena, looking for potential troublemakers. For a moment, his eyes lingered on Throgg himself. The Shattered Hand ogre did not look happy. Malus could guess the reason. Deep down, Throgg was something of a traditionalist, and Malus was perverting the ways of the ogre, the laws of the Gordunni, to serve and suit his own needs. Or in any case, to serve and suit the needs of the Hidden. In the end, Malus knew it was this last notion that prevented Throgg from challenging his master: the ogre had pledged an oath to serve the cause of the Hidden. Throgg lowered his head in submission.

No one else stepped forward. The double threat of the previous Gordok's killer and the Shattered Hand ogre was more than enough incentive to keep the rest in line. Malus raised his sword one last time and shouted, "Gordok is dead! Long live Gordok!"

And as one, the Dire Maul Gordunni shouted, *"LONG LIVE GORDOK!"*

Dawn was approaching. There was light in the east.

Aram looked down at the pouch in his hand.

I have a life debt of my own now, he thought.

As if reading his mind, Makasa said, "We will share this burden, brother. The compass of your father *and* the seed of Thalyss."

He looked up at her and tears welled in his eyes. Was he mourning the loss of Thalyss, or of Greydon Thorne, or was he grateful for the loyalty of his new sister, Makasa? Even he wasn't sure. It was probably all of it. Everything. He felt supremely tired and leaned against her. She put an arm around him, and they were silent for a time.

All that remained was to get out of the wyvern's nest and down off the mountain. There were none left among them who spoke Taur-ahe, let alone knew the words of permission, but Aram was confident enough in One-Eye's gratitude to ask the wyvern through gesture, pointing, and pantomime if she would fly them down at least as far as the northwest slope of Thousand Needles.

* * *

Old One-Eye squinted at Aram crossly for not observing the proper forms. But what other choice did she have? She had to get them out of her nest one way or another. That meant eating them, pushing them off the cliff, or acquiescing to the boy's request. She looked over at her cubs, happily roughhousing, and thought about the painful months she had gone without laying her eye on them inside their thorny prison. Aram had been right. She was too grateful to the boy to do anything but aid him.

Once Thalyss was dead, Makasa had carefully removed the crossbow bolts from his back. That was the tradition of her people. *For how could a soul rest if he must carry the cause of his death with him forever?*

Hackle had found this quite odd. The tradition of *his people* called for them to eat Thalyss. After all, the night elf was carrion now. The gnoll suggested as much to Aram—who briefly looked quite appalled.

But Aram didn't get upset; he put a hand on Hackle's shoulder and said, "That's, uh, not the kaldorei way."

Together, the four young travelers carefully wrapped the druid up in his robes. Aram put on his father's coat, now stained with some of the night elf's blood. *I've lost too many people on this voyage,* he thought, quite determined not to lose anyone else.

The lesson that Makasa and Thalyss had tried to teach him—that you cannot save everyone—had not truly sunk in at all. Despite the losses, he wouldn't let it sink in. *Not now. Maybe not ever.*

Aram and Murky climbed up onto One-Eye's back. Makasa and Hackle handed Thalyss up to them, then climbed up behind.

Aram checked one more time to confirm that the acorn pouch was safe in his coat pocket, that the compass was safely tucked under his shirt, and that his sketchbook was securely stuffed into his back pocket. *Yes*, he thought, *I have many burdens.* Then he leaned forward to whisper into the wyvern's ear, "He'll want to lie in soft earth, in good soil, where things may grow. Can you take us somewhere like that?"

Aram had no idea if she could understand him—but he could have sworn Ol' One-Eye rolled her one eye. He assumed that from Makasa's place in back, she had been unable to catch it. This made him smile just a little, as the wyvern barked a command to her three cubs—presumably to stay put—before spreading her wings and taking to the sky . . .

CHAPTER THIRTY-FIVE
THE LAST MILE

One-Eye's flight arced gently to the southeast as she gradually descended from atop Skypeak, down the last mile toward the border of Feralas with Thousand Needles and a verdant slope just west of the flooded canyon.

Suddenly, something grabbed Aram and yanked him forward, nearly flipping him right over the top of the wyvern's head. Caught off guard, he let go of Thalyss and grabbed two fistfuls of mane. Once secured, he looked back to confirm that Murky, Hackle, and Makasa still held the night elf's body. Then Aram looked down to see what was *still* attempting to pull him off One-Eye's neck.

It was his shirt! No, not his shirt—*it was the compass* beneath his shirt, pulling hard on the chain around his neck and straining against what remained of the torn, stained, and ragged fabric that covered his chest. Without thinking, he reached up with one hand and pulled the compass out. He let go of it, bracing himself again by grabbing the wyvern's mane with both hands.

Behind him, Makasa shouted, "Aram?"

He didn't answer. The compass was pulling—and pulling hard—just a few degrees to the south of Old One-Eye's current heading, as if it had a mind of its own.

And then the clasp on the chain snapped! The compass flew off, passing close enough over One-Eye's good right eye to startle her into a brief dive.

Before she had completely recovered, Aram shouted, *"FOLLOW THAT COMPASS!"*

He instantly thought it a ridiculous thing to say—especially to a beast who might not even understand the words—but the wyvern *hated* to be startled and had no issue with giving chase to whatever it was that had even momentarily upset her. She wasn't sure what had zipped past her, but she *was* sure she would kill and eat it. She veered south.

The only problem was that their quarry was such a little thing. It was easy for the boy and the one-eyed beast to lose sight of it.

Aram scanned the air, spotted the compass, pointed, and shouted, *"THERE!"*

She turned her head back and grunted at him. He had to lean way forward over the wyvern's head so she could actually *see* where he was pointing.

Makasa, whose own view was partially blocked by Hackle, shouted out, "What's going on?! Did you drop the compass?!"

"No, it flew away on its own!"

"Don't take that tone with me, boy!"

He realized she thought he was being sarcastic, and if he hadn't been out of reach, he knew she'd have slapped him on the back of the head.

Aram didn't care. He was desperately trying to maintain focus on the little compass. By this time, it was heading steeply down, angling toward the base of a waterfall. One-Eye tucked her wings and dove down after it—as the sun chose just that moment to rise over the eastern edge of the canyon. The glare caused Aram to briefly shut his eyes and look away.

When he looked again, he couldn't immediately find the compass. Then a flash of light—perhaps the sun reflecting off the compass's brass setting—caught his eye. He saw a second flash of light, farther down, on the ground just to the left of the falls. *What could* that *be?*

He wasn't sure—but the first light beelined directly toward the second, and both reminded him of something, something . . .

The wyvern saw the lights, too, and maintained her steep and fast descent.

Murky screamed, and Hackle howled. Makasa remained silent.

Aram saw the first light hit the second light *and* the floor of the canyon; they were close enough to see a cloud of dirt poof up from the impact.

Long after it seemed too late, One-Eye extended her wings, which caught the air and arrested their dive. Still, *this* landing wasn't gentle. She put down hard on her rear feet, with her body at a forty-five-degree angle. The force of the contact shook the elf's body loose from the trio holding him. Thalyss thumped brutally against the soft ground.

Aram quickly slid off the wyvern.

Makasa was right behind him. "Aram!"

"The compass flew off on its own," he said again, but this time she could tell he meant it.

The sound of the falling water was almost deafening. He glanced up at the falls, and the artist in him briefly registered them as magnificent. But they couldn't hold his attention. Not now.

Twenty feet from where the cascading water fell to earth, Aram soon found a small crater in the soil, and, at the bottom of it, half-buried by dirt, he found the compass. The crystal needle was spinning in circles and glowing brighter than it ever had before. Carefully, with Makasa and One-Eye both looking over his shoulder, Aram lifted up the compass. As soon as One-Eye got a good look at it and saw it was a piece of inedible metal, she harrumphed and turned away. But Murky and Hackle joined Makasa as Aram felt something hard on the underside of the compass's metal housing. Aram turned it over. It was another glowing shard of crystal, like the needle, only slightly bigger. Tentatively, he poked at it. It slid around to the front of the compass, resting just on the glass above the needle, which suddenly stopped spinning. Now, both crystals—needle and shard—pointed southeast.

Still tentative, Aram touched the glowing, diamond-like sliver . . .

The Voice of the Light called to him: "Aram, Aram, it is you who must save me!" The Light got brighter and brighter, but this time Aramar Thorne did not turn away . . .

"Aram! Aram!" Makasa was shaking him out of his stupor.

He looked down at the compass. Neither the needle nor the new shard was glowing anymore. Slowly, he turned to look at Makasa. "It's calling to me," he said quietly.

She didn't understand, but she took him seriously. "What? What's calling?"

"The Light. I'm supposed to save the Light." Somewhere in the back of his mind, he knew he couldn't be making much sense to her. None of it made much sense to *him*. But it *felt* right.

With something approaching clarity, he could see why his father was so determined to protect the compass. Greydon had said it would lead Aram where he needed to go. Aram had assumed that meant home to Lakeshire. Now, that seemed not simply unlikely but even a little ridiculous. Something larger was at stake. Something so important, Greydon Thorne had wanted his son ready to face it, had been training him to face it before time had run out. This Light-That-Needed-Saving was now Aramar's responsibility. It was another burden, true. Yet it also felt like an honor, a great privilege, which his father had bestowed upon him. Aram no longer wondered why Greydon Thorne had brought his son aboard *Wavestrider* or why he had given him the compass instead of throwing it into the sea. Whatever anger, whatever resentment Aram had once felt toward the man had completely and forever melted away. And in his heart, Aram thanked his father for having that much faith in him. In the Greydon-son and in his sister Makasa Flintwill.

The compass needle once again pointed southeast. *Was there another shard of crystal there? Perhaps it lay hidden somewhere along that path?* Thalyss had theorized that the compass was tracking someone or something heading from south to north. Now, Aram thought it more likely that their trek with the ogres had brought them close enough to this particular sliver of the Light to attract the compass's attention. With the sliver found, the compass was back to pointing in its original direction, southeast toward Gadgetzan. He'd promised Thalyss to take the acorn to Gadgetzan, just as he'd promised his father to safeguard the compass. He told Makasa, "All roads lead to Gadgetzan."

She nodded and repeated, "All roads lead to Gadgetzan."

Hackle said, "To Gadgetzan."

Murky said, "Mrgle, mrgle."

A sulky One-Eye merely harrumphed again.

*   *   *

"The boy?" Malus asked.

"I can't be trackin' him tru da sky, mon," Zathra said, scowling with undisguised frustration.

The Hidden had triumphed over the Dire Maul Gordunni. Malus ruled the ogres as their new Gordok. Yet, despite these victories, none of them was particularly cheerful.

None except Valdread. The Forsaken removed his hood to reveal his stretched grin. "Tsk, tsk, tsk," he said. "So the young squire and the compass have escaped us again. Even got away with the ever-impressive Flintwill and our murloc leverage."

"I tink I killed da elf," Zathra said.

"Perhaps," said Valdread. "But night elves are notoriously difficult to kill, so it's hard to say for sure. Still, the boy's not short on allies. I believe he has a gnoll with him now. And, let's see, am I forgetting anything?"

"Enough," Malus said, not amused.

Valdread ignored him. "Oh, yes, that's right. *He has a wyvern!*" The baron laughed heartily at that. It was a somewhat chilling sound, and it dislocated his jaw for him. But he quickly clicked the bone back into place and said, "He may even have four!"

"What now?" Throgg asked gloomily.

Malus considered this for a time. Finally, he said, "From the beginning—aside from the detour here, which wasn't by choice—they've maintained a fairly direct heading. Toward Gadgetzan. That's where they're going. That's where we'll go. If we don't catch up to them en route, we'll find them in the city. We'll send out the ogres, too."

"Whole clan?" Throgg asked.

"Yes, all of them. Empty Dire Maul and scatter them across every deer trail, mountain path, road, and waterway to help us search. These ogres belong to me now, and that means they're not Gordunni anymore. They're Hidden. So we might as well make decent use of them."

Throgg looked miserable and angry but nodded his acquiescence.

Malus continued. "We all rendezvous in Gadgetzan." He turned to Ssarbik. "Send a message to your sister on the *Inevitable*. I want the ship to meet us there."

"What if you're wrong?" the arakkoa asked bitterly.

"I'm not."

"And what if the boy uzzezz the compassss? What if he findzz shardzz of the sssword?"

"Then we'll have that many fewer to secure ourselves."

Ssarbik spoke to Malus with his mind. *"Our masster will not be pleazzed."*

Malus scowled his silent response. *"No one said this would be quick. Tell him the game isn't over yet."*

"Ukul."

"Hackle."

"Ukul . . ."

"No. HACK-le."

"UK-le. Ukle."

"Close enough," Makasa said, stopping Murky and Hackle's exchange before it drove her to kill them both.

Aram was drawing Old One-Eye in his "magic" book, having acquired what he guessed was her permission, through pantomime and a flip through the pages, to portray the wyvern's likeness. It wasn't at all clear whether or not she understood. But she didn't fly off and, in any case, remained still enough for him to sketch her well. He gravely thanked her for the honor.

For good measure, he sketched in her three cubs as well. He tried to draw them from memory, but as he hadn't seen enough of them to have any solid recollection, he instead wound up drawing three little two-eyed One-Eyes.

When finished, he displayed the illustration to her, again on the off chance she might be pleased with the result. Maybe she was. Maybe she wasn't. But she seemed to be in an unusually cooperative mood—or perhaps she still felt some obligation toward the boy. At his mimed request, she was now digging a large, deep hole in the soft soil where Aram had found the crystal shard.

While she worked, he worked . . . on the memory sketch of his father. It had given him much trouble previously, but now he found his recollection of Greydon's features had improved considerably. Perhaps he understood his father more now. Perhaps, as his mother had once advised, he had found the Greydon Thorne within himself. Or at least a shard of him. He wasn't

Old One-Eye
and Her
Cubs

AYAM

sure he'd ever quite complete the drawing to his own satisfaction, ever quite do justice to the man. But now he could look at it and not feel ashamed. Good magic, indeed.

When One-Eye was done digging, Makasa and Hackle lowered the night elf into the grave. Aram thought he should try to say a few words over the body, but before he could speak, the wyvern used her tail to begin pushing the earth back into the hole.

So Aram waited. He looked around him. A slight breeze played through the leaves on the nearby trees; they swayed gently. A bored Hackle was furiously scratching his neck with a hind leg. But Murky was very sad and attentive—*until* he spotted a spider advancing down a web and lunged for it. He missed the spider and was left spitting out the sticky web with no little difficulty. Makasa just shook her head, appalled.

Once the wyvern had finished tamping down the earth, Aram gathered the others around. He began: "I don't think there's much to say. Thalyss lived a long life, and we were only a very small part of it. But in that short time, I believe Thalyss made a conscious choice to care about each and every one of us. I believe he would be glad we were here with him at this moment. Glad we were here together. My father once said there are all kinds of families. And I believe Thalyss helped us forge this one out of sweat, blood, and a little magic. Oh, and I believe Thalyss would have liked this spot, surrounded by green and under good clean earth." He lowered his head.

Then, struck by an afterthought, Aram suddenly leaned

forward and spit on Thalyss's grave. "But a little moisture never hurts," he quoted.

Makasa stared. "You spit . . . *on his grave?*" she whispered, as if afraid the kaldorei might hear her.

"Um, yeah." Only now did it occur to him how disrespectful that must seem. He spoke quickly. *"But it'll help things grow! And I really think it would have made him smile."*

"Everything made him smile," she said, her scowl lifting only slightly, like a ray of sunlight peeking out from behind a stormcloud.

Aram shrugged. "Exactly."

Murky spit, too, though perhaps he was still trying to get the spiderweb out of his mouth. But Hackle took it as custom and spit on the grave. All eyes turned to Makasa. She met Aram's gaze . . . and spit.

Old One-Eye yawned then. She seemed impatient to go. The thought occurred to Aram that traveling by wyvern would certainly get them to Gadgetzan faster. But he already felt like he had pushed his luck with the great beast. So Aram thanked One-Eye and said good-bye, and they watched her lift off and soar away toward her nest and her young.

Aram looked around. There didn't seem to be much reason to linger. The compass and chain, its clasp crudely repaired, were back around his neck. He checked the needle. Then he pointed the way for the others.

"Gadgetzan?" Makasa asked.

"I think so," Aram replied, tucking compass and chain back

under his shirt. "The compass'll let us know if we need to make any other stops along the way." He felt for the purple leather pouch inside his coat pocket, where the crystal shard was stowed alongside Thalyss's giant acorn.

"It is . . . intriguing," Makasa said.

"Oh, at least that," he agreed.

They started walking downhill alongside the runoff from the waterfall, which was sparkling in the distance. The rain forest was opening up into the wide, bright vista of the great flooded canyon as they finally stepped across the border into Thousand Needles.

They. Aram, Makasa, Murky, and Hackle. Even Aram thought it an odd group. Yet somehow he knew they all belonged together.

Out of nowhere, Makasa said, "You better not be putting me in that blasted book."

It was only then Aram realized he was still holding his sketchbook in one hand. He wrapped its oilskin back around it and stuffed it in his back pocket, saying, "I promise I won't sketch you unless you ask me to."

She nodded, satisfied. They walked on for a time in silence. And then she said, "I *might* ask you. I've heard it's good magic."

Aram looked up at his sister, and they smiled.

GREYDON THORNE

A. Thorne

ACKNOWLEDGMENTS

First off, I'd like to thank my old friend, Andrew Robinson, for making the initial introduction that led to this astounding gig.

Thanks also to James Waugh and the brain trust at Blizzard: Stephane Belin, Michael Bybee, Samwise Didier, Cate Gary, Logan Laflotte, Logan Lubera, Chris Metzen, Byron Parnell, Matthew Robinson, Robert Simpson, Jeffrey Wong, and the Lore Team.

At Scholastic, I'd like to thank my original editor Elizabeth Schaefer for her support, Associate Publisher Samantha Schutz for ably jumping in when Elizabeth set sail on her own travels, and Jenna Ballard, Katie Bignell, Rick DeMonico, Danielle Klimashowsky, Charisse Meloto, Monica Palenzuela, and Maria Passalacqua for their help bringing things home.

At the Gotham Group, thanks to Tony Gil, Ellen Goldsmith-Vein, Julie Kane-Ritsch, Peter McHugh, Julie Nelson, Hannah Shtein, and Joey Villareal. At Bay Sherman, Mike Sherman and Baerbel Struthers.

Appreciation also to my *Rain of the Ghosts* AudioPlay partner, Curtis Koller, and to my *Shimmer & Shine* work family—Farnaz Esanaashari, Carin-Anne Greco, Michael Heinz, Elizabeth Jordan, Julie Kinman, Crystal Leal, Ian Murray, Dave Palmer, Jackie Sheng, Pragya Tomar, Chad Woods, and especially Andrew Blanchette, Dustin Ferrer, Rich Fogel, Kevin Hopps, Cisco Paredes, and Stephanie Simpson—for their patience with my sea chantey, etc.

A word of gratitude to the "tall women" who helped inspire Makasa Flintwill: Jennifer L. Anderson, Vanessa Marshall, and Masasa Moyo.

And, of course, extra special thanks to my real family: my large extended clan of in-laws, laws, and outlaws—especially my parents, Sheila and Wally; my siblings, Robyn and Jon; my wife, Beth, and my amazing poppers, Erin and Benny.

ABOUT THE AUTHOR

Greg Weisman has been a storyteller all his life. He's best known as the creator of Disney's *Gargoyles* and as a writer-producer on multiple animated series, including *Gargoyles*, *W.I.T.C.H.*, *The Spectacular Spider-Man*, *Star Wars Rebels*, and *Young Justice*. In addition to writing the first two books in the World of Warcraft: Traveler series, he's written several comic book titles—including *Captain Atom*, *Gargoyles*, *Young Justice*, *Star Wars Kanan*, *Mythic Legions*, *Mecha-Nation*, and *Starbrand & Nightmask*—plus two young adult novels, *Rain of the Ghosts* and *Spirits of Ash and Foam*.

Don't miss the thrilling continuation of Aram's journey!